Cheri Giaque

C0-ASI-345

THE HANGING TREE...

In the dim twilight Vonnie looked out from the balcony onto the grounds of Hazard House. Looming in the darkness was the large oak tree—its sinister branches stretching out as if to seize her.

She knew the history of the tree. During the American Revolution a spy had been hung there. Stories were told of other deaths as well, yet the tree still stood—a grim sentinel of death.

Suddenly Vonnie's heart started pounding and her legs went limp. A figure was emerging from behind the tree. It was a creature—ghost-like and eerie—and she was moving slowly and deliberately toward the house. Horror-struck, Vonnie's screams pierced the darkness . . .

HAZARD HOUSE

by Paulette Warren

POPULAR LIBRARY · NEW YORK

All POPULAR LIBRARY books are carefully selected by the
POPULAR LIBRARY Editorial Board and represent titles by
the world's greatest authors.

POPULAR LIBRARY EDITION

Copyright © 1972 by Paul W. Fairman

PRINTED IN THE UNITED STATES OF AMERICA

All Rights Reserved

CHAPTER ONE

The conference was routine, the whole of it going down on tape. So Vonnie had only to put the important parts down in her book—those parts she thought Keith might want for quick reference later—statements such as the pompous big wheel of Enterprise Associates Inc., Leo Haywood, had just made:

"Mr. Elwood, we feel that twenty-five-thousand is a generous fee for the research we're asking."

Vonnie glanced at Keith, wondering if he agreed. When he made no objection she assumed that he did.

She could not be sure however because Keith had seemed off somewhere in space during most of the conference. Those lapses of his! Vonnie had witnessed them several time during the two weeks of her new job as his secretary. But this was the first time he'd wandered off mentally during a business conference.

Shifting her position slightly, Vonnie dropped her pencil to the polished, hardwood floor of the conference room. The sound of metal meeting wood was not startling, but it rang sharply in the waiting silence.

Keith blinked, threw Vonnie a quick look, and said, "The inaccessibility of the property is the main problem, gentlemen."

"But then again," Haywood countered, "the rugged terrain is the principal asset."

George West, the Associates' publicity director, retrieved Vonnie's pencil, thus getting a quick scan of her shapely legs as he straightened. His smile as he returned it, suggested an intimacy which did not exist; or rather, perhaps, one he dared hope for.

Vonnie's cool but pleasant thank you, did not further those hopes a bit. She was used to having men smile at her in that fashion and knew exactly how to react.

Getting back to business, West frowned at his notes and said, "Hazard House has a rather sinister background, I understand. You might research that. It could be good color material for publicity releases after we get the ski lodge going."

"*If* we get it going."

This from Victor Poole, the comptroller. Vonnie made a mental note to remind Keith about Poole; a cunning little man—type cast for the role of penny pincher—he had been the negative voice from the start. She was sure that Keith would want to remain aware of that fact.

"Regardless of the seemingly favorable aspects," Poole went on, "launching a project of this scope onto virgin ground is always a risk."

"But Victor," Leo Haywood said gently, "one

hardly creates a ski lodge on any other kind of ground."

President Haywood was obviously the key here. A big, handsome, gray-haired man, his final decision and his alone would stand. Vonnie did not particularly like him. His attitude was too transparently false. He deliberately posed as only one of the voices present, ostensibly allowing free discussion and dissent. Thus, he made a game out of it, enjoying his power—while the others present were engaged solely in trying to guess his position in the matter at hand in order to be on the right side.

The conference went on. Vonnie was secretly amused. A small-town girl lately arrived in big, bustling Manhattan, she'd assumed that tycoons engaged in spending millions revealed brilliant minds when laying vast financial plans. So far, she'd seen no sign of this.

Here assembled, for example, were the moving spirits of a multimillion-dollar organization. They were making arrangements to risk several of those millions in building a ski resort in the hills of New York State. And of whom did they consist? A confirmed egoist in command who was mainly interested in preening his own feathers. A sour little comptroller who would have called government bonds a speculation if he thought it would please Haywood and several cautious associates who were vying with each other to come up with Haywood's previously-arrived-at-intentions concerning the matter at hand and thus make the "correct" decision ahead of the others.

These and a lecherous public relations man who could undress a girl with a single sweep of his eyes.

Perhaps, Vonnie thought, she was being too harsh with these gentlemen. It didn't really matter however. She was an observer, not a judge, and—as Aunt Madge had openly stated—"Child, you've inherited your mother's gift of laughter and your father's disrespect for all that's sacred."

Aunt Madge had been Vonnie's sole family since her fourteenth year when her parents were taken from her. A huge, comfortable woman, Aunt Madge wore frankness and cynicism like an overcoat she seldom removed. And perhaps some of this had rubbed off on Vonnie. Mainly, however, Aunt Madge had been the only rock to which Vonnie had clung while being buffeted toward destruction by the storm of grief when she was fourteen and her mother and father crashed in an old jerry-built plane. (Her father had bought it as a souvenir from World War I and had not had the good sense to leave it on the ground!)

Perhaps, at least—as Aunt Madge had said—it was a good age to lose loved ones if they had to be lost. Vonnie had been old enough to remember them and still resilient enough—"filled with the sap of youth" as Aunt Madge put it—to bounce back and go on with life. Still, the bouncing had been long and painful and it hadn't been until well into Vonnie's fifteenth year that Aunt Madge could refer to Lee and Helen in conversation.

There wasn't a jealous bone in Madge's vast bulk

but she did remember her sister with wistfulness and wonder.

"It was hard to believe that Helen really belonged to us," Madge would say, and during such reminiscences would reveal her more tender side as well as her poetic. "She was a golden person—all light and laughter—so I suppose it was natural that a golden man would come and find her, even in such a little one-horse town as Wilton." Then she would look at Vonnie to add, "And I suppose it was natural that they should have a golden child."

These revealing moods were rare, though. Mostly, Aunt Madge guided and raised her niece with harsh kindliness. And Vonnie thrived on it. Aunt Madge guided her through the confusions of early romances, shooing boys off the porch when necessary and convincing Vonnie that she didn't have to meet the competition by being overeager or submissive.

This had not been too difficult because she had an apt pupil in Vonnie who had inherited a great deal of her mother's independence. Helen had waited, unmarked emotionally, until her mid-twenties, and when Lee, who was later Vonnie's father, came along, it was as though she were expecting him . . . So much for heredity.

. . . Haywood slapped the table sharply. "Okay," he said, "it's a deal. I'll have the contract drawn up immediately for your approval. You'll go up there and make a complete survey—from the condition of the mansion itself to the attitude of the local people on having a ski resort in their midst. And make it complete. We don't want to be stopped cold for any reason after we've poured money into the thing. Agreed?"

"Agreed," Keith said, "except for one point."

"And that is . . . !"

"The fee. Twenty-five thousand isn't satisfactory."

"What's your idea of the price?"

"Exactly double. Fifty thousand and I'll pay my own expenses."

"I should hope so," Poole murmured, his eyes on Haywood.

Vonnie's first thought was that Keith did not want the deal. His demand could have been for no other purpose than to force Haywood to turn thumbs down.

So she was amazed when Haywood merely smiled and looked at Poole with what might have been interpreted as gentle pity.

"Agreed," he said, and held out a regal hand to Keith . . .

As the latter explained to Vonnie a short time later in a small bar nearby: "You've got to understand those clowns."

"But double the fee they offered! I'd have sworn you were telling them you didn't want the assignment."

"On the contrary. I need the business. But twenty-five grand for a job like that is ridiculous. If I'd gone along, there would have been no contract. Haywood would have changed his mind. He'd have figured I was stone broke and was grabbing at anything I could get."

Sipping her sherry thoughtfully, Vonnie conceded

that she might have misjudged these people with whom she'd been so suddenly thrown into contact.

"I guess," she said, "it takes nerve to survive in the business jungle."

"Jungle?"

Vonnie laughed. "That's what my Aunt Madge called it when she warned me against coming to the big city. She warned me against a lot of things."

"She must be quite a gal," Keith said.

But he spoke vaguely now, that abstract look taking over. Again his mind had gone elsewhere.

This was as close to sociability as Vonnie had come with her new boss. After the conference in the Associates' lush offices and with her pocket tape recorder safely stowed away, they had left, only to have Keith spot the cocktail sign and say, "I need a drink after that. Come on."

Keith gulped the last of his martini and looked at his watch. "No need for you to go back to the office. It's after four. We'll get a cab. You're in the Village, aren't you?"

Vonnie could only nod, her last phone conversation with Aunt Madge flashing through her mind:

"Two hundred dollars a week! Why, child! That's insane. You know what you'll be expected to do for it, don't you?"

Vonnie knew nothing of the kind and told Aunt Madge so; that her fears were strictly small-town fantasies, not big-city reality. And Vonnie's arguments were logical and convincing—at least to herself.

But now—here it was; decision time. She could see

12

Aunt Madge's stern visage, declaring in her abrasive voice: "All right, now you've got yourself into a situation, let's see you handle it."

These were her almost panicky thoughts as she followed her employer into the street. She could find no coherent protest as he raised his hand and brought a cab to a skidding halt. He opened the door and she got in.

Then he slammed the door, pushed a five-dollar bill at the driver, and said, "Take the lady where she wants to go," turned immediately on his heel and strode off in the other direction.

As the cab sped south, Vonnie sat back and tried to sort herself out. Being a normal female, her ego had suffered. It was nice to have had the problem removed, but it was disturbing to have been treated like a kid sister. She had to think back and recall the odious Mr. West's lustful attentions in order to reassure herself.

Then she laughed. "Aunt Madge, darling," she murmured, "if you knew, I'll bet you'd be actually disappointed—a man showing no interest whatever in your beautiful niece."

Then, as the cab wound through the curious little streets of Greenwich Village, Vonnie faced a less humorous but more serious question:

If Keith's inclinations had been different, what would I have done? What would my decision have been? . . . The correct one, of course. And I would have been diplomatic enough about it to save my job. After all, I'm twenty-four years old and not quite the

13

little small-town girl I appear to be. I worked in Des Moines, Iowa, for a whole year, and Des Moines isn't exactly a whistle-stop village . . .

But then again, she mused as the cab pulled up in front of her building, Keith Elwood is a terribly attractive man . . .

Now that the immediate danger was past, Vonnie could allow herself the excitement of daring thoughts . . .

An attractive man.

But one with mysterious problems that made Vonnie's job a continuing puzzle—and who had turned her, she admitted with some guilt, into a snoop . . .

CHAPTER TWO

Vonnie March had come to her present status as an established Manhattan career girl by doing everything wrong; at least, by doing the exact opposite of everything Aunt Madge drilled into her after Vonnie finally made her stand:

. . . "Aunt Madge, I'm twenty-four years old and I've never been out of the state of Iowa. I'm tired of commuting back and forth between Des Moines and Wilton and I want to see something of the world before I need bifocals."

"All right. I certainly can't lock you in your room. Of course I could but the neighbors would talk. So remember, if things don't go right, I am as near as your closest telephone . . ."

There was far more, of course:

. . . "Now dear, when you get to the city go immediately to the Martha Washington or the Barbizon or some other women's hotel. There are several reputable establishments in New York where men are barred and a girl is reasonably safe."

"Yes, Aunt Madge."

"Another thing. Check with the Better Business Bureau for the names of some reliable employment agencies. It would be just like you to give your money to some fly-by-night outfit ready to be indicted for fraud and theft."

Vonnie could not quite figure out why that would be "just like her." She had never demonstrated a tendency to be that gullible. But she said, "Yes, Aunt Madge," and didn't make a point of the matter.

Then, when Vonnie boarded the bus enroute to the airport, Aunt Madge tempered the whole thing. "You'll be all right, dear. I'm sure of it. Your guardian angel and I are good friends. You'll get special treatment."

And indeed, that appeared to be the case. Upon arriving in New York, Vonnie took the Carey bus into the East Side Terminal from Kennedy Airport. When she climbed into a cab, she felt so self-confident and delighted with all the rush and bustle she said, "The Waldorf Astoria, please."

She'd seen foreigners and glamorous jet-setters on TV arriving at that famous hostelry and told herself, "I'm just as glamorous as anybody else, so why not?" And perhaps her guardian angel was hovering about because Vonnie got a room without an advance reservation.

Then, instead of checking with the BBB or anybody else, she went to Times Square and put an ad into the *Situations Wanted* column of the *New York*

Times after which she bought a copy and answered an *Apartments to Share* ad which took her to a quaint little street in the Village.

She was met by a pleasant-faced, middle-aged lady who said, "I'm sorry, dear, but I couldn't accept you as an apartment mate. You're too young and attractive. You'd have too many young men pounding on the door."

"I'm sorry you feel that way. It's such a nice apartment. If you change your mind, would you call me?"

The lady called the next morning.

"Oh, you *have* changed your mind?" Vonnie said.

"No. But I just got word—my sister is ill in London and needs me. So as long as you were the first one to answer my ad, you may have the whole apartment if you want it."

Rent-controlled, beautifully serviced. Perfect. In fact, even Vonnie began to wonder about Aunt Madge's personal friendship with her guardian angel.

Only one thing was missing, though Vonnie did not know it at the time. There was no small inner voice to warn: *You're going to need a guardian angel before long, darling. Oh, how you're going to need one!*

But, for the time being, the fabulous luck went on. And the morning after, there was a reply waiting for Vonnie at the *Times* office.

The letterhead read: *Keith Elwood—Consulting Engineer.* She went to the address on Madison Avenue near the Lever Building and found a man in his mid-thirties whom Aunt Madge would have classified as "handsome as sin." But he was as nervous as a cat.

"So uptight," Vonnie thought, but was intrigued from the very first instant.

Instead of interviewing her across the big, shiny desk, he paced the floor, sat on the window sill, peered down twenty floors into the street, and frowned a great deal.

"Do you know what a consulting engineer does?" he asked.

"Why, I suppose he gives other people advice on engineering problems."

"That's about right. I'm an industrial engineer. It covers a lot of territory."

"I'm sure it's a broad field."

"Would you object to foreign travel?"

"Why—why no. I see no reason why I should. I wouldn't care to live abroad permanently, though."

"You say you worked for a lawyer in Des Moines?"

"Yes."

His look was not always abstract, as though he were miles away. He had sharp blue eyes—unique with his jet-black hair—eyes he could bring around like twin daggers and hurl straight into yours.

"Why did you leave?"

"I got bored. I wanted to try a big city—see if I could fit in."

"Shorthand . . . typing?"

"I'd be glad to demonstrate my speed—"

An abrupt wave of his hand cut her off. His manner irritated Vonnie. She wanted him to pay attention to the interview and worry about his personal problems later.

"I'll take your word for it. You aren't planning to get married or anything like that, are you?"

"Hardly. I don't know a soul in town—male *or* female."

"Anybody waiting for you back home in case you get lonely?"

"No one."

He paced clear around the office this time, then he stopped, skewered her with his eyes and asked, "You aren't on drugs are you?"

Vonnie gasped and half rose from her chair.

"Oh, sit down . . . sit down. I just had to be sure. Is two hundred a week okay?"

Vonnie gasped again. "Quite all right," she managed to reply.

"Then you might go to work on those files. They're in a mess. It's been almost a month now."

That last was a bit cryptic but Vonnie asked no questions. She went to work on the files and found that her new employer had not exaggerated. They were a mess indeed; correspondence jammed into the drawers—in total confusion.

The relationship remained singularly uncommunicative. Keith Elwood came and went in whirlwind fashion, leaving Vonnie to spend much of the time alone in the office. There were letters once in a while, sent off to various places around the world. Through these and what she found in the files, Vonnie learned that Keith analyzed and advised on diverse business and industrial projects. Had acted as consultant in the introduction of a grocery chain in Taiwan; selected the site for a plush motel in Caracas, Venezuela, and supervised the building personally. But he had also advised against projects—on the basis of his experience, training, and instinct.

As to the immediate office situation—why things were in such a mess—Vonnie found only a series of canceled checks for two hundred dollars made out to a Sarah Hall. There was a social security number but no address for Sarah.

Further proof of Keith's generosity emerged at the end of Vonnie's first week. He came to the office that morning and stayed long enough to check the mail and write out Vonnie's check.

"I don't quite understand," she said. "The withholding tax—"

"Oh, that," he said as though it were a petty bother. "It goes in every three months—I think. Figure it out when the time comes and take it out of the working fund. That and Social Security. Too much bother deducting from your check. I'll pay it over and above the two hundred. But you'll have to do the figuring."

A suspicion—and not necessarily faint—sprang into her mind at this moment. The overgenerosity; the vaguely unbusinesslike manner in which she was hired. Did it mean that a far more intimate relationship was expected—?

If so, there'd been no hint of it to date. Quite the opposite. Vonnie, thoroughly feminine, was well aware of her attractive legs and seductive torso. Far more so, it seemed, than was her employer. This did her ego no good at all. Even though Vonnie had always been completely sensible about such matters, being totally ignored in that department was not flat-

21

tering. Obviously, something other than business was disrupting Keith Elwood's life. Vonnie wanted to ask point blank what it was, but naturally she wouldn't dream of doing such a thing . . .

Keith looked vaguely around the office that morning and asked, "Is everything going all right?"

"Yes, I think so. Of course I still can't answer telephone inquiries very intelligently."

"That's all right. You'll get orientated into the business in due time. How's the filing?"

"All done except the locked drawer at the bottom of the steel cabinet. Do you want me to—?"

Again he cut her off with that peremptory wave of his hand. "That one's okay. Leave it alone."

His tone was almost harsh; enough so to anger Vonnie. Did he think she was going to attack the drawer with a crowbar?

Then he smiled—he had one of the warmest smiles Vonnie had ever seen—and rushed out with a quick compliment: "You're doing fine. Keep it up."

Alone again, she decided *doing fine* to Keith meant obeying orders without comment and asking no questions. At least, she had asked no questions and she got the impression that it pleased him. It was on this basis that she began putting together certain pieces of a mystery.

There was Keith's checkbook which she dug into for figures on withholding taxes and Social Security payments. She found these easily because Keith had made notations on all outgoing items. For that very reason she questioned two check stubs, one for eleven hundred and fifty dollars and the other for five thousand, neither of which bore a notation or a date. The sequence of other dated items, however, showed them to be a little over a month old. She could have dug through the jumbled bank statements in search of the canceled checks, but that seemed too downright sneaky.

Still, she wondered if it would be wise to call the items to Keith's attention on the theory that he had overlooked making complete entries. She decided against this, at least until she'd been around long enough to really sink her teeth deeper into her job.

Then she unearthed two more scraps of the puzzle while finishing off the back filing. One was a receipted bill for the eleven hundred-odd dollars dated roughly a week later.

It was from the Westfall Funeral Home.

And, finally, stuffed in the back of a lower file drawer, she found several partially used sheets of stationery. They appeared from their condition to have been originally slated for the waste basket. Why Keith had thrust them into the file cabinet, Vonnie couldn't imagine; except that his actions were erratic enough—as she'd observed—to have mistaken one for the other.

A quick check after flattening out the sheets, told Vonnie they were repeated attempts to finish a letter. Done in her boss's strong, masculine hand, they showed that he'd had trouble, even to the point of slashing an underlined *damn!!!* under one of the attempts.

They were all addressed to Mr. & Mrs. Ralph Hall, and one—presumably a first attempt—said, *I am enclosing a small check in the hope that you will—*

Keith evidently thought that too impersonal as later efforts indicated:

I understand and share your grief in the death of—
Please believe me when I say that your tragic bereavement—

Each of the sheets demonstrated a new effort on Keith's part to reflect what had certainly been a loss to him as well as to the Halls. Vonnie would have liked to have seen the final letter. She felt that it could be assumed until proved otherwise that death had separated Sarah Hall from her job with Keith Elwood. An answer of sorts, but one that raised any number of new questions. How had Sarah died? It had certainly been sudden and unexpected. What had the relationship been? Even as she wondered, Vonnie realized that none of it was any of her business. Still, she could not help wondering.

Then, at the beginning of her second week, Vonnie got her first non-routine order. Keith arrived around ten that day. He went quickly through the mail and started to leave. He stopped at the door, turned, and said, "Oh, I want you to do something for me—find out all there is to know about a place called Hazard House."

"Hazard House?"

"It's an old mansion somewhere up in the lower Adirondacks. Somewhere near Big Moose Lake, I think. Check a town named Burton's Forge."

"What's—what's to know about it?" Vonnie asked helplessly.

"The place has quite a history, I understand. A hundred or so years old. Built by an old coot named Haz-

24

ard. Try the public library and give me a rundown."

With that he was gone, leaving Vonnie to wonder, as usual, where he did spend so much of his time . . .

The imposing, block-long New York City Public Library daunted Vonnie as she approached it. She could not help comparing it to Cedar Point's neat little red building—a gift long ago from Andrew Carnegie—where Molly Sims knew every book in the place and frowned at you when you brought one back with a spot on it.

She expected difficulty, what with nothing to go on but the name Hazard, so she was pleasantly surprised to find that this was quite enough. Three history books and a volume on New York State genealogy revealed a fascinating story.

John Hazard, the founder of the line had been a man of surprising contrasts: apparently a devout churchman on the one hand, he was also a student of the black arts on the other.

During the years leading up to the Civil War, he made the bulk of his fortune as a slave trader out of Charleston, South Carolina. Then, when the war clouds began to gather, he sold all his holdings and came north with his wife, Rachel, whom he had met and married in Cuba a short time earlier.

There was only one reference to Rachel, this in a book on Southern slavery in which the writer referred to her as a "woman of color."

Once clear of his Southern connections, John Hazard appeared to seek seclusion. He moved into what was then an almost inaccessible forested area some eighty miles north of Manhattan and built Hazard

House, a mansion which—according to another historical volume—"still stands as a confusing example of architectural experimentation; a haphazard mixture of classic Georgian, Ionic splendor, and Moorish symbolism; all in all, a brooding monstrosity. It was rumored that Hazard consulted astrological tables when building the house and that it somehow conformed to the signs of the Zodiac."

Intriguing, thought Vonnie.

From what more she could gather, Hazard's move to the north was a correct one so far as his personal fortunes were concerned. By making the move, he accurately predicted who the victor would be in the War Between the States and put himself in a position to profit thereby. This he did by lending money to northern borrowers at fine rates of interest, remaining in semi-retirement and venturing forth only at intervals, but always to augment his fortune. As an example, he took sides against the mighty Cornelius Vanderbilt when the wily old Commodore fought for control of the Erie Railroad.

Anyone with a grain of sense would have known that Vanderbilt would destroy such upstarts as Daniel Drew, Jay Gould, and James Fisk for daring to cross him. But all logic went by the boards and the Commodore was soundly beaten for the first and last time in his robber baron career.

After this victory, John Hazard withdrew completely from the clique although he was most cordially invited to participate in other and greater financial forays. But his business acumen was proved by the fact that none of these turned out very well.

Later, John Hazard did participate in a cattle deal with the wily Daniel Drew of Carmel, New York; in which "Uncle Dan'l" banked all the profits. A short time later Drew's fortunes collapsed and he died a poor man.

An encyclopedia featuring genealogies revealed tragedy in John Hazard's life. Rachel bore him two sons and a daughter, the sons dying in young manhood in places far from home. Only dry statistics and brief statements attested to this so there had to be a great deal left unstated. Did the sons flee Hazard House at the first opportunity? Had they been disowned and sent away? Or had they left with parental blessing?

Vonnie found herself wondering about many things relative to John Hazard and his spectacular life. She sensed things not referred to by the historians.

When she left the library after collecting Keith's data, and walked out onto busy Fifth Avenue, she found that she had become so immersed in the lore of the past that the present was a mild shock. She had half-expected to find the New York of an earlier century—horse-drawn carriages, soberly dressed people, the tiny buildings of a hundred years before.

Then her return to the present brought a warm surge. How fortunate to be alive in the present day! How drab and colorless the world of John Hazard and his contemporaries.

As the light changed at the corner of Fifth and Forty-second Street and a New York cop waved her across with an appreciative look at her legs, she could chuckle to herself at being so susceptible to fanciful images conjured up from musty old volumes . . .

That evening she stayed late at the office, transcribing what she had learned into a readable profile of John Hazard.

She was surprised when the phone rang at seven o'clock. It was Keith.

"You don't have a home phone, have you?"

"No—I'm sorry. I've applied, but it will take a few days."

"Uh-huh. I called to tell you to be on time tomorrow morning."

Vonnie bristled. Keith certainly had a way of ruining a girl's day! What right had he to imply that she was unreliable? She had been in the office every morning before nine. He certainly deserved to be told off!

But, instead, Vonnie angered herself even more by meekly replying, "Of course."

"We've an important appointment with an outfit down the street—Enterprise Associates."

"What time will they be here?"

"They won't. We'll go to see them at one-thirty."

Vonnie didn't ask why being in at nine was so important with the appointment not until afternoon, but Keith did deign to be vaguely enlightening.

"I want to go over that material you got at the library today. You did get it, didn't you?"

So terribly irritating in his approach. The way he put things! The tone of that last implied she'd forgotten all about it and was thus a source of great irritation to him.

"I was there most of the day," Vonnie said evenly. "That's why I am here in the office now. I'm working over my notes—getting them ready for you."

"Okay—see you in the morning."

He hung up and Vonnie slammed the phone down.

There was one thing she'd certainly learned during her short tenure. Her erratic boss would be the easiest man in the world to hate! Not a single word of commendation for a job well done. Only the implication that she had to be watched carefully and telephoned at all hours to remind her of her duties.

And now she was angrier than ever because she found herself close to tears.

That brought her up sharply. Was she going to let emotionalism drive her away from what promised to be a very interesting job? Also, a well-paying job? After all, a good secretary did not demand her own standards from her boss. A good secretary's worth was measured in her ability to cope; to take an employer as he was and learn to live with him.

Live with him! That brought the realization that she hadn't the least idea where he did live; which made her mind click to the point of consulting the telephone book. And there he was: Keith W. Elwood, Consulting Engineer—with two addresses; the one where Vonnie was slaving her heart out and another on East Seventy-third Street where he was probably rolling in luxury while she burned the midnight oil for him!

Vonnie slammed the phone book back on its stand and the racket helped bring her back on an even keel. She stared at it, smiled, and then laughed . . .

She took a bus home, resolutely forgetting all about Keith Elwood and turning her mind to her own affairs. The way things had worked out, she was going home to a completely furnished apartment, having purchased the furnishings, lock, stock, and barrel, from Miss Prentice. The transfer had practically wiped out her savings but she could use ninety percent of what she'd bought and she'd been saved the frustrations of shopping for furniture, drapes, and all the rest of it.

Also, her somewhat rash act had been symbolical. She had a stake in New York City now. She had a lease and an apartment and all that went with it. Thus she had cut herself off completely from running back to Aunt Madge the first time she suffered an emotional upset.

I'm here to stay, she told herself grimly as she made a salad and scrambled two eggs.

It wasn't until she finished her dinner that her thoughts went back to Keith Elwood. Fed and rested now, she could view him with less hostility. Poor dear! Something traumatic was bothering him, and a man with a load on his back was entitled to consideration. Whatever was bothering him would straighten out later and things would be better.

With that thought in mind, Vonnie showered, washed her pantyhose, and went to bed with a paperback novel—*Murder on the Subway*—left behind by the London-bound Miss Prentice.

It quickly put her to sleep.

And she slept well the whole night, except for a peculiar dream which came during the early morning hours.

She was waiting at the curb on Fifth Avenue for a carriage she knew would come . . . for the man who would be riding in it was John Hazard. He was exactly as she knew he would be, huge, dour-faced, a raven-black beard and bold eyes with no friendliness in them. She got into the carriage and then—the way it can be in dreams—they were at their destination: a vast room lit only by a single flame in the center of a design on the floor. The design marked the twelve houses of the Zodiac and a tall, striking black woman Vonnie knew to be Rachel, John Hazard's "woman of color," waited there beside the flame.

The woman extended her hand and Vonnie took it. "Come and see," the woman said and Vonnie looked at the sign of Leo the Lion and the symbol of the sign, a great beast, came alive and roared and stalked off into the gloom.

"See," Rachel repeated and pointed to the sign of Taurus, whereupon a bull materialized from the symbol on the floor, pawed at the circle, and backed away.

"What does it mean?" asked Vonnie.

"You were born in Leo . . . you will die in Taurus."

The fire flared brightly, awakening Vonnie from sleep. She opened her eyes and found herself staring into the street lamp outside her window.

What a ridiculous dream, she thought. All that ancient history in the library had had its effect. How odd that she actually *was* born in Leo. August the eighteenth. This occurred to her as she drifted back to sleep . . .

Vonnie was at her desk by 8:55 the next morning. Somewhat grimly, she awaited nine o'clock. It arrived and passed and the outer door did not open.

At a quarter after, the knob rattled and Vonnie put a cold look upon her face. Keith was going to be reminded of her punctuality and his own tardiness; this even though it was a boss's hereditary right to arrive when he pleased.

The door opened and a little blond head was poked inside. There was a pert little face under the mop of hair and a question was asked in a broad Brooklyn accent:

"Are you the new girl here?"

"Why, yes. Won't you come in?"

"Thanks. I brought you some coffee."

"Why, that's sweet of you!"

"I'm Beverly Kowalski from down the hall. I been on vacation for two weeks, and did I have a time!"

Appearing to be totally familiar with the office, Beverly pulled a chair up to Vonnie's desk and took coffee cartons out of a brown paper bag. She smiled warmly at Vonnie, obviously ready to become an instant old friend.

"I went to Miami with a girl friend and is it a place! You ever been there?"

"No, I'm afraid not."

"You ought to go. You really ought. Men? They're crawling all over the place!"

"I'll have to go sometime."

"You'll just love it. Do you take sugar, dear?"

"No, just black, thank you."

"I didn't get your name."

"I'm Vanessa March. But I've been Vonnie since I was a little girl."

"It's a nice name. Like the English movie actress. You're taking Sarah's place for good?"

"I hope to."

"I'm glad. Mr. Elwood had a couple of temporaries in but they were awful. That poor man! I wanted to come in and help but Mr. Frazier—that's my boss down the hall—he said no. Not that Mr. Frazier's an old bear or anything like that. He just said I'd mess things up even more—not knowing Mr. Elwood's system. That poor man! And poor Sarah!"

"I really know very little about her," Vonnie said. "I've only been here two weeks and we've been very busy."

Beverly leaned close, darting her eyes in two directions as though she were imparting top secret information.

"She died, you know."

"I was aware of that . . ."

"The poor girl! Well, not a girl exactly. She was over thirty, I think. And toward the end she looked older. And that poor man! He just put up with everything."

"What was the cause of her death?"

33

"You didn't hear?" Again there was the conspiratorial gesture. "Drugs. She took an overdose. They called it too many sleeping tablets by mistake, but I don't think so. Mr. Elwood found her here one morning out cold. She was in a coma. He rushed her to a hospital but she never came out of it."

Much was explained but many new questions were presented. Vonnie was shamefully eager for more information but could not bring herself to make direct queries to her new-found bosom friend.

"Mr. Elwood must have thought a great deal of her."

"You mean were they having an affair?" Beverly considered this wisely for a few seconds, then shook her blond wig in the negative. "I don't think so. Sarah wasn't that kind of a girl. I mean, well, she wasn't sexy if you know what I mean. She was very intellectual. She always had weird books with her and she wore her hair straight back in a bun. You got beautiful hair. Is it your own?"

Vonnie unconsciously raised a hand to her deeply bronzed head. "Thank you. It's mine but I don't take very good care of it. It's darkened a great deal in the last couple of years."

Beverly was a born sensualist, eternally conscious of her body and the bodies of others. Her nervous hands kept going from her breasts and sides to her thighs where she smoothed her skimpy miniskirt and allowed her fingers to caress the smooth nylon of her pantyhose.

Evidently feeling that an apology was due, she said, "I don't wear purple pantyhose to work as a rule. Mr.

Frazier doesn't like wild colors. But I had runs in everything else this morning."

"They're very attractive," Vonnie said.

"Dave likes them—he's my boy friend—but not in Miami. I mean he told me no sexy clothes in Miami, not even miniskirts. Can you imagine? What did he want me to wear—flour sacks?"

"I think I can understand his point of view."

"Uh-huh. Jealous." Beverly sighed. "I guess we'll get married when he gets out of school. But Miami sure was groovy."

"Maybe you can go there for your honeymoon."

"I don't think so." Beverly considered the problem and then added cryptically. "A different part of town, maybe." Then she bounced up off her chair. "I've got to get back. Mr. Frazier's due and he doesn't like the office empty when he comes in."

"It was sweet of you to bring me coffee."

"Don't mention it. If you're going to be here permanent maybe we can take turns."

"I'm sure we can."

At the door, Beverly turned back for a moment. "You ought to ask Mr. Elwood about Sarah. She was a way-out character . . ."

After the door closed, Vonnie thought about that. Ask Mr. Elwood? She sincerely wished that she'd been blessed with that sort of a personality; an openmindedness akin to Beverly's. A week in any office and Beverly would no doubt know every detail of her employer's life, private and otherwise. Vonnie was sure that her own inability to thus communicate was misinterpreted as snobbishness.

Perhaps I should take a course in how to go about satisfying my curiosity, she thought. They teach everything else in a big city. I'm sure I could find a class.

Then Keith turned the knob and swept into the office, bringing his erratic, electric aura with him. And, of course, by that time, all of Vonnie's plans relative to the cold greeting and the stern mien had melted. She was her usual calm, beautiful self, her usual smile in place.

" 'Morning, Vonnie. This is going to be a busy one. Let's hope it turns out all right."

"One-thirty, I believe you said."

"Right. In the meantime, you can take a few letters . . ."

Thus had passed the morning of the day Keith got the Hazard House contract. The day Hazard House and all it would mean to Vonnie was officially introduced into her life . . .

CHAPTER THREE

"Have you got a car?"

"No, I haven't."

"We'll use mine then. I'll rent you one when we get up there."

"You're taking me with you?"

Keith glanced at Vonnie sharply. "Of course. You told me you didn't object to traveling."

"Oh, I don't. But I supposed you'd want me to stay here and mind the office."

"The answering service will do that. We just check with them once a day."

"When do we leave?"

"Tomorrow morning." Keith puzzled for a few moments over the details. "Can you drive?"

"Oh, yes."

"Then you can pick up my car tomorrow morning. I keep it in the Radio City Garage. Show up at my place about ten."

It was more amusing than frustrating that while he'd never mentioned a word about where he lived, he obviously expected her to know.

"You'd better make reservations up there. It's a small town but you can never tell about accommodations."

Vonnie had learned enough about Keith Elwood and his ways to know that questions irritated him. Her job was to obey directives without a lot of conversation; to carry them out correctly even though she had only instinct to go on.

In this case, she had a little more. Keith had mentioned Big Moose Lake and Burton's Forge. Big Moose Lake was listed in the books she'd researched but not Burton's Forge.

Also, the historians had noted a settlement called Lamphere in the vicinity, and a trading post named Narragansett Bluffs. But she sensed these were long vanished, at least under those names, since the French and Indian War of pre-Revolutionary days.

On an atlas she found that Lamphere did still exist —a small circle on the map denoting a town. But it was much farther from Big Moose Lake than Burton's Forge, marked by a heavier circle. But then there was Big Moose Lake, a town on the shores of a blue spot on the map marking the lake itself.

The name Hazard House, or even Hazard, was conspicuous by its absence.

She checked the phone book, found the New York State Tourist Bureau and was about to ring them when she suddenly remembered the American Express directory of restaurants and hotels in Upper

New York. It was on Keith's desk and it yielded a name—Big Moose Lake Lodge. As good a place as any to start, so Vonnie dialed the number.

A man answered. Vonnie said, "I want to arrange accommodations as close to a place called Hazard House as possible."

The man was confused. "Lady, this is Big Moose Lake Lodge. I don't know of any motel by that name."

"It isn't a motel; it's a very old house—a mansion somewhere in your neighborhood."

"Wait a minute. I only came to work here last week. I'll ask somebody."

There were long, silent moments of delay after which a female voice came on the wire.

"You were inquiring about Hazard House?"

"Yes."

"But it isn't open. It isn't even a hotel."

"I know that. What I'm trying to do is reserve accommodations as close to Hazard House as possible."

The woman's knowledge was as vague as the man's who had just come to work there. Vonnie had stirred some interest however, because the woman spoke to someone else near the phone.

"She's asking about Hazard House."

"What for?" the off-stage voice demanded.

"How do I know?"

"Ask her. Maybe somebody gave her a bum steer."

"All right—madam, were you planning to stay at Hazard House?"

"No. I understand that it's a very old mansion which has been closed for years. Is it nearby to your lodge?"

"How far would you say, Art?" the woman asked Mr. Off-Stage.

"Ten miles, maybe. But tell her she'd have to ride a mountain goat to get there."

"It's about ten miles, miss."

"Then I'd like to make two reservations. One for Mr. Keith Elwood and one for Miss Vanessa March."

"That's two separate rooms?"

"Of course."

Vonnie couldn't tell from the woman's tone whether she approved of joint occupancy or not.

"That will be on American Express."

"When will you arrive?"

The details were completed and Vonnie was rather proud of herself for having handled the thing so efficiently. There'd be no compliments from the boss, though. Such efficiency was expected of her . . .

Vonnie was wide awake at five o'clock the next morning. "You ought to be ashamed of yourself, Vonnie March," she murmured. "You're acting like a country girl waiting for her first trip-to town. Better start acting your age."

Well, she thought in self-defense, it is exciting. And I *am* a country girl. I worked in a whistle stop called Des Moines out in Iowa and it was a lot different than New York City.

Her bag was packed, emptied, and repacked the

night before, so, with nothing to do, she tried to go back to sleep. She failed.

The time passed somehow and after forcing herself to stay in bed until seven, Vonnie arose, showered, dressed. She donned a pale blue blouse and a deeper blue midiskirt that showed her legs a sensible distance —some two inches—below her shapely knees. Then she brushed her dark, coppery hair until it glowed.

She finished and turned from the mirror, but only to pause suddenly and look back as a quick image of Beverly Kowalski's purple pantyhose flashed through her mind.

Just what that had to do with it was obscure, but Vonnie went suddenly into action. In a few minutes she was stripped to her bra and panties. Then began dressing all over again.

She pulled on a pair of skin tan pantyhose and got out one of her three miniskirts, the lavender one, after which she wriggled into a black turtleneck sweater which fit like her skin.

Now she stepped back to gauge the new image; found it to her liking. Sleek legs and thighs encased in glamorous almost-nothingness . . . the black turtleneck revealing gifts God and her parents had given her in bold detail.

Hardly Raquel Welch, she mused, but will do. And now she was ready to bet a week's salary that Keith Elwood's eyes would no longer bore through her to study the wall on the other side.

A last look before she picked up her suitcase. "If you've got it, flaunt it, darling," she advised herself, and went outside to hail a cab . . .

The service was good at the Radio City Garage; so good, from an appreciative attendant, that Vonnie was driving away while two men who'd come in ahead of her were still waiting; also, at the impressive high-rise which was Keith's place of residence where a uniformed doorman touched his cap and awaited orders.

"I'm meeting Mr. Elwood," Vonnie said.

The attendant indicated with a look that he considered Mr. Elwood a lucky man.

"He's on the twenty-first floor, miss. Go right on up. I'll take care of the car."

Whisked higher in the sky than she'd ever been in Iowa, Vonnie pressed a button beside Keith's door. In a short while the door opened and Keith appeared. For a moment, he seemed to be wondering who she was and what she was doing there.

"Am I early?" Vonnie asked.

His eyes cleared. "Oh, no. Right on time. Come on in a minute. I'll be right with you."

He rushed away to let her enter by herself. Vonnie walked in slowly. It was a beautiful apartment. The foyer was papered in red with thick, red wall-to-wall carpeting underfoot. Half of one wall was mirrored, the rest was hung with richly framed French prints.

The living room into which Vonnie turned was sunken—down three steps—then up again to a kind of curved indoor terrace which gave a breath-taking view of the East River and what lay beyond.

Some might have considered the place too showy; even garish; a movie set rather than a home. To Vonnie it was plain fantastic. She had no time to form a more considered opinion before Keith rushed in from somewhere. Vonnie was posed on the terrace and as she turned, Keith stopped and stood rubbing his chin.

His gaze was squarely upon her. But she then realized he was looking through her: out the window, over the East River and at whatever lay beyond.

"Guess we're ready," he said. "Let's go."

He picked up the suitcase waiting in the hall and as she followed him out toward the elevator bank he called back, "Slam the door. It'll lock."

The attendant was waiting in the lobby to snatch Keith's suitcase and rush it into the trunk. Keith got in behind the wheel and if the attendant hadn't hurried around to open the door for her, Vonnie would have been left to climb into the car by herself.

As Keith pulled away and crossed Fifth Avenue to enter a winding road through Central Park toward the West Side Highway, Vonnie stared grimly through the windshield and held one thought firmly in mind. She was getting two hundred dollars a week for an interesting job . . . was not required to punch a time clock . . . didn't have a gimlet-eyed boss looking over her shoulder from nine to five . . . there were no scheming underlings trying to intrigue their way into her position.

So what was wrong?

Nothing.

Nothing but outraged vanity.

So cool it, she told herself, and have done with these childish frustrations.

Vonnie patted her hair into place and said, "It's a nice morning."

"Uh-huh. Where are we going?"

"Why—why to Hazard House. I thought—"

"Are we going to live there?"

"Oh. The reservations. I made them at a place called Big Moose Lake Lodge. It's about ten miles from Hazard House."

"You couldn't find anything closer?"

"I don't think there is any place closer. The woman I talked to said I'd have to ride a mountain goat to get to Hazard House from the lodge."

"Wild country, eh?"

"I assume so."

They lapsed into silence. When it became unbearable, Vonnie said, "A girl from down the hall dropped in on me yesterday morning. She works for a man named Frazier."

"He's a patent lawyer."

"Her name is Beverly. She's a nice little thing. Friendly."

"I think I've seen her around."

"She told me your last secretary, Sarah, died. I'm sorry."

He was a long time in answering; so long that Vonnie thought there would be no reply. Then he said, "That's right. An accident. Sleeping tablets."

Before Vonnie could comment on that, Keith swerved the car into a filling station. They were on Saw Mill River Parkway now and while the attendant stood waiting for the tank to fill, Keith said, "Have you got an upstate map?"

The attendant brought it and Keith handed it to

Vonnie. "Plot a course north from Lake Carmel," he said.

Vonnie began studying the map and by the time they were a mile from the gas station, she said, "We should get onto the New York Thruway."

"Okay, we'll go through Stormville to Taconic and pick up the Thruway from there."

Obviously, Lake Carmel was going to be a stop-over point. Vonnie wondered why, but would allow her nails to be pulled out with red-hot pincers before asking.

They drove straight through Carmel, a quiet, clean little town and on out to the lake beyond, where Keith pulled abruptly into a narrow blacktop road, obviously private, and stopped in front of a beautiful old mansion in the center of several acres of neatly barbered lawn.

"I'll be right out," he said, and hurried toward the front door. It opened and he vanished inside.

Vonnie, seeing no reason why she shouldn't stretch her legs, got out of the car and drew in a lungful breath. It was wonderful—the first place which reminded her of Iowa. The grass had been recently mowed and the smell, like no other in existence, put her back into Wilton's town square where Cecil Wentworth rode his battered old mower across the common and produced that same, heady aroma.

Kentucky blue, Vonnie thought. She was a girl who knew her grass and was surprised that they would use that particular variety here in the more vigorous climate.

She had been looking at the blazing-white, newly

painted mansion for some sign of identification and found none. Then, as the door opened and Keith hurried forth, she spied the neat little sign by the porch. Hardly larger than a shoe scraper, its neat gold letters read: *Morton Rest Home*.

They departed as they'd come, drove on through Lake Carmel on Route 22 and got onto Taconic Parkway where they boomed on north.

It was Vonnie, as usual, who broke the silence. "I assembled the data I got on Hazard House at the library. The place dates back over one hundred years to pre-Civil War days. John Hazard was a Southerner who came north."

"Did you get much on the house itself?"

"It appears to have been built by a crazy, mixed-up architect. All kinds of styles worked in. It should certainly be big enough for a ski lodge."

"There's lots more to it than that."

"Such as ski runs?"

"And access."

"From what I learned, that could be difficult."

"The attitude of the local people is important, too."

"I'd think they'd welcome the development. It would bring business."

"Mostly. But these days a small group can raise hob. They organize and make a big row and find a judge who'll give them an injunction."

"Let's hope the people of the area will welcome progress."

"Are you getting hungry?"

"No, not particularly."

"We can stop if you want to."

"I think we should get there as soon as possible."

Vonnie felt gratified. It was the first time since she'd known him that Keith had shown the faintest interest in her needs or desires.

But there was more to come. After another period of silence, he glanced across at her and said, "I've been meaning to tell you. You've done a pretty good job."

Not giving herself time to be overwhelmed, Vonnie replied, "Thank you. I've made a special effort because you were more than fair."

"What do you mean by that?"

"The way you hired me. A few questions. You didn't ask for references. You took me on practically as a stranger."

"I needed help."

"I can believe that. From the shape the office was in, you must have been desperate."

"Sarah was with me for five years. It was only the last six months that she—well, went bad."

"From what I've been able to gather, you were very considerate."

"It was partly my fault. I should have seen what was going on."

Vonnie contrived to look as interested as possible, hoping Keith would expand on that. Instead, he kept his eyes glued on the road ahead and lapsed into silence.

Vonnie pondered the ordeal he must have gone through, recalling the question he'd so abruptly asked her during that interview: *You aren't on drugs, are you?*

She now saw the question as less personal; a sort of

protest, cried out by Keith against his own involvement with tragedy.

All her resentments died at that moment. She would have been petty indeed to have retained them in the face of this new knowledge.

"Where did you say that exit is?" he asked.

"It's called Kattagat. According to the map, it's about twenty more miles. Then we take Salt Lick Road around the lake and right into the town."

He received the information in silence. A few more miles unwound behind them.

"You know, I'm married," he said.

"No, I didn't."

"I should have told you."

"There was no reason why. I mean—" Vonnie wasn't quite sure what she meant. With a small, uncertain laugh, she added, "You were interviewing me when I came for the job. Not the other way around."

"Okay," Keith said. He straightened his shoulders as though she'd helped him somehow, then reached over and gave her a comradely, open-handed slap high on her thigh. "We'll get along fine."

Vonnie blinked and choked off a cry of protest. She looked down at herself and saw a red expanse under the thin nylon about the size of Keith's palm.

Hoping for at least a little warning of such effusion in the future, she pointed to the overhead sign coming up, and said, "That's our exit."

"So it is."

As they threaded into Salt Lick Road, Vonnie pondered the comparative wealth of information Keith had poured out during the ride.

So he was married. Nothing startling about that. A personable, wealthy young man of his caliber certainly would be. And for all her immaturity as she chose to call it, she had certainly not nurtured the shop girl's dream of marrying the boss. Her resentment had been for other reasons; for being so systematically ignored. A girl didn't have to be lovelorn to expect reasonable treatment as a human being.

It now occurred to her that she had not met Mrs. Elwood that morning in Keith's apartment. But, more than that, she had sensed Keith as having been alone there; not only that morning but during the whole time of their association. There had been no calls home from the office; no calls to the office from a Mrs. Elwood; no word from Keith when he left during the day as to where he would be if she called.

Vonnie automatically associated that with the morning's stop at the rest home in Lake Carmel. It was not too wild a supposition to place Mrs. Elwood in that white mansion and shape a dozen new questions. Perhaps . . .

"That must be it," Keith said as they rounded a turn in the narrow road, saw an expanse of blue water ahead, and a low, rambling log structure flanking the shore . . .

Vonnie took in the sylvan picture with some relief. On the basis of her difficulty in locating it, she'd envisioned an isolated establishment where she and Keith would be the only guests, ogled and whispered about by scandal-hungry rustics.

This was not the case. A sizable neon sign over the

archway leading into the parking lot proclaimed the lodge in bright red letters. There were two dozen cars parked in the lot. Guests lounged on a shoreside terrace and several boats dotted the lake. And aside from appreciative looks from a uniformed bellhop, nobody paid any attention to them when they entered.

The bellhop extended his hand. "If you'll give me your keys, sir, I'll get your bags."

A middle-aged, efficient-looking woman presided at the desk. Keith gave his name and she thumbed through some cards. Then she glanced up as though recognizing Vonnie.

"Oh, yes. You're the young lady who called to ask about Hazard House. I'm Miss Stone. I talked to you."

Vonnie nodded. "Yes. I made two reservations."

Diplomatically turning her attention to Keith, she said, "I have two on the forest side, third floor with adjoining bath, sir."

He shook his head. "We'd like two baths."

"If you'll just register, sir." She handed Keith the pen. "Then I'll give you two on the lake side. Second level. I'm sure you'll be very comfortable."

Vonnie waited, hoping against hope that Keith would not be absent-minded and sign Mr. & Mrs. Elwood. He didn't. He wrote his own name in bold strokes and then handed Vonnie the pen. It was with marked satisfaction that she wrote her own name, well aware that the efficient Miss Stone was watching every move.

But even if Keith had blundered, Vonnie felt that Miss Stone would have been neither surprised nor shocked. Big Moose Lake Lodge, while no doubt thoroughly respectable, looked like a place where sophistication was the key; where the management did not pry into personal affairs.

The bellman arrived with the two bags and Miss Stone handed him two keys. He led them up purposely crude stairs into a timbered corridor with thick wall-to-wall carpeting where he unlocked a room, put Keith's bag inside, and then went on to the next door. Either by design or mere chance, Miss Stone had put them side by side.

Keith turned off into his own room and Vonnie followed the bellhop on into hers.

Once inside, he brightened immeasurably, favoring Vonnie with the gleam of his white teeth and the glow of his personality. He was about her age, in his mid-twenties, and wore his young virility and youthful confidence like banners. And with true feminine perversity, Vonnie—who had deliberately dressed to make herself attractive—now resented his admiration.

He drew the drapes, fussed with the combination radiator and air conditioner, and turned on his most intimate smile.

"Anything more I can do, miss?"

"Nothing," Vonnie said sharply, and held the door pointedly as he brushed by her into the corridor.

She opened her suitcase, then closed it again and went out onto the terrace. The view was lovely. She had never seen such a clear-blue lake. Several motorboats rocketed over its surface. It seemed to Vonnie that all this augured success for the ski lodge. The area had already been opened up to tourists and vacationers.

Then she noticed something of interest. Balconies protruded from the whole lakeside wall of the lodge. The majority serviced single rooms while a few were for double occupancy. One of these double balconies serviced both her room and Keith's.

Vonnie did not know whether to be amused or annoyed. One thing was certain: Miss Stone as a matchmaker was not easily discouraged.

A knock on the outer door brought Vonnie from the balcony. She opened the door and found a child of perhaps ten waiting there; a lovely little creature with long, golden hair and the most expressive blue eyes Vonnie had ever seen. The girl was simply dressed in a plain gray shift. She wore no stockings and was barefoot.

"Would you like to buy some flowers, Miss March?"

The child extended the bouquet of small, blood-red roses she was carrying; the same variety, no doubt, that Vonnie had seen bordering the road into the lodge.

"Why, yes. I'd love to," Vonnie said. "Won't you come in?"

The little girl entered. Vonnie closed the door and asked, "How much are you charging?"

"Only ten cents."

"Why, I think they should be worth more than that. Wait 'til I get my bag." The child remained where she was, not moving a muscle until Vonnie returned.

"How about fifty cents? They're lovely roses."

"Thank you."

"My name is Vonnie, dear. What's yours?"

"Abigail."

"What a nice name. Do you live near the lodge?"

"At Burton's Forge."

There was an empty vase on a corner table in the room and Vonnie went to the bathroom to fill it with water.

"Do you know of a place named Hazard House?" she called.

Abigail did not answer until Vonnie had returned and placed the roses on the table.

"It's over near Satan's Grove, beyond the grave-yard."

"I'm planning to visit Hazard House. Is it difficult to find?"

"That depends on which way you go."

"Perhaps you could show me the easy way?"

"I can show you."

The child puzzled Vonnie. It seemed that she should have been tanned from the summer sun—hardier-looking, as befit children with the opportunity for outdoor living. But Abigail's complexion resembled the palest ivory. Her skin was flawless, her features classical in their perfection. Also, she had a deeply serious mien out of place in one so young.

"I'd appreciate that very much."

"Tomorrow?"

"Perhaps. Where can I get in touch with you?"

"I'll be around."

It was so very odd. Each time, before replying to

Vonnie or answering a question, the child waited, her head slightly tilted as though listening; as though some unseen person were telling her what to say.

"When I answered the door," Vonnie said, "you called me Miss March. How did you know my name?"

"Patience told me."

"Patience?"

"I've got to go now. Goodbye."

With that, the child opened the door and went swiftly out.

Immediately, Vonnie saw the two quarters lying on the table. She picked them up and ran to the door. "You've forgotten your money," she called.

When she opened the door, the corridor was empty. Vonnie frowned in both directions. The lobby was forward of the room but there was a back stairway leading onto a terrace along the service road to the kitchen.

Vonnie went to the rear and looked down. Though the way was visible clear to Salt Lick Road, there was no one in sight.

Turning in the other direction, Vonnie went down the front stairs until she could see the whole of the lobby. Miss Stone was still at the desk. She looked up alertly.

"Was there something, Miss March?"

"A little girl. Did she just come down?"

"No. No one has come down in the last five minutes."

"This little girl knocked on my door and sold me some roses."

That obviously annoyed Miss Stone. "*Sold* you flowers? Why, that's ridiculous. We have flowers everywhere."

"Well, she didn't sell them actually. She left the money I paid her on the table. That's why I'm trying to find her."

"I'm glad you reported it, Miss March. We don't allow our guests to be annoyed that way."

"It was no annoyance, really."

"She must have run out the back way."

"Thank you," Vonnie said and turned to retrace her steps. Then she turned back. "By the way, is your first name Patience?"

"No. It's Lucinda." Miss Stone paused to glance about, her usually firm mouth twisted into a half-grin. "Don't tell anybody, though. I like Lucy a lot better, although that's not any great shakes of a name either."

"I'll keep your secret. Do you know anyone named Patience?"

"No, I think not. It's a quite old-fashioned name. I don't think it's used much anymore—except perhaps over around Burton's Forge."

"That's where the little girl said she lived."

"Those little scalawags! I hope they're not going to start getting in our way."

The bellhop opened the front door at that moment, leading two new guests in, and Lucinda Stone turned to business.

Vonnie went slowly back to her room. It had been so strange. That ethereal-looking child appearing seemingly from nowhere and vanishing the same way. Had she actually forgotten the fifty cents, or had she

56

returned it? It had been clutched in her slim little hand so she'd had to deliberately put it on the table.

Vonnie closed her door and crossed the room to return the two coins to her purse. Then she turned and looked at the roses and stood frozen . . . staring.

The flowers had wilted.

Wilted, yes, but that was hardly the word to describe what had happened to them. Vonnie approached the table almost fearfully. She reached down and touched one of the petals, now faded to a dull brown. It shattered under her finger.

Without knowing why, Vonnie drew back, clutching her finger as though she'd burned it. A breeze from the patio touched her back. Like a cold finger. She whirled about in time to hear laughter and see that there was no one else in the room. She ran to the balcony and looked out. It was empty.

At that moment, there was a knock on her door. She crossed over and opened it, half expecting to find the corridor empty also.

Keith stood waiting. He wore trunks and a robe and his feet were encased in bath slippers.

"Hi. Thought you might like to take a swim and lounge in the sun before dinner. It's too late to do much of anything else today."

Vonnie stepped back and held the door open.

"Come on in."

As he did so, Keith eyed her curiously. "Something wrong?"

"Do I look as though something were wrong?"

"Pale, I'd say. A little upset."

Vonnie pointed. "Those flowers . . ."

57

Keith crossed over and looked carefully as though he didn't want to make any mistakes.

"They're dead."

"Yes."

"Ring for the bellhop. Tell him you want fresh ones. Those must have been here for a month."

"They've been here no more than fifteen minutes."

Keith's frown demanded further explanation.

"A little girl came to the door and sold them to me."

"And you *bought* them?"

"They were fresh then."

Keith studied the flowers closely. "Couldn't have been. They must have been at least wilted. Ready to go. You just didn't notice."

"Were you on the balcony a few minutes ago?"

"No," Keith replied. "I haven't been out there at all. Why?"

"I thought I heard someone."

"You're not supposed to get nervous until after dark . . . when there's a storm and howling wind. How about that swim?"

There was such a change in Keith—his becoming aware of her as a person this way—that she hated to disappoint him.

"I'm sorry, but I didn't anticipate any time for recreation on this job. So I didn't bring a suit."

"Maybe there won't be much. But we can get a little sun and have a drink or two."

"I'd like that. And I do have some shorts."

"Okay," Keith said, and strolled out onto the balcony.

Vonnie opened her bag. She was lucky to have even the shorts with her—a pair of red hotpants and sunglasses she'd seen in a Madison Avenue window on the way home one night. She'd included them in her packing through the same impulse which had put her into the miniskirt when leaving her apartment.

She changed quickly in the bathroom, donned a loose-fitting white blouse, and presented herself on the balcony.

Keith's expression showed a definite change in mood. Obvious appreciation. But his voiced compliment was meager. "Nice," he said. "How about those lawn chairs down there? Or would you rather be in the shade?"

"I could use some sun," Vonnie replied.

They went down and found two chairs and Keith motioned to a white-coated attendant who presided at a nearby portable bar.

"What will you have?" he asked as the youth approached.

"I think I'd like a whiskey sour," Vonnie said. She'd almost asked for her usual dry sherry, but decided to live it up a little. With a smile she recalled Aunt Madge during their discussion of alcohol in general.

"I guess one drink of hard liquor never hurt a girl—but just one," Aunt Madge had counseled.

With the drinks on a small lawn table between them, Vonnie stretched out her arms. "This place is just too beautiful for words," she exclaimed. "It's hardly conducive to work. We should have signed in at a New England boarding house with windows looking out on a blank wall."

59

"You ought to have time for a little fun," Keith replied.

"With whom? I don't know a soul around here."

"People do get acquainted."

Vonnie glanced over quickly. Was he warning her off: telling her not to expect any social breaks with him? This angered her. If it was a warning, why did he feel that she needed one?

"I'll have plenty of time for social activities when I get back to the city," she said, trying to keep sharpness out of her voice. "I'm here to do a job—whatever is expected of me—and I'll give it my whole attention."

Vonnie had taken her dark glasses off for a better look at him. Now she put them back on and stared off across the lake.

Keith peered out at the sun through his own shades. He pulled at his ear thoughtfully and said, "I seem to rub everybody the wrong way lately."

Vonnie's reply was on the tip of her tongue. Then she held it back, realizing this was a time to choose her words carefully.

"You do seem to have something on your mind," she said slowly. When he didn't answer, she went on: "Of course I understand. Your last secretary's death must have been tragic."

"Did that little blonde down the hall tell you about it?"

"She mentioned it, but in a most sympathetic way. I think I mentioned it to you on the way out."

"So you did. She told you it wasn't just sleeping tablets?"

"That meant nothing. She wouldn't have been in a position to know."

"On the contrary. She got to know Sarah pretty well. It was sleeping tablets that finished her. But not an accident. She took them deliberately."

"She must have been greatly troubled."

"She had a—well, she had a problem. I didn't realize it. I just brushed it off. I should have taken it more seriously and tried to help her."

She was in love with you, Vonnie said silently. She was in love with you and knew it was hopeless and probably never told you.

"It's over now. You can't go on feeling guilty."

"I feel guilty, but that's not all of it. I just have bad luck with women."

He was still squinting at the sun, his drink untouched. Vonnie's "Oh?" sounded a little ridiculous in her own ears; as though she'd asked what else was new.

"I told you I was married."

"Yes."

"That place we stopped off at. They're taking care of Valerie there."

Vonnie found scant satisfaction in learning that her surmise had been correct.

"I'm sorry," she said.

"We had a child three years ago. A son. He died. Valerie was never right after that."

"How tragic!"

He jerked his glasses off, reached for his drink, and downed half of it at one gulp.

"It looks as though you'll be around awhile," he said, "so I figured I'd better tell you."

"I appreciate your confidence."

"Another reason—you may be working alone up here off and on. I'll be running down there at times."

"I understand."

Vonnie wanted to say more. With all her petty resentments forgotten, she wanted to tell him what a good person he was; even to voice the hope that the next girl he got involved with would be an asset rather than a burden. But of course she held her peace.

Then, feeling that perhaps the subject should be changed: "That little girl who came to my door. I keep thinking about her."

"A real little con artist—selling dead flowers."

Vonnie wished he hadn't mentioned that. The shock of those dead blossoms had gone deep. And because she had no explanation, she didn't even want to think about them.

"She lives in a place called Burton's Forge. I gathered from something Miss Stone said that it isn't the best community around."

"Did you ask her about Hazard House?"

"I did. That's what I wanted to tell you. The girl may be of help to us. It seems there are two ways to get to the place. She promised to show me the easiest one."

"Good. One of your jobs will be to get around and meet people. We've got to find out what the local attitudes are. Troublesome minorities could bug us plenty if we rub them the wrong way."

"Have you formed any ideas yet about the feasibility of the project?"

"Haven't tried. I'm keeping an open mind. First thing, we'll check out the town and rent a hill buggy of some kind. We'll need it in country like this. Then we'll take a look at Hazard House."

Keith finished his drink and came suddenly to his feet. "I think I'll try that lake. Hold down the fort. Order yourself another sour."

He was off, down the hill, moving in long strides as though he were either trying to get away from something or catch up with something else.

Vonnie watched him. His good points far outweighed his annoying ones, she thought. He would be an easy person to become attached to. But the girl who did latch onto him would have to have a great deal of understanding . . .

"Hello."

The voice came from over Vonnie's shoulder. She removed her glasses and twisted around.

"Abigail! Where on earth did you come from child?"

"From over there." She pointed vaguely toward Salt Lick Road.

"You left so suddenly. I tried to find you. You left your money." When the child did not reply, Vonnie said, "The flowers died."

"I know. Rachel made them die after Patience sent them."

"I don't understand."

"I don't either. That's just the way it is."

"Who is Patience?"

"She's my friend. She wants to meet you. She wants you to come to her."

"But she doesn't know me. I don't know her."

"She knows you're here."

"I'll certainly be happy to meet her. But about you —there was something Miss Stone, the room clerk said. Are you forbidden to come here?"

"I don't know. I've never been here before."

"I'll tell you what. You stay with me and it will be all right. Would you like to have dinner in the big dining room?"

"I can't stay. I have to go." Abigail pointed toward the lake. "That's the man you're with, isn't it?"

Keith was just coming out of the water, shaking his head like a spaniel.

"Yes," Vonnie said. "He's my boss. We're up here to look at Hazard House—to see if it would make a good ski lodge. What do you think, Abigail?"

Abigail did not reply. Vonnie waited. After a pause she said, "Do you think it would be a good idea?"

When there was still no answer forthcoming, she twisted around to look. Abigail was gone.

Vonnie sat up and turned completely around.

The child was nowhere in sight . . .

CHAPTER FOUR

It was the afternoon following her talk with Keith on the lawn.

"Hello," Abigail said.

Vonnie looked up from the lacy frond formation she was examining and frowned in perplexity.

"Good heavens, child! How you do keep popping up."

"Aren't you glad to see me?" Abigail asked solemnly.

"Of course I am, but you behave in such odd ways. I never know what to expect. Like just now. Where did you come from?"

"Out of the woods."

That morning they'd gone on into the town of Big Moose Lake and found it large enough for their needs. There was an auto rental agency that functioned during vacation months where they rented a serviceable looking jeep. Vonnie also bought a pair of boots and a pair of riding britches that looked as though they would take heavy going.

They got back to the lodge a little after noon, when Keith found a message waiting for him; one which called him back to the city. He'd lapsed into his uncommunicative mood and told Vonnie only that he would be back by noon the next day if not sooner. Then he took off, leaving her to herself. A hike in the woods did not seem too much out of order, so she dressed for it and here she was, a mile or so into the woods from the lodge; only now, she was no longer alone.

"It's just that you always manage to startle me, Abigail. But no matter. Were you going anywhere in particular?"

"I came for you."

"But how on earth did you know where I'd be out here in the woods?"

"Patience told me."

"Child, is there any such person as Patience?"

"Yes."

"The lady at the lodge never heard of her."

"That doesn't mean Patience doesn't exist. Even if she's different—"

Vonnie regretted her words. "Of course it doesn't." After all, Miss Lucinda Stone had never heard of Abigail.

"You said Patience wants to meet me?"

"That's why I've come."

"Shall we go back to the lodge and get my car?"

"We won't need it."

"But they said Hazard House is ten miles from here."

"We don't have to go that far. It's this way, through the woods."

"You're sure you won't get us lost?"

"Oh, no. I never get lost."

As Vonnie followed the child through the woods, she realized her question had been stupid. A native of these hills—one who seemed to be able to appear and disappear at will—would certainly know her way around.

The going was hard, or would have been if Vonnie hadn't had Abigail for a guide. The mystifying child slipped barefooted between rocks and around brambles where Vonnie scratched her new boots and accumulated stubborn cockleburs on her jodhpurs.

Vonnie lost all track of distance and was ready to question the trip when they breasted a rise and she found herself looking down into a saucerlike hollow filled with flourishing weeds and the dried stalks of other weeds from many a summer season.

The silence was broken only by the faint hum of bees foraging amid the yellow blossoms on the tall stalks. There were grassy sections in the hollow, but wind and dust had blighted the color, dulling it into grayish shades.

But there were other things down there; things that made Vonnie gasp, "Why this is a graveyard!"

"It's where Patience is buried. That was a long time ago. A hundred years."

"But you said she existed."

"She does. Just because they killed her doesn't mean that she no longer exists."

Vonnie had difficulty finding words. "Abigail," she cried, "someone has been deceiving you cruelly—telling you things that aren't true."

"You don't understand, Miss March. Patience said you wouldn't. You see nobody knows about Patience except Grandpa and me."

"Grandpa? And what does he say about her?"

"He tells me not to talk to her. But he's talked to her himself."

"Two of a kind," Vonnie murmured helplessly. "What does Patience want of me?"

"I don't know. I think she wants you to help her."

"Tell her I'm sorry but I wouldn't know how—I wouldn't know how to begin."

"Maybe she'll tell you when she talks to you."

There can be times in a person's life when the reality of a situation is less of a shock than that same situation viewed from the oblique aspect of fantasy. Had Vonnie been able to look into the future and see what was about to happen, she would have doubted her own sanity.

But now that the moment had come, she found herself believing her senses as the last anchor to which she could cling. If they were betraying her, all was lost.

It began when Abigail changed before her eyes; not in physical form; her little-girl structure remained the same. But there was a sort of psychic distortion which aged the child. Her eyes were the same, yet they had aged, became adult, expanded in years and knowledge. The childish innocence of her face was washed away as though by tears which had long since dried.

She had become a ten-year-old adult.

"I am Patience," the new Abigail said.

Vonnie's words came without thought. They sprang from some deep source within her where hidden knowledge had remained deeply buried all the years of her life.

"This is monstrous!"

"You must help me."

"I'll help the child if I can."

"That is why I am here. To save the child."

"From whom? From what?"

"I protect her from Rachel."

"Why do you come to me?"

"I have searched for you."

"That is no answer."

"I must leave now. The child can stand it only a short time. Help me protect her from Rachel."

"What could *I* possibly do?"

There was no answer. Vonnie stood there, frozen, as the transformation she had seen in Abigail reversed itself. So slowly did she return that Vonnie could not be sure it was happening. Abigail's eyes were closed and Vonnie reached toward her.

Then she quickly drew her hands back. Some instinct warning her this was not the way.

While she waited, Vonnie sensed other manifestations, more subtle but no less believable. The graveyard with all its tumbled neglect, its rotted and tilted markers, its melancholy mien, had stopped in time.

Had frozen, as solidly as she herself had frozen during the supernatural performance.

There was a chill all about her as though the graves had opened to release their fetid threat upon the living air.

Then it was over. Abigail opened her eyes and looked about uncertainly.

"I must have fallen asleep."

"I think you did, dear. How do you feel?"

"I feel all right. But—"

"But what, darling?"

"Was Rachel here?"

"No. I don't think so."

"Then Patience?"

"Yes—Patience."

This seemed to relieve the child greatly. "I'm not afraid of Patience. But if Rachel comes, she'll take me away."

"Are you sure of that?"

"Yes, I'm sure."

"But how can you know?"

"I just—know."

There came a sound of breaking brush, footsteps. Vonnie lifted her eyes to the crest of the rise and saw a tall, bearded man looking down at her.

Vonnie opened her mouth to speak but the man lifted a quick finger to his lips and shook his head in warning. Abigail had been paying no attention. Her gaze was fixed on the wooden marker beside her.

"This is Patience's grave," she said. "See?"

With that, she traced the name and the dates worn down so long ago.

The man obviously did not come upon an unknown situation. As nearly as Vonnie could discover, he was telling her silently that Abigail's return to her normal self was a touchy thing and to be handled carefully.

He watched in silence for a short spell, then came down the slope.

Abigail heard him now, and turned.

"Grandpa."

"Yes, child. I've been looking for you."

"I'm sorry."

"It's all right. We must go home now."

"I'm sleepy, Grandpa."

"I'll carry you."

He lifted Abigail into his arms, laid her head upon his shoulder and she went quietly to sleep. Only now did the old man turn his full attention to Vonnie.

"You handled yourself very well. I'm grateful."

"Thank you. But, purely by chance. I don't understand any of this."

"I'm sure you don't. And I'm sorry you were drawn into it. But I guess it was inevitable."

"I'm sure you won't think it cruel of me when I say that I'd like to withdraw as soon as possible."

"Are you quite certain of that?"

There was the look of a patriarch about the old man. As straight as a reed on a windless day, his look of fragility was belied by the way he held Abigail effortlessly in his arms unaware of her weight.

"Yes. I am quite sure. Mainly, I think, because there is nothing I can do to help. Somehow, I've blundered into a—well, I won't say an unbelievable situation, I can't say that. Because I was here and I have faith in my own senses. I'll call it a delicate situation where I could be of no help whatever."

"I'm afraid it isn't as simple as that, Miss—"

"March. Vanessa March."

". . . Miss March. Your involvement was inevitable."

"On the contrary, it was accidental. I was walking in the woods and met Abigail . . ."

"It was not the first time."

He had young blue eyes which at first seemed incongruous in his ancient face. But after a short time there was the impression that this was right; that the face would have been wrong without them.

"No," Vonnie said. "Abigail came to my door at the lodge and sold me some roses." Vonnie shivered though the air was sultry under a storm-poised sky. "They withered instantly."

"She was not there by chance."

"She seems to come and go out of nowhere. It was almost as though she materialized—"

"Hardly."

Vonnie passed a weary hand across her brow. "I'm sorry to appear rude, but I'm really not at my best just now."

"Of course. You want to get back to the lodge and rest. I'll show you the way."

"You have Abigail to take care of. I'll have no trouble."

"You just keep going downhill from here. Eventually you'll reach Salt Lick Road."

"Thank you. I gather that you are Abigail's grandfather."

73

He nodded. "Not by blood. But I have looked after her for a long time."

"She is a very sweet child."

As he looked down at the sleeping head, Vonnie saw much in his eyes. Frustration, sadness, compassion.

"She is a star-crossed child, that's certain. Again I want to thank you. My name is Jason Leopold. I am a Hungarian Jew." He paused and now his gentle face reflected humor. "At least I was once. What I am now is a moot question."

"If I was of any help, I am glad," Vonnie said. "And now if you'll excuse me . . ."

"You are interested in Hazard House, I believe?" He waited.

"Yes," he continued, "Abigail told me. I may be of some help to you there. When you are rested I suggest you drive over to Burton's Forge. You'll find me there."

"Thank you. I shall."

"I'll expect you."

With that, he turned and moved back up the slope. Somewhere, Vonnie was sure, he'd found the secret of youth—an inner youth which allowed him to carry Abigail as though she were a feather while he moved, sure-footed, up a rocky, treacherous hill . . .

Finding her way back was not difficult. With a little practice, she decided, she might have real mountain-climbing talents. She found Salt Lick Road and began walking toward the lodge, but her mind was still back in the graveyard where a new world had been opened to her.

When I get back, she told herself, I won't believe it. I won't believe any of it because I don't want to. I don't even want to accept that old man's invitation to visit Burton's Forge, because I'm afraid of the things I might learn. Shakespeare said it, I believe: There are more things in heaven and earth than are dreamed of in our philosophies. All right. Maybe that's true. But is that enough reason to go poking around trying to find out about them? . . .

Nobody came along to give her a ride, so she walked the mile from the edge of the forest to the lodge. I'll drive to town and buy a bathing suit, she decided. A very daring bikini outfit. Then I'll swim and lounge and have a drink and perhaps meet some of the other guests. An attractive bikini certainly ought to do it unless they're all married.

Trying to lighten her mood thus, she arrived. But to find that there would be no trip to town and no bikini.

"Oh, Miss March," Lucy Stone called as Vonnie entered. "There's an urgent phone call for you. Mr. Elwood. He left a number."

Vonnie took the slip, read the number and then a curious notation: *Call privately. Collect.*

She took that to mean by public phone, not through the lodge switchboard. There was a phone booth in the lobby, so she followed instructions and called from there. A woman answered by repeating the number, thus giving no clue as to where Keith was.

He came on the wire and got immediately to the

business at hand: "There's something I'd like you to do for me. Do you feel up to a trip into the city?"

"Of course. If that's what's to be done."

"Good girl. You'd better drive that hill buggy into town and trade it for a bigger car. It would be rough, riding into New York. Then I'd like you to go to the office."

He stopped, as though debating the rest of it. Vonnie waited a while before asking, "Are you still there?"

"Yes. What I want you to do is open that locked drawer in the file cabinet."

"I don't have a key."

"Don't worry about that. Just get it open. There are some small tools in the closet on the floor. If they aren't what you need, borrow a crowbar from the super. In the drawer you'll find a green metal box. It's locked but you can leave it that way. Take the whole box with you and drive back to Big Moose Lake. I'll see you there tomorrow."

"Very well. I'll get started right away."

"Good girl," he said, then broke the connection.

Certainly a cryptic assignment, but Vonnie hardly thought of that as she went back to dress for the run to New York. It was the "good girl," warmly stated twice, that occupied her mind. Such effusions from Keith Elwood were overwhelming.

She started to think about the mysterious box in the locked file drawer only after she was in the jeep on her way to town.

Then, on her way to New York in a pretty little green sports car which seemed to have rabbits under its hood, she considered things on an overall basis. The prime objective, the sojourn into the hills and an appraisal of Hazard House, kept getting pushed aside. When, if ever, would they finally get down to it?

She had done good work, personally, but this was by chance rather than design. She'd found there was an easier way to the mansion than was generally known. And, also, she had been offered help by a native who would certainly know his way around in those perilous woods.

As to the other thing—the weird experience in the abandoned cemetery—she just refused to think about that. Perhaps she had heard the last of Patience and Rachel and the whole eerie business. At least, for want of more comforting assurance, she wanted to believe that . . .

There was no trouble at the office except that she had to park in a tow-away zone and take her chances. She went directly upstairs and without further help— a large screw driver was in the closet—she applied leverage and the drawer gave as though eager to surrender responsibility for its mysterious contents.

The green metal container was of standard lockbox size, easily handled. She tried it and found that it was indeed locked. But, she told herself firmly, she would not have opened it even if it hadn't been. Then why had she tried it? There was no answer for that either. She certainly didn't want it falling open on the trip back.

All of which reflected a mood of general excitement. All this mystery. She could only thank her stars

—or perhaps Aunt Madge's friend the guardian angel —that she had not been harnessed to a dull nine-to-five job.

As she headed out the West Side Highway, she pitied all the other secretaries who had to stay in town . . .

The return trip was uneventful. When she got back, she found that the storm which had been hovering over the cemetery had come and gone, freshening everything; making the lodge and its surroundings even more lovely.

She stopped to take the box to her room and hid it on the very top shelf of her closet where she covered it with the extra blanket a thoughtful management had provided. Then she drove on into town and got the hill buggy back.

Now all she could do was compose herself and wait until Keith arrived. There might be further revelations. She parked the jeep and went to her room, looking forward to a shower and some complete relaxation. She turned on the shower and stepped back out—to catch a sudden movement at the balcony door.

She whirled.

"Hello," Abigail said . . .

CHAPTER FIVE

"Child! Where on earth did you come from?"

"I was waiting for you."

"And, as usual, I suppose, no one saw you come in?"

Abigail's look was grave, doubtful. "You aren't glad to see me?"

"Of course I am. Did Patience send you again?"

"No. I came all by myself."

"But your grandfather took you home. Won't he be worried? It's after sundown."

"He went to Lamphere to sit with Judge Adams."

"All right. I'll tell you what. I'll take my shower and then we'll go down and have dinner. Would you like that?"

"Yes."

While Abigail's acceptance was mildly stated, the brightening of her lovely little face indicated a hunger for the people and places she so rarely saw. Thus it occurred to Vonnie that giving the child a normal, enjoyable evening would be of greater help than participating in the weird mumbo-jumbo revealed at the graveyard.

"Fine. Give me ten minutes. Would you like to look at one of those magazines? They have nice pictures."

Abigail obediently picked up a magazine and sat primly down to wait.

Vonnie showered and when she came out, wrapped in a bath towel, Abigail hadn't moved. Speaking from the dressing room off the bath, Vonnie asked, "Do you go to school, Abigail?"

"Yes. We have a school at the Forge. Miss Melany teaches us."

"How many of you children are there?"

"Thirteen. The older ones go to high school in Big Moose Lake—some of them."

"But not all?"

"The rest go to work, or maybe they leave home."

"Tell me about your mother and father."

"I only have Grandpa and Melissa."

"You don't remember your real parents?"

"No."

Vonnie thought it best not to pry further. She had a strong urge to do some questioning about Patience and Rachel but vetoed that also. The child deserved that consideration during her evening out.

"All right," Vonnie announced a few moments later. "I'm ready."

She came out into the balcony room and Abigail's eyes widened in admiration. "You're awfully pretty, Miss March."

81

"Thank you. And why don't you call me Vonnie? Everyone else does."

Not feeling particularly adventurous that evening, Vonnie had gone back to her midiskirts; a tweedy one with a yellow sweater under a utility jacket gave her a woodsy look.

Abigail's smooth brow wrinkled in worry. "Will the lady downstairs let me stay?" she asked.

"The lady downstairs certainly will," Vonnie replied firmly.

And perhaps it was the foreknowledge of Miss Stone's attitude concerning Burton's Forge children that gave her a certain belligerence as she led Abigail downstairs. And perhaps it was that belligerent look that caused Miss Stone to straighten her face into a pleasant smile after one quick frown when she saw them.

Vonnie gave her a quick good evening and led Abigail on into the dining room. It was only a third full, so there was no waiting.

An attractive miniskirted teenager who looked to be doing summer work, took them quickly to a table and had the breeding to be not the least curious about the drab little figure who walked close to Vonnie and held tightly to her hand.

But then, when they were seated, Vonnie's heart dropped into her shoes as a good-looking young man in a state trooper's uniform—one she hadn't previously noticed—got up from his corner table and moved in their direction. Could Lucy Stone possibly be so hard-hearted as to expel a helpless little girl from her dining room?

The young state trooper wore a pleasant enough smile. It was directed at Abigail.

"Well, young lady. Fancy meeting you here. You're out on the town, I take it."

"Hello, Mr. Jackson," Abigail said solemnly.

The smile he turned on Vonnie was positively brilliant. "I'm Bill Jackson," he said easily. "I apologize for barging over, but Abigail and I are old friends."

Vonnie silently apologized to Lucy Stone. The fact that she could have even suspected Lucy of being so cruel certainly attested to her own tight nerves.

"I'm Vanessa March," she said. "I'm happy to meet any friend of Abigail's. Won't you sit down?"

"You're sure I'm not intruding?"

"Not in the least."

Bill Jackson pulled up a chair, tickled Abigail's ear in a gesture which brought not the slightest sign of a smile, and said, "You're staying at the lodge?"

"Yes," Vonnie replied. "I'd invite you to have a drink but—"

"Oh, the uniform. Think nothing of it. I'm off-duty. And I will have a drink. But I'm buying."

Bill Jackson had influence. The barest lifting of his finger brought a waitress—a carbon copy of the schoolgirl hostess except that her uniform was different.

"What will you have, Miss March?" Jackson asked.

"If you insist, I guess I'll have a whiskey sour. They're very good here."

"They certainly are. Everything at the lodge is the very best. Meg, bring me a scotch and water. And maybe we can dig up a Shirley Temple for our other lady?"

"I'll see what I can do," Meg dimpled, and was off.

"Here for a vacation?" Jackson asked.

"Well, no—not exactly. But it's certainly an enjoyable place."

He brushed a lock of Abigail's straight golden hair back and now asked the question foremost in his mind. "And how did you two get to know each other?"

An odd mood descended upon Vonnie. Perhaps Bill Jackson's engaging manner had something to do with it; that coupled with a release from tensions she'd been under. At any rate, it was a puckish mood.

"Why, didn't you know, Mr. Jackson? I'm an old Burton's Forge native."

"You're kidding."

"Oh, yes. I grew up there and then went out into the world . . ."

He shrugged ruefully. "Ask an impertinent question and a guy gets the answer he deserves."

Vonnie laughed. "I'm sorry. What really happened was that Abigail turned up at my door with some flowers and we've been friends ever since."

"She's hard to resist," he replied. "And I'm not Mr. Jackson. Ask for me that way around here and you'd get blank stares. I'm Bill—sometimes Jackson—usually not."

"I'm not Vanessa either. I'm Vonnie."

"Well, I'm glad that's settled. You say this isn't exactly a vacation for you?"

Vonnie recoiled at the question. The acquaintanceship was a trifle short for such inquiries, even though Bill Jackson's manner took all the sting out of it. But then, she thought, why not? She'd been instructed to sound out the natives. Now she was being given an opportunity.

"I'm up here with my boss to make an evaluation on opening a ski resort."

"Oh? And where would it be located?"

"We're going to check on Hazard House. We hope it can be transformed into a ski lodge."

The waitress had come back and was handing out menus now. As Vonnie opened hers, Bill Jackson spread his so as to share it with Abigail. He seemed to have taken over the child's supervision completely, but still Vonnie did not feel superseded. He obviously had a warm interest in Abigail.

"What would you like, toots?" he asked. Then to Vonnie. "Incidentally, this is on me."

"Oh, no! I insist—"

"But it would be a waste of money if you bought. On me, it's all free. Local graft." With that he turned back to Abigail before Vonnie could again object. Abigail had been staring fascinated at the bright colors of her Shirley Temple. Bill hooked the maraschino cherry out of the glass and popped it into her mouth.

"I think it ought to be roast beef for you, honey. Get some meat on your bones."

Bill Jackson seemed to have a mind that could work in two directions at once. The orders were given and he rambled on with Abigail and then said in almost the same breath, "It's a novel idea."

"What idea?" Vonnie asked.

"A ski lodge up there. There are slopes for two ideal runs, but—well, I don't know."

"Do you see difficulties?"

"The access could work out all right. It would take a load of money. But the house itself . . ."

"Do you think it isn't large enough?"

"It's not that. I'm surprised that it's for sale."

It suddenly occurred to Vonnie that she had not been briefed in that area. Did Enterprise Associates own the house? It hardly seemed likely that they would spend fifty thousand dollars for a survey if they had doubts about being able to take possession.

"Have you looked at the place yet?"

"No, we haven't. We've been here a very short while and my employer was called away."

"Then you've seen nothing of the country."

"I took a walk in the woods."

It was Vonnie's impression that she'd seen more of it than many old residents, but she didn't go into that.

"I've got to take this one home," Bill Jackson said. "How would you like to make a quick visit back to your old plantation?"

"Do you mean Burton's Forge?"

"Uh-huh." Bill Jackson grinned engagingly and got an answering smile.

"I haven't seen the old folks for a long time."

"Okay, if you don't mind being seen riding in a police car."

"I'll carry a sign reading, 'I'm Innocent!' That should quiet the gossips . . ."

It was dusk when they started, Abigail wedged warmly between them in the front seat. Heavy shadows were already falling over Salt Lick Road but Bill Jackson was in no hurry to switch over from his parking lights. He drove with a sure hand, but to Vonnie it was like riding into dark, mysterious depths. She could not help wondering what the old abandoned cemetery would be like at this hour. The thought brought a shiver.

"This tyke is really something," Bill said.

Vonnie glanced down and saw that Abigail was fast asleep, her head trustingly against Bill's side.

"She's fantastic," Vonnie replied. "Like a sweet little ghost. She keeps popping up from nowhere."

"You should feel honored—having her seek you out. She's usually as shy as a wild deer."

"I could learn to love her quite easily."

"If you think she's fantastic, you should meet the old man who takes care of her."

"I have," Vonnie replied without thinking.

Bill Jackson glanced over sharply. "Is that so?"

Having broken her reserve, Vonnie saw no reason for not going on—at least up to a point.

"Abigail found me out in the woods early today. I got the feeling she was looking for me. She promised to show me a short cut to Hazard House when we first met."

"Did she?"

"No—at least we didn't get there. She led me to an old cemetery out in the wilderness. I'm sure nobody's been buried there for generations."

"I know the spot. Abigail has a talent for seeking out weird places."

"It was certainly weird. Anyhow, we met her grandfather there—at least the man she calls Grandpa. She fell asleep, so we talked. They are not blood relatives."

"He's quite a guy. And there's quite a story behind Burton's Forge. It's a historical spot—rich in Revolutionary lore. But things changed—the place got cut off and a religious sect moved in there. That was a long time ago, and the Burton's Forge people degenerated if you could call it that. They became secluded, hill-billy types, staying off by themselves—living off the land. As long as they bothered no one, they weren't bothered."

"Were they in any way involved with the first Hazard—John Hazard, who built the mansion?"

"I can't really say. I don't know much about the old boy—John Hazard, I mean. But this Jason Leopold turned up some ten years ago. Nobody knew quite why. He was some kind of a psychic investigator—or so the story went; a man recognized internationally. Why he decided to settle at Burton's Forge, nobody will ever know. Not that we aren't glad he did. He sort of adopted the place; pulling it out of the mud. Bringing the standards up. They're still isolated and suspicious of outsiders over there but Leopold has done a lot—gotten the kids into schools; taken personal charge of children with either no parents or no sure knowledge of who their parents were."

Bill paused to glance at Vonnie. He didn't want to

shock her but he still wanted her to understand the earlier moral level of the community.

"He sounds like an amazing man."

"How did he impress you?"

"Well—amazing."

Bill turned on his headlights. Now they rounded a turn and the lights picked out a number of jerry-built hillside huts descending helter-skelter down to the edge of a narrow dirt road.

The dim light of oil lamps shone in the windows. A more depressing spectacle, even when shrouded in night shadows, Vonnie could not imagine.

Bill pulled up in front of the largest and neatest of the houses and immediately the door opened and a tall, gaunt woman came out.

"I brought your wandering child back," Jackson called out cheerfully.

The woman came forward and he lifted Abigail out and into her arms.

"We're obliged," the woman said. "Jason would have been out hunting her as soon as he gets back. He's away."

"Melissa, this is Miss Vanessa March. I think she'd want you to call her Vonnie."

"I'm proud to know you," the woman said in the same, grave voice Abigail used.

"I too, Melissa I hope I may see you again."

"We're obliged," the woman repeated gravely and turned toward the house with the still-sleeping Abigail in her arms.

"They're good people to get on the right side of," Bill explained as he turned the car. "They're a minority and don't appear to count for much but on a project like Hazard House they could make it succeed—or stop you."

It seemed that Bill's statement could stand clarification but Vonnie didn't press for it.

"You seem to be on the good side of them."

"They trust me, I guess. I don't look down my nose at them. That way, when one of their people gets into a ruckus and I have to step in, they trust me. They know he'll get a square deal."

"That's saying a lot. Is Abigail some special child to Leopold?"

Bill frowned over that one. "I think she's a special child, period. I can't say quite how. I mean you can see it but you can't explain it. Even the other kids here in Burton's Forge seem to understand it. They can be rough little urchins but Abigail is always handled like something fragile. They stand in awe of her."

"You say they were a religious sect at one time?"

"Something like that. There's a flat stone somewhere around, nobody knows where for sure, that they used for sacrifices many generations ago. Human sacrifices some say, but I doubt it."

"Around the time of the Civil War and before?"

"I imagine. But enough of Burton's Forge. I want to talk about you?"

"I'd make a pretty dull subject after the colorful characters we've been discussing."

"Not to me. Now tell me all about yourself."

Vonnie laughed. "Well, when I was a little girl, I always wanted to know what was on the other side of the rainbow."

"We'll leave those early years until later. Let's start with right now. Is anybody waiting for you in New York?"

"My landlord. The rent will be due the first of the month."

"No one with long-term designs on your person?"

"Why do you specify long-term?"

"Because that can make it difficult to compete. I'm not too worried about short-term."

"You move awfully fast, Mr. Jackson."

"I have to. I'm in a dangerous business. Some hijacker going through could knock me over anytime. In this day and age, any guy you stop for a license check may have a shotgun trained on you."

"Good heavens! You don't make yourself sound like much of a long-term gamble."

"Wups! bad salesmanship. Tell you what. We'll stick to the really-short-term. Like I'm a passable dancer and we've got a few interesting spots hereabouts. Does the idea of a bit of pub-trotting turn you on?"

"I should get back to the lodge in case there's an emergency phone call."

"Do they come often?"

"Well, hardly ever in the middle of the night."

"Then it's a deal."

"I'll have to change."

"I'd never allow that. If you looked any better I'd lose you at the first stop."

"You're not very sure of yourself, are you?" Vonnie teased.

"Surer than you'll ever know, angel," he replied as

he pulled up in front of a neat white cottage behind a trimmed lawn under two towering trees. "Here we are," he announced. "Home at last."

"What is this? Am I going to meet Mother already?"

"I've been alone for three years now—since my father died."

"I'm sorry."

"I stopped off to get out of this monkey suit. If you walk in like a cop, you can cool a spot off. Come on in."

"No, I'd rather not."

"Afraid?"

"I don't think so. It's just that it's such a beautiful night I don't want to miss any of it. I want to sit in that swing I see and look at the moon."

"Okay, I'll change and then come out and help you . . ."

Bill Jackson was evidently a man who needed music. A hi-fi went softly on with the lights. All the windows were open and from her seat in the old-fashioned suspension swing, Vonnie could hear him moving about, whistling cheerfully now and then with the music.

She leaned back and looked up into the dark sky and realized how completely she was enjoying herself. The night blotted out the immediate past; dropped like a curtain over the absurd things of the day; things such as a possessed child in a lonesome cemetery and a mysterious trip to the city to pick up a still more mysterious metal box.

The lights and the music went off and Bill Jackson

came clumping across the porch. The moon revealed him as wearing slacks, an open-collared shirt, and a sport sweater. Obviously there was no formality around Big Moose Lake . . .

The evening, from Vonnie's point of view—and obviously from Bill Jackson's—was a huge success. They visited several places, some loud, some dreamy. Vonnie downed several whiskey sours with no other effect than to feel wonderfully happy.

Finally, arrived back at the lodge, Miss Stone, still on the desk, appeared to approve highly of them. She was bent over in front of the desk with a dust tray and whisk broom as they passed. Bill fetched her a hearty whack on her bottom that straightened her. Her look said murder but it was all show. Vonnie could see that attention pleased her.

What a wonderful place! What fine people! Why couldn't the whole world be this way?

At the door, Vonnie had scant time to consider the problem of inviting him in. Would that lead to problems? Bill took the load off her mind by reaching for her after he'd unlocked the door. Then, there in the hallway, he enfolded her and kissed her in the same masterful manner in which he would probably handle a major crime.

Vonnie found herself cooperating. This was not the first time she'd been kissed. But it could have been the first time she became a wholehearted partner in the operation.

When common decency finally insisted she draw back, Vonnie murmured, "Thanks for a wonderful evening. I don't know when I've enjoyed myself so much."

He gave her a final quick smack as though to say she'd been a good girl and winked broadly. "See what I mean about short-term relationships? No problem at all."

Then with a "see you tomorrow," he was off toward the lobby.

Vonnie went inside and closed the door behind her. She felt light as a feather; as though she would never again need sleep. Perhaps, she thought, it was all those whiskey sours, but she knew it was not.

Ready for bed, she stood for a little while on the balcony. The moon was down and the sky was like black velvet sprinkled with diamonds. Vonnie looked across at the dark window of Keith's room and felt a surge of guilt. She had not thought of him once, not even a single second, during the whole evening.

This called for a little soul-searching relative to Bill Jackson. Meeting a man and feeling as she did after a single date pointed to only one thing. A schoolgirl crush. That was hardly becoming for a girl who liked to see herself as a mature woman. Vonnie had no trust whatever in the love-at-first-sight business. True, solid love was slower in coming. It started with affection and grew. Aunt Madge had taught her that.

"If those two hadn't literally thrown themselves into each other's arms, things might have been different. They were practically two strangers married to each other . . ."

That was how she described the romance of Vonnie's parents. Aunt Madge had always called it tragic because of the tragic manner in which it ended.

Vonnie had puzzled over this judgment and finally got what she thought was Aunt Madge's meaning; that if they'd taken their time and gotten to know each other better, the tragedy would have been averted.

"Things that start in tempest end in tempest," Aunt Madge had declared more than once.

This now caused Vonnie to ponder. How could a person know? Sudden attraction does not announce itself. So if it comes, do you run away from it? She finally decided she was taking things far too seriously and turned from the balcony toward bed . . .

As she did so, the mood of the night and her own mood changed. She was not alone. Someone was there in the room. She had turned on only one small table lamp so the room was full of shadows. She saw no one but so positive was the feeling of no longer being alone that she called, "Yes? What is it?" as she stepped into the room.

There was no reply, yet there was an answer of sorts. A chill. It was as though a powerful air conditioning unit, far too large for the room, had been turned suddenly to maximum. A wave of frigid air swept over her.

"Please!" she murmured helplessly.

An icy wind swept past her, chilling her bare legs, raising goose pimples on her thighs; this even though she noted vaguely that the hem of her shortie nightgown did not move.

The sob which arose in her throat came unconsciously.

"Oh, please . . ."

There, on the table where she had placed the vase, she saw the outline of the withered roses.

But she'd thrown them out! She'd thrown them into the waste basket—and they had been carried away! Who had brought them back? And why?

Then it was over. The strange darkness was again penetrated by the light from the table lamp and was doing so now again.

The deep shadows were gone.

Also, the frigid wave of bone-chill.

Vonnie passed a hand over her thigh. She had definitely felt the goose pimples rise but now, only an instant later, her skin was again velvety smooth. They could not possibly have vanished so quickly.

A manifestation of the spirit? Had nothing physical really happened?

It seemed the only possible explanation.

The empty vase on the table lent confirmation to the idea. Vonnie crossed over and picked it up. What qualities did it have other than those put into it by the glass blower? None.

The whole frightening episode had sprung suddenly from her mind, to vanish as quickly.

But the traumatic effect remained.

"I'm going home!" Vonnie sobbed and lunged for the telephone.

Miss Stone, the eternal, the unsleeping, answered. Vonnie, forcing control into her voice, said, "I want to put through a call to Wilton, Iowa."

She gave Miss Stone the number and code and waited, still fighting to regain control of herself. The phone rang at the other end, three times, then Aunt Madge's blessed voice.

"Vonnie! Child! How are you? I've been worried."

"Why, Aunt Madge?"

"I expected to hear from you. One phone call! No letter. Not even a postcard."

"I'm sorry, Aunt Madge. I've just been so busy."

A gusty sigh came over the wire. "I understand. That's how it always is. The young go off and forget the old."

"That's not true. I think of you every day."

"Well, that's a blessing. Too bad you aren't tele-pathic. You could save telephone bills. How is that job going?"

"Oh, fine—just fine."

"Do you like New York City?"

"Very much. It's frightfully crowded. The streets are jammed. The buses just crawl along."

"How on earth can you like such a place?"

"It's so busy. So vital."

"Well, I'm glad everything's all right with you. But remember what I said: I'm always here."

Vonnie could find no words to express her grati-tude for that, so she didn't try.

"You'd better hang up now, dear. Long distance is expensive. Write me a letter. And call collect the next time . . ."

Vonnie put the phone down and got into bed. That firm, confident voice from the wilds of Iowa had changed everything.

Not really, however. Vonnie had reversed herself while waiting for that voice. She'd given the number with every intention of telling Aunt Madge she was on the way. So what had changed her in those few seconds?

I couldn't run away like a scared kid and leave Keith to fend for himself. I could never forgive myself.

The phone rang. Vonnie picked it up. It was Miss Stone. "Did you get your party all right?"

"Yes, thanks."

"I'm glad. Sometimes the wire isn't very clear up here in the hills."

"It was fine."

Miss Stone seemed loath to ring off. "By the way, did you have a nice evening with Bill?"

"Very nice."

"You got the child home all right?"

"Yes, we took Abigail back to Burton's Forge and then Bill changed his uniform and we went a few places."

"He's a very nice young man. But he *is* a policeman."

"What could be wrong with that?"

"Nothing, except being a policeman's wife is hard. A girl would never know. Her husband could be brought home in a box anytime."

"Lucy! Are you ever the pessimist!"

"A girl has to face facts."

"Well, we haven't set the wedding date yet. I may change my mind . . ."

Lucy Stone got an incoming call and Vonnie lay

back in bed. It occurred to her that if Lucy was matchmaking, she was pretty clumsy about it.

But her call had cheered Vonnie. The lodge was a sophisticated place, but the people were reliably small town . . .

CHAPTER SIX

With no word from Keith the following morning, Vonnie had breakfast in the dining room and then went for a stroll in the bracing morning air. The weather was holding miraculously; even Miss Stone admitted that, and advised Vonnie to take advantage of it.

"A really big summer storm can flood the streams and make the land soggy for days."

She wandered down to the lake, crossed over Salt Lick Road to wander amid the tall pines of the forest edge. The birds were conversing sociably—all in all it was an enchanting scene. Then realizing half the morning had passed and perhaps Keith was waiting for her, she hurried back to the lodge.

The lobby was empty as she entered. No one was present except a young college-type room-clerk to whom Miss Stone had finally relinquished her post. The young man smiled her way, then he disappeared through a doorway—to attend to something or other.

Vonnie was about to go up to her room when she heard a faint voice and realized the phone booth was occupied by someone inside crouching low over the transmitter.

The booth was so situated that Vonnie could see only the man's back and she was about to move on when his head turned slightly and she saw it was Keith.

Vonnie walked over toward the booth from behind so Keith did not see her and it was thus that she inadvertently became an eavesdropper. With the booth door slightly open and Keith totally immersed in his conversation, Vonnie did not have to strain her ears:

"I've *got* to do it, Brad, I've got to know . . . What does it matter now? It matters a hell of a lot to me . . . Look, old buddy, I'm not asking you to get involved. I'm just asking you to do your thing for me. You won't have to testify in court . . . Yes . . . like you said, whatever I find out, it won't make any difference now. It's just that I've *got* to know . . ."

Vonnie suddenly realized her position. Standing there in the open obviously listening to someone else's conversation . . . unthinkable! Like a child escaping with a stolen cookie, she retraced her steps, keeping Keith's hunched shoulder before her till she got to the dining room door where she ducked inside, greatly relieved.

She passed through and out the patio door and circled the lodge to reenter through the front door. The phone booth was now vacant.

She ran quickly upstairs and into her own room.

103

Immediately upon the sound of her door closing, there came a knock on the door joining the two rooms.

"Vonnie?"

"Yes, Keith."

She opened the door and stopped dead; he looked awful. His eyes were dark circles sunken from lack of sleep. A growth of beard—that his face had not felt a razor in some time.

"Oh, there you are. Everything been all right?"

"Yes . . . except that I've worried about you."

Keith moved back into his room. Vonnie followed. He passed a mirror, peered into it and running a hand over his jaw, he muttered "Need a shave."

"More than that. You need sleep."

She watched as he peeled off his shirt. He went into the bathroom and turned on the faucet. Through the open door Vonnie saw him take a razor and cream from the cabinet.

"I'll be all right after a shave and a shower."

"But you haven't slept since you left here, have you?"

"No."

"Then you've got to get some rest."

"Later, maybe. There's something I've got to do first."

Vonnie went closer. She stood at the bathroom door, then said, "Keith, you're killing yourself. Whatever's troubling you is none of my business and I'm not prying, but you've got to slow down."

"Later . . ."

"Later nothing. Whatever it is you must do—can't I do it for you?"

He braced his hands against the edge of the sink and thought it over. "No," he said finally. "I'd better take care of it myself."

"Please let me try!"

He squeezed out shaving cream and lathered one jaw and said, "All right. Maybe you can. It's a delivery that has to be made."

"I'll do it immediately."

"Did you ever hear of The Davidson Research Institute?"

"I don't believe so."

"It's located in a town called Bensonhurst not far from Syracuse. An old college buddy of mine works there—Walter Sims. That box you picked up from the office. I want it delivered to him."

"I'll start right away."

"You can look the town up on the map. From here, with a lot of country roads, it might be a three or four hour drive. You'd better take my car."

"I won't start, though, until I see you in bed with the *Do Not Disturb* sign on the door. Have you had anything to eat?"

"Haven't taken the time out. But I'm not hungry."

"I'll see that some breakfast is sent up while you're showering. And I want you to eat it."

Vonnie went down personally, ordered the meal and brought it up herself. When she got back to Keith's room, he was still in the shower.

She went to the curtain and called out over the

sound of the cascading water. "Your breakfast is on the table. I'm going in to change. Knock on my door where you're through."

The tan pantyhose and the miniskirt were the handiest and Vonnie got into them almost without thinking, her mind solely on Keith. She was hired as a secretary but seemed to be functioning more as a nurse. Somehow, she was going to have to find out what was tearing Keith apart and try to be of more substantial help.

When she was ready to go and the knock had not come, she tapped on the door, then peeked in. He was stretched across the bed, sound asleep. Vonnie went in and threw the extra blanket over him and moved the untouched breakfast out of reach. Then she hung the *Do Not Disturb* sign on the door and would lock and bolt it from the inside when she left.

Now her touchiest problem. Getting the metal box down, she put it on her bed and frowned. Then she made her decision and went back to get Keith's keys off his dresser.

There were a dozen but she had no trouble finding the one which belonged to the lock on the box. She thrust the key in and turned it. After a moment's hesitation, she lifted the lid. A laid-over white cloth hid the contents.

She did not have to go any farther, she fully realized, but she was only human and the temptation was too great. She laid back the top fold of the cloth.

Nestled underneath was an empty glass tube, a heavy rubber band, and a vicious-looking hypodermic needle.

At that precise moment she heard Keith's heavy breathing stop. Vonnie's heart almost stopped also as she replaced the cloth, closed the box and turned the key. In her own ears the turning of the key sounded like boulders thundering down a hill. But then Keith went back into his gentle snore and Vonnie's relief almost weakened her knees . . .

She took a last look around, put the box under her arm and let herself quietly out of her room . . .

The clerk was not at the desk and while Vonnie waited the front lobby door squeaked. She turned and saw Bill Jackson, again resplendent in his uniform, striding in.

"Not checking out, I hope?" he said.

"No. I'm waiting to ask about maps. I've got to drive to a town called Bensonhurst."

"What for?"

"To run an errand for my boss. Did you ever hear of the place?"

"Is it an emergency?"

"Not exactly. Do you know where Bensonhurst is?"

"Sure. About three hours from here as the crow doesn't fly." He stopped to grin as he pulled at one ear. "But this being an emergency, I can help you out. Come on."

He seized her hand and started back toward the door. Vonnie had no recourse but to follow unless she dug her heels in and demanded to know what he had in mind.

She didn't get around to asking questions, however,

until they were in the patrol car pulling into Salt Lick Road. Then she found the breath to demand, "What is this? What are you planning to do?"

"Send you the way the crow goes. What's in the box?"

"I have no idea," Vonnie calmly lied.

"Looks like loot. Are you a bag woman?"

"I never ask questions."

"I checked, but there weren't any wanted posters out on you."

"You're impossible!"

Taking his eyes off the road, he turned his bold gaze on her, starting at her knees, going up her thighs and higher until he was considering her gold-burnished hair.

"You're not so bad yourself."

"I'd still like to know what this is all about."

He promptly turned on the siren. "What did you say?"

"I said I'd like to know what this is all about."

"Can't hear a word. That damned thing makes too much noise."

Shortly thereafter, Bill turned into a blacktop drive that led to a neat little red brick building Vonnie identified as a State Patrol Station. The door opened and another uniformed man came out.

Bill pushed his cap back and said, "Errand of mercy, Jake. This is Florence Nightingale. The serum she's got in this box has got to get to Bensonhurst fast."

Jake was eying Vonnie with obvious appreciation,

but if he believed any of what Bill had told him, his face did not reflect it.

"Somebody sick in Bensonhurst?" he asked Vonnie.

"I'm to deliver this to the Davidson Research Laboratory."

"One of their rabbits is sick," Bill said.

"Okay," Jake said. "We'll call it a test flight," and went back inside.

Bill drove around the station and some hundred yards out to where a helicopter was being puttered with by a man in coveralls.

"A run over to Bensonhurst, Sam," Bill said.

The other young man looked at Vonnie appreciatively "Have you got a requisition?" he asked.

"A test flight," Bill said. "I understand the carburetor's been coughing."

"I'll find out. If you'll just crawl in, Miss."

"You don't have to stay, do you?" Bill asked.

"No. I just have to find a man named Walter Sims," Vonnie said.

"I know Walt. He flies model airplanes at Bryan Flats when he gets the time. Say hello for me. I'll pick you up back here in an hour . . ."

Twenty minutes later, Vonnie was deposited on a huge lawn beside the Davidson Laboratory, a sprawling one-story building with an antiseptic look about it. Minutes later, Vonnie was ushered into Walter Sims's office. Sims looked out the window and said, "Cops. Keith isn't in any trouble, is he?"

"Not with the police."

109

Sims looked at Vonnie with speculation, considered for a moment, and said, "I know about the other."

It was on the tip of Vonnie's tongue to reply, *Well, I wish you'd tell me.* But she held her curiosity in check and said, "Bill Jackson arranged to get me over in the helicopter. He sends his regards."

"That crazy fuzz. He'll find himself transferred to the North Pole one of these days . . ."

The trip back was as swift and Vonnie found Bill waiting for her. "I'll run you back," he said. "Then you'll have to fend for yourself until tonight. I've got to do some patrolling."

As the car wound back toward the lodge, Vonnie regarded him frankly. "This is an awful lot of service for one goodnight kiss."

"I expect to get more than that, angel."

"Oh, you do, do you?"

"Uh-huh. I'm going to marry you."

"Then you'd better hurry. Walter Sims says you're going to be transferred to the North Pole."

"He's a worrier. Nice guy, though."

"He and my boss went to college together."

"Walt's the dedicated type. Takes life too seriously."

"Somebody has to."

"Well, he's the guy for it. But about your boss. You've never said much."

"I told you why we're here."

"I mean about him personally. Is he gone on you?"

"Hardly. At times, he doesn't know I exist."

Bill was glowering at the windshield. "It's not fair

110

—having to compete with the guy who pays your salary. It gives him a big edge."

"I told you. We're as platonic as a pair of Greek statues."

The scowl turned to a grin. "Then it's all cozy with thee and me."

"I didn't say that. I just told you how things are with my boss and me."

"Well, we'll thresh it out later tonight. Get your cute little fanny out of here now and let a man do his job . . ."

As Vonnie entered the lodge, she found herself moving reluctantly. Somehow, the only really pleasant hours she'd had at Big Moose Lake were spent with Bill Jackson. Also, the saner hours, though some of his antics bordered on the insane.

Am I falling in love? Vonnie asked herself and tried to consider it—without qualifications, whys, or wherefores. His kiss was thrilling, his masculine warmth and roughness attractive. Then she tried to compare this with her regard for Keith. But there was, actually, no honest way of doing this. The two men were so different and her relationship with Keith had so many different aspects. Loyalty, concern, pity—it was difficult to sort these out or try any exact labels to fit her feeling for him.

Back upstairs, Vonnie found—as she'd hoped to—that Keith was still deep in sleep. That left her with the day to herself.

But what to do with it? She was beginning to feel

guilty at the way things were going, though it was through no fault of hers. Still, there was a fifty-thousand-dollar job to be done and they seemed as far from starting it as at the signing of the contract. She had to concede that taking on the assignment had been a mistake what with the personal trouble plaguing Keith. It would have been of some comfort to know exactly what that trouble was. Lack of knowledge added to her sense of helplessness.

She was forced to concede also that while Keith left nothing to be desired as an employer—she clung to that conviction loyally—still a streak of unstability in him made for a precarious future. Visualizing Bill Jackson under the same degree of pressure, she was sure he could meet his problems more forcibly.

But the comparison was unfair . . . they were two different people . . .

She wandered onto the balcony, pondering the cryptic conversation she'd heard at the phone booth. What could it have meant? The contents of the box had been obvious to her although she knew nothing of drugs or even met anyone under their influence. It was a drug-user's kit: the drug container, the rubber band for raising a vein for the injection, and the hypodermic needle so necessary to the addict.

But why had Keith sent them to his friend in a research laboratory; and especially if the answer Keith sought was no longer vital. For that matter, what was there to discover? It would not take a chemical researcher to tell what had been in the glass container. Obviously the kit had belonged to Keith's ill-fated secretary. Keith himself was certainly not a user. It was known that Sarah had been an addict, so why all the secrecy surrounding the kit? Why had it been locked away?

Vonnie knew she could only wait—if answers indeed she ever got at all. And also to wonder why she dwelt so single-mindedly on Keith and *his* problems, rather than those terrifying experiences she herself had gone through.

She realized, while not clearly defining it to herself, that she was a little like the frightened ostrich with a sand pile handy: she did not want to think about the cemetery experience, the dead roses, or the frightful chilling there in her own room. And if she never got the answers to those conundrums it would not bother her a bit . . .

So there was still the afternoon ahead of her . . .

"Hello," said Abigail . . .

Vonnie turned almost wearily to see the child standing just inside the corridor door. This time, her reply was different.

"I won't ask you how you got in here, Abigail. That's beginning to sound too much like a part of a broken record."

"I came up through the lobby," Abigail replied solemnly. "Miss Stone saw me but she knew me from dinner last night and didn't say anything."

"Well, at least there's nothing supernatural about that. Did you come to spend the afternoon with me?"

"You said you wanted to see Hazard House. I said I'd show you an easy way to get there."

"Today? This afternoon?"

"If you want to."

Vonnie didn't want to. She wanted to stay very close to the lodge, out of harm's way, and hope that nothing would get in the way of her spending the evening with Bill Jackson. But she could hardly give that to Abigail as an explanation, so she said, "I'd like to see Hazard House. Will we be back before sundown?"

"If we don't stay too long."

"All right. You can look at a magazine while I change . . ."

Back in the boots and heavy riding britches, Vonnie took Abigail to the parking lot and they climbed into the jeep.

"Which way, honey?" she asked as they approached Salt Lick Road.

"You turn the other way—away from town. We go about two miles. I'll tell you when to turn."

As they settled into the run, Vonnie said, "Abigail. Tell me about Rachel."

"She's—bad."

"Do you know her as well as you know Patience?"

"I don't see her very often. Patience always keeps her away from me."

"Patience is stronger than Rachel?"

"I don't know."

"What does Rachel want?"

"She wants—" Abigail stopped and pointed on ahead. "You turn there—into the woods."

Vonnie braked the jeep and moved forward slowly.

She saw nothing that looked like a turn or an intersection.

"Where, dear?"

"There—into those green bushes."

"But there's no road."

"There is a road. It's just covered up."

"Well, if you say so," Vonnie murmured doubtfully, and nosed the jeep in where she'd been directed.

The bushes parted. Vonnie lowered her head behind the windshield to avoid whipping branches and they pushed on through.

The clump was some twenty feet thick, after which it vanished and the faint, grass-covered impression of a narrow roadway appeared on ahead.

"The bushes are in the exact center of the road entrance," Vonnie said. "It's almost as though someone planted them there."

"Maybe somebody did," Abigail replied. "I don't know."

"Is this a secret road?"

"Maybe. Nobody uses it. Nobody ever goes to Hazard House anyway."

"Where is the other road?"

"It goes in from over on the other side. It goes around Whiskey Mountain—the big one you can see from the lodge."

Vonnie recalled the green cone which stood out over the lower hills surrounding the lodge on the forest side. It wasn't very high as mountains went but it dominated the area and gave indications of hard going.

"What an odd name for a mountain," Vonnie said.

"It's because some moonshiners used to hide in the caves there. That was a long time ago, though."

At least Vonnie was learning something. She'd always thought moonshining was native to the Kentucky mountains and the Big Smokies of the South. Evidently New York State had had such troubles also.

The road onto which Abigail directed her remained constant though it did wind interminably. As she navigated its twists, she was proud of having discovered something of value to Keith and the ski project. A road not clinging to a mountainside would certainly reduce costs.

"How much farther, dear?"

"A little ways now. There's the graveyard."

Vonnie looked down from the ridge to which the grassy road clung and saw the saucer-shaped indentation where people of long ago had buried their dead. The high sun shimmered down on it, distorting the air with heat waves.

Still Vonnie shuddered.

"No one has been buried there for a long time, has there?"

"Grandpa says about fifty years. Not since the new road was built the other side of the lake."

"Why do people stay away from Hazard House. It's an interesting place, I understand. I'd think people would come to see it."

"Rachel doesn't want them to."

There was no time to inquire further because the jeep negotiated a turn in the road and the forest ended abruptly.

On ahead, covering a circular area of some twenty

116

acres, there were no tall trees; only low saplings and struggling young seedlings. The pines of earlier growth had been cut away.

"There's a rain coming," Abigail said, but Vonnie scarcely heard her. She was getting her first view of Hazard House.

It stood on the far side of the circular area, on a rise that dominated its surroundings. A monstrosity. That was the only word Vonnie could think of. The writer who had called it a mad mixture of many styles had not exaggerated. The crowning feature was a Moorish tower in the center of the structure; a graceful enough dome if it had been located in some other place, in entirely different, less incongruous surroundings.

What had once been a broad driveway circled up to a porch that ran half the length of the building's width and above that an open terrace supported by a dozen pillars in the Ionic style.

The rest of the mansion could be described only as a piecemeal combination. There were two wings which bore no resemblance to each other, one after the sparse, plain design of early New England, the other ornately carved gingerbread and rococoed, giving it a semblance of the opulence of the great Southern plantation dynasties.

But that was not all: The sky had changed in the past few minutes; black afternoon clouds had gathered in response to the heated air currents; black thunderheads, rolling through to cool the land.

And now, as Vonnie gazed at the house John Hazard built, the clouds overhead split, letting the sun

117

through. It came as a single blazing ray, spotlighting the house as though by some celestial lighting expert.

This enhanced the darkness round about and the house stood out like a brooding, macabre creation out of a painting by Gustave Dore.

The sight held Vonnie spellbound but had no effect on Abigail. "We'd better get inside, or we'll be soaked . . . with no top on the car," she said.

"Of course," Vonnie agreed, and sent the jeep down across the weed-strewn circle toward the mansion.

The first raindrops were spattering the windshield as they stopped at the great porch and dashed for shelter. Just as they got in under the pillar-supported roof, the storm broke, rain came crashing down.

"We just made it," Abigail said.

"By an eyelash. How long do these rains last?"

"Not very long, usually. Do you want to go inside?"

Actually, Vonnie would have preferred to stay where she was. "What about Rachel? Would she resent our intrusion?"

"She can't really hurt us. Come on. I'll show you the circle."

It would have been impossible to move the great front door. It was massive and its hinges had long since rusted solid. But it stood ajar barely leaving room for them to slip by.

Inside, enough light revealed a long, narrow room, probably a reception hall in other days, with another door beyond. It also stood open. Moving confidently, Abigail led through to a large court of Moorish design. It was circular with the tower standing directly overhead. A lower roof supported the base of the tower but, above that, the tower stood open, forming a high ceiling for the court.

But the floor of the court was more interesting: Mosaic tile wrought into a huge astrological pattern, it had stood well the test of time, the vari-colored design was still comparatively bright, the astrological signs clearly discernible.

As Vonnie gazed, she was sharply reminded of her dream the night before she and Keith came north. How clearly it flashed back into her mind! So starkly, she expected to see the Lion in the Leo segment to materialize, roar menacingly, and vanish back into the gloom.

"It's fantastic," Vonnie murmured quietly.

"It had something to do with their religion," Abigail said.

"It's so very clean. I'd think there would be a foot of dirt on it after all these years."

"No, Grandpa comes and cleans it every six months."

"Why on earth would he do that?"

"He gets paid. It was in the will or something. Like he told me there's a big building in Chicago where they have to lead a cow through once a year; things the men who build places say have to be done in per— in perp—"

"In perpetuity," Vonnie said.

"Yes."

"That's very interesting. I'd like to talk to your grandfather about it."

119

"I think he'd tell you."

"Have you any idea who owns Hazard House?"

"I don't know. Rachel did once, I guess."

"Rachel!" It suddenly dawned. "Why, she was the wife of John Hazard! The man who built Hazard House."

"Yes."

"And Patience?"

"Patience was their daughter. I guess Rachel still owns Hazard House."

"Rachel! That's nonsense. Rachel has been dead for almost a hundred years!"

"I don't know. Maybe Grandpa can tell you."

Vonnie had been tense during this entire weird visit; more than even the bizarre findings justified. Now she realized why: Abigail's seizure in the graveyard.

What if it came again, here on this fantastic place? Here with Jason Leopold not present to lend his experience and give aid?

This fear in mind, Vonnie drew the child close. "I think we'd better go, dear."

"Don't you want to see the rest of it?"

"Some other time."

"The rain hasn't quite stopped."

"I know, but there's a top to the jeep. I'll put it up and we'll soon be dry as tinder."

They went back onto the porch. The rain was subsiding. Vonnie got partially drenched putting up the top. Then she motioned Abigail from the porch and pointed the jeep toward the lodge.

In her haste there had been more than fear for the child. Something was there in the court; a presence watching; the air thickening around her. And Vonnie had found herself cringing from a blast of frigid air she was expecting.

Then, as though Abigail sensed her thoughts, speaking calmly, almost dreamily, she said, "Rachel was there. She didn't like us to come."

"I'm sorry," Vonnie said, shaking somewhat. "Perhaps we should have waited for an invitation."

"It was all right. Patience wouldn't let her hurt us."

"Abigail, do you actually believe Rachel, who has been dead for so long, actually could hurt us?"

"I don't know. I was afraid of her at first but I'm not afraid anymore."

"You're a very brave little girl."

"No. Patience always comes."

How grotesque! thought Vonnie. A child clothed in almost glowing innocence not fearing one shade because another was there to protect her.

The sky cleared as they approached Salt Lick Road. As they pulled onto the blacktop, a state patrol car rounded the bend ahead and came toward them. It stopped beside the jeep and Bill Jackson got out.

"I've been looking for you," he said.

"Is anything wrong?"

"No. I just don't like to have you get too far out of range. Where've you been?"

"Gadding around in the woods. Abigail is a wonderful guide."

"Where are you going?"

"Back to the lodge . . . sir. With your permission of course."

"Not this one," Bill said. Reaching in he lifted Abigail out of the jeep.

"Kidnaping is a federal offense. I'll report to Mr. Hoover as soon as I get back."

"No dinner tonight for you, young lady," Bill sternly told Abigail. "I'm taking you home on working time. I'll be courting tonight and I don't want any kids around."

Abigail did not seem averse to the idea and Vonnie was just as happy to return to the lodge alone. Keith might be awake and having the child on her hands could be clumsy.

"See you around eight," said Bill.

"I don't know. I may have things to do. You'd better phone."

"I'll phone and then see you at eight."

The patrol car moved on. Vonnie watched it go. She suddenly felt lonely there in the deep shadows with the sun lowering down behind the pines . . .

CHAPTER SEVEN

Bill Jackson called, but earlier, around seven: "Sorry as the devil, angel. Can't make it tonight. Extra patrol duty."

"I'm sorry, too, Bill," Vonnie admitted. "I hope it isn't punishment for that trip to the laboratory."

"Not unless Jake broke his arm to see that I got the extra duty."

"There was an accident?"

"He hit a deer on the way home—or almost did. The deer dived into the road and Jake slammed into a tree avoiding it. Freak accident. Busted his wing."

"Tell him I'm sorry."

"Okay. I may stop off late in the evening if I'm around there."

With that he hung up and Vonnie went back on her balcony to sit down to think about him. She had become greatly attracted to Bill, but exactly why? What was there about him that drew her?

One thing was his even temperament. Nothing seemed to distort his cheerful, matter-of-fact outlook on life. He was the first man she'd ever met who could be cheerfully angry, cheerfully happy, and probably cheerfully blue.

It seemed that whenever she saw him, Vonnie wanted to sit close to him and absorb his self-confidence and zest for life.

Then, too, he was in such contrast with the frightening aspects of the Big Moose Lake country which seemed to be driving her into a whirlpool of darkness. One thing was sure; with Bill's happy image in her mind the other things had a hard time pushing through.

Keith had still been sleeping when Vonnie got back from Hazard House. Even now, his window was still dark. She hoped he would sleep straight through until morning.

As the last glimmers of twilight threw silver nets across the lake, Vonnie consciously put Bill Jackson from her mind to concentrate on Keith. Not wishing to be in the least evasive, she asked herself point-blank if he too was not on drugs. She decided not. His actions, no matter how puzzling, were not those of an addict as she visualized them.

Keith was a highly sensitive individual, there was no doubt about that; even neurotic. He was a person, Vonnie sensed, who could be sent up the wall by emotional trauma. And with his physical health seemingly good, that remained the only logical answer: he was up to his ears in an emotional problem.

Trying to think logically, Vonnie now decided that

125

it was something that had happened recently. It had to be, because as a compulsive neurotic, Keith could not have built a career where he was trusted with fifty-thousand-dollar assignments by hard-headed business people such as Enterprise Associates. Therefore, she could only hope his problem would be solved so he could apply himself to the job at hand . . .

With the sky now turned to black velvet studded with sparkles, her mind descended to her appetite. It was high time for dinner. Then it turned out that Bill's extra duty had come at a propitious time because her phone rang. Lucy Stone put a man on whom Vonnie recognized instantly.

"Mr. Leopold!"

"I am in the lobby, Miss March. I came on over in the hope of catching you."

"Yes?" Vonnie said uncertainly.

"My time is pretty well occupied but I think it a good idea if we have a talk, so I thought I might give you dinner."

"That's sweet of you. As a matter of fact, I was just coming down."

"I'll be at the bar."

When she got downstairs she was in for another surprise. She expected to find her dinner companion freakish in comparison to the lodge clientele; a little like John the Baptist invading one of Caesar's elite Roman dinners.

Such was not the case. His gray beard was very much in evidence but otherwise he more than fit into lodge picture. He wore a gray flannel suit needing no apology, a white shirt with a blue tie, and the manner in which he got off his stool to greet Vonnie could not be seen better at the Waldorf.

"Nice of you to see me," he said. "Would you like a drink here or shall we take a table?"

"I'll leave that entirely up to you."

"Then let's sit down." As he motioned to the hostess, he also raised a finger to the bartender. "Have my scotch sent to our table, please," he directed.

Seated at the corner table he chose, he looked about the dining room pensively. "It's been a long time."

"A long time?"

"Yes, since I've patronized a restaurant like this. I think of the Viennese restaurants once in a while."

"With any urge to go back?"

"No. At one time I thought that the knowledge I sought had to be pursued in the world's great centers of culture. I was mistaken. I may spend the rest of my life here in the woods."

"Your activities at Burton's Forge seem to take all of your time."

"I range around. The Forge is a sort of hub—a central location."

"Bill Jackson spoke of you," Vonnie said. "He mentioned you as being interested in psychic manifestation, but from other things I've seen and heard, I'd call you a humanitarian."

"We go where destiny leads us," Leopold said, "but I am making no sacrifices, believe me. If anything I have undertaken became boring I would abandon it."

"You find the Burton Forge people interesting then."

"As a community, they are highly sensitive people.

I dare say that if the Duke University specialists invaded the Forge with their ESP know-how, they would be amazed."

"Then shouldn't you do something about it?"

"I can give you two answers to that: First, I have no intention of sharing my guinea pigs with anyone. But the reply I like best is that I won't have those people probed and gaped at and made generally unhappy."

"I think the second reply is the correct one."

Leopold kept the conversation general until they'd ordered and their dinner was before them. Then he said, "This is a pleasant, restful setting. It's too bad we are going to have to discuss serious matters."

"I think you're referring to Abigail?"

"I'm referring to you."

"If you hadn't brought these more serious matters up, I would have done so. I need advice. I've had no experience with the supernatural before . . ."

He lifted a quick hand. "That word is not right in the meaning it is given. There is no such thing as the supernatural if you mean occurrences beyond natural law. All law is natural. We call things we cannot understand supernatural when the thing to do is increase our understanding."

"And that's what you've spent your life doing?"

"To the extent of my meager abilities."

"Then perhaps you can tell me; am I in danger here?"

"No more so now than you would be in danger anywhere else."

"You mean it—they—whatever you are referring to—would follow me?"

"Probably. Now that it has found you."

"But what sort of evil—?"

"I don't like that term, either. I prefer *destructive*. Evil for some can be good for others. Destruction profits no one."

"Are you talking about the dead?"

"A comparative term, but about people who have lived on this plane of existence—yes."

"And are now living somewhere else?"

"Those are my conclusions from what I have seen and researched. The situation at Hazard House goes back a very long way."

"To John Hazard himself?"

"To his wife, Rachel. She was a Haitian woman who literally enslaved Hazard through his love for her. From the time he met and married her, he was no longer his own master."

"How tragic!"

"From one point of view the situation had its advantages. Hazard had been only mildly successful prior to that—even in the lucrative slave trade. But afterwards he could make no mistakes. It was she who brought him north and directed his every move."

"He built Hazard House for her?"

"Rather, she built it for herself. The woman would probably have been adjudged mad by today's standards. Of course madness is also a comparative word. I believe people are normal or abnormal based on the intensity of vital force they are able to absorb. Rachel's capacity was many times normal."

"I've noticed that some people are more keenly sensitive to outside forces than others. Is that pertinent to your theory?"

"Definitely. Some people go completely to pieces because of the death of a loved one for instance. Others are much less affected."

"The difference is usually attributed to individual strength of character, is it not?"

"There are many views opposed to mine, Miss March."

It was on the tip of her tongue to suggest that he address her less formally. Then she hesitated. It seemed impertinent somehow. Familiarity, such as calling her Vonnie, seemed alien to this remarkable man.

"If I understand you correctly, you must be in great fear for Abigail."

"I would of course prefer not to have her involved, but I hope she is in no great danger. The two opposing forces, Rachel and Patience, have found Abigail to be a perfect medium through which to manifest back onto this plane of existence. I am unable to keep them from channeling their vitality through her. I can only play one against the other as much as possible."

"But what are they after? What do they want?"

"I can only theorize on that. In my opinion, Patience wants release. She is being held by the destructive Rachel through power she cannot cope with alone."

"It's all so fantastic!"

Jason Leopold smiled briefly for the first time. "And so unbelievable?"

Vonnie stirred her coffee, staring into its depths as though seeking an answer. When she didn't find it, she lifted her eyes. "A few days ago, I would have said yes—totally unbelievable. But by saying so now, I would have to call myself abnormal. And I'm not prepared to do that."

"A sensible conclusion."

"In all truth, Mr. Leopold, I can't say that I am ready to accept your explanations, either—not completely."

"I would not want you to. I suggest you use what I've told you as material upon which to base your own investigations; as guideposts for your own research."

"I'm hardly a researcher and there is one thing I think I shall never understand."

"And that is—?"

"Why me? People have come to Big Moose Lake by the thousands since Hazard House was built. Why did Patience select me?"

"I don't know, Miss March. My true knowledge of what lies beyond our senses is too meager. Only the experience of death itself could possibly prepare me to know."

"Another thing. Abigail said Patience sent her to my room with those roses. How did she know I was there?"

"The answers to that is less difficult. While these invisible entities function from a base of power, a core so to speak, there is no reason why they cannot range far more widely."

"And the roses—why did they wither so quickly?"

"I can only suspect. If you care to check the public library in Big Moose Lake, you will find a curious volume. It was written some seventy-five years ago by a Dame Barbara Goody—and was written in longhand. Dame Goody, a self-admitted witch, put down a great deal of the local lore—witchcraft, black magic, the like—and she had some things to say about Rachel Hazard. Among them, that Rachel could grasp a bouquet of fresh flowers and wither them into dried petals with one look from her terrible eyes. That is a reasonably-close quote."

"Then Rachel was there too!"

"It is not impossible."

"One thing you said just can't be true: *that there is no escape for me*. Surely if I went to, say Florida, or California—far from this base of power—they would not be able to follow."

It was Leopold's turn to study his coffee cup. He took somewhat longer than Vonnie. Then he admitted, "You have strong logic on your side. In fact, you may be entirely right. However, I am hoping that you will stay voluntarily."

"Why should I?"

"Because I am far from infallible. I told you that I don't believe Abigail is in danger. But I could be wrong. She is a fragile vessel for the transmission of Rachel's kind of power."

"Then what you're really doing is asking me for my help . . ."

. . . "Oh, there you are."

Vonnie raised her eyes as Keith came toward the

table. He looked much better, rested, no longer haggard.

Jason Leopold arose from his chair and Vonnie made the introductions. "This is the gentleman I told you about from Burton's Forge," she said.

Keith was immediately interested. "I think you said Mr. Leopold might help us on the Hazard House project."

"I'd be happy to do what I can," Leopold said.

"Mind if I pull up a chair?"

"Of course not," Leopold replied. "Have you had dinner?"

"It's a little late for me. I think I'll just have coffee and maybe a piece of pie." Seating himself, Keith asked, "What's your idea about turning Hazard House into a ski resort. Does it sound feasible?"

"There's certainly a great deal in its favor, Mr. Elwood."

Vonnie interrupted. "I've had a rather heavy day and I'm beat. I think I'll leave you two to your discussion and go upstairs."

"Go right ahead," Keith said heartily. "Get a good night's sleep. Tomorrow we go into high gear."

Vonnie thanked Jason Leopold for the dinner and left the dining room. She *was* tired but her prime urge was to get off by herself to think. Everything Leopold had told her was boiling around in her head.

But once inside her room, she was thinking about Keith. He looked a great deal better than when she'd put him to bed. The rest had sharpened him and he'd gone into the talk with Leopold with brisk directness.

Still, he had displayed the same brittleness, the same

hair-trigger alertness which she'd found unnatural from the very beginning; as though he'd been conditioned to expect a sudden blow and was tensed for it.

As she pondered the situation she realized how impossible it would be to tell him all that had happened to her in the past thirty-six hours. She was positive he would brush it all aside as a complicated product of her imagination.

But if he did react differently, and if he did take her seriously, she would only be piling her personal problems onto the load he was already carrying.

The best thing, she thought, would be for Keith to confide in me. I could do a better job for him in all departments if I knew exactly what's tearing him apart.

He had shown indications of opening up to her but they were only indications. She could only wait and hope for the best . . .

The phone rang twice in the next fifteen minutes. The first call was from Walter Sims. Lucy Stone had not seen Keith enter the dining room so when he didn't answer, she routed the call to Vonnie.

"Keith is having dinner downstairs, Mr. Sims," Vonnie said. "I'll have your call transferred to the lobby."

"No. Don't bother. Just tell Keith to call me when he has a minute. I'm leaving the lab now. I'll be home in half an hour."

"He has your home phone?"

"Yeah. Tell him he can call up to midnight." Sims

hesitated. "Or he can wait until morning if he wants to."

After the connection was broken she considered her reaction to the call. It seemed that Sims had shown relief at not finding Keith at Vonnie's end of the wire; as if he dreaded talking to him. If she was right, what distressing news could he have concerning the contents of the metal box? But she would relay the message.

She resolutely put the whole thing from her mind. It was really none of her business and she was annoyed with her new tendency to overanalyze, to measure the tone and quality of people's voices and try to read gravity into them.

A short time later, the second call came.

"Where were you?" Bill Jackson demanded.

"Where was I when?"

"Half an hour ago. I called."

"I was downstairs having dinner with a gentleman."

"Who?"

"Jason Leopold."

"Good lord! Is that old kook on the make for you?"

"He's not an old kook, and I find him fascinating."

"Where is he now?"

"Still in the dining room having coffee with my boss."

"What are you doing?"

"Sitting here waiting for my engagement ring—what else?"

"I hadn't planned to give you one."

"Oh, so your intentions weren't honorable from the very beginning! And after I've given you the best twenty-four hours of my life!"

"Those were the best?"

"You cad! Never speak to me again." There were a few long moments of silence after which Vonnie asked, "Are you still there?"

"I was just thinking."

"About what?"

"About your much-quoted Aunt Madge. Do you think she'd approve of me?"

"Of course she wouldn't."

"It's a gamble. It really is."

"What's a gamble?"

"Giving up my valuable freedom only to find I'm not approved of."

"By the way, aren't you supposed to be patrolling the roads and earning your pay?"

"I stopped off here to have a sandwich at Lorraine's. Can't you hear the juke box?"

"I certainly can. And I think I hear people laughing and living it up. Who's Lorraine?"

"She owns a joint over here on the south side of the lake."

"A place you didn't take me."

"Overlooked it."

"Well, see that you pay for the sandwich. I don't want you taking favors from that hussy."

"Are you going back downstairs?"

"I'm going to bed."

"See that you do. Goodnight, angel . . ."

This was another new experience for Vonnie; her

rapport with that crazy, mixed-up state trooper. Men were not strangers to Vonnie, but never in her life had she met one with whom she had fallen into such an immediate affinity; whom she did not have to measure her words beforehand and could say almost whatever came into her mind.

Of course, the gift of easy communication was his. She had merely responded—too easily? It was natural to wonder, but Vonnie really didn't think so.

She could only be grateful that he was there. However heavy her thoughts or great her fears, a few moments of contact with Bill, even over the phone, and her spirits went up like a balloon.

Am I in love with him?

Vonnie refused to answer that question. Instead, she tried to visualize his reaction if she were to tell him about the withered roses, the scene at the graveyard, and her discussion with Jason Leopold.

He would react differently than Keith because, for one thing, he would be more interested. But his disbelief would no doubt be the same. She could not see him, with his matter-of-fact outlook on life, accepting anything he could not see, feel, taste, or smell.

But what was wrong with that? What was wrong with being normal? And when he said, *Angel, it's all in that dizzy head of yours*, who could prove he would not be right.

We are always ready to judge other people, she thought. I've labeled Keith an unpredictable neurotic but never had the least doubt as to my own solid mental state. What would a psychiatrist say if I told him about my recent experiences?

Now the phone rang for the last time that evening. It was Jason Leopold.

"I hope I didn't awaken you. I just wanted to thank you for having dinner with me."

"I should thank you. Did you and Keith have an interesting talk?"

"Very. We hit it off very well. He has some heavy problems?"

"He works very hard," Vonnie said somewhat sharply.

Confidences had gone quite far enough for one evening, so if Jason Leopold was fishing for information Vonnie had no compunction about disappointing him.

"Goodnight," Leopold said. "We'll talk again."

"I'm sure we will."

Some minutes later Keith tapped on the door, saying, "If you're in bed, don't get up. I'll see you in the morning."

Vonnie was grateful. She'd had enough for one day and wanted only to sleep and banish the depression which was settling over her.

Still, it was nice to know that Keith was just next door. His presence just beyond the wall made any chilling blast from unnatural sources less likely.

But would it make any difference if Rachel chose to exert her power? . . .

CHAPTER EIGHT

Big Moose Lake was a clean little town with nothing of historical atmosphere about it. It was a new town, not more than twenty-five years old. It sprang up in answer to a need for a town in that exact spot once the proper roads were built and vacationers had found the lake.

Vonnie had no trouble finding the library. It was a neat, red brick building on Main Street and she thought of Mr. Carnegie with his thing for giving away libraries and she felt quite at home. But then she saw the cornerstone and realized that it only looked like one of his donations. Mr. Carnegie had been long gone while Big Moose Lake was still a wilderness.

But once inside, she could still have been back in Wilton—except that the woman behind the desk didn't look Midwest. She looked primly New England.

"Good morning," Vonnie said, "I've come to look at a book you have—or so I've been told."

The woman took in Vonnie's boots and riding britches; didn't seem to know what to make of her.

"A manuscript, really—written by Dame Goody about Hazard House."

This brought a frown. "Who told you about the manuscript?"

"A Mr. Leopold—Jason Leopold. I'm staying at Big Moose Lake Lodge and I'm quite interested in Hazard House."

The name Leopold brought even greater doubts. "Did Jason say the manuscript was available for inspection?"

"Well, he implied so. He didn't say that it wasn't."

"Do you have a library card?"

"No, I'm sorry."

"I suppose it doesn't matter," the woman mused. "You couldn't take the manuscript out in any case. It's too valuable."

"I'm sure it is. But may I look at it here—over there at one of those tables."

The woman remained reluctant. She said, "Well, I suppose so. Do you know Jason well?"

"He's not an old friend. I met him only recently."

"What is your interest in Hazard House?"

Vonnie hid her annoyance. The woman had no right to question her. But, then again, she could withhold the manuscript.

"My interest is general you might say. From what I've heard, John Hazard and his family must have been very interesting people."

"Very well. If you'll just wait at that table, I'll bring the manuscript."

There was further annoyance—a leisurely delay while the prim librarian took care of a small boy who brought back an armload of books. She checked them in, asked the little boy about his mother and sister, then returned the books to their stacks.

Vonnie could only surmise that the lady resented outsiders.

With no one else arriving for service, the manuscript was finally brought to the table, carried respectfully on the palms of the librarian's hands.

It had been given expert care. It was encased in a heavy plastic binding in loose-leaf fashion with each page carefully inside a lighter plastic.

"Be very careful," the librarian cautioned. "We have been offered ten thousand dollars for this manuscript."

That last seemed a faint gesture of friendship so Vonnie took advantage of it. "Who was Dame Goody?"

"A witch, I believe. Anyhow, she came here from Salem, Massachusetts, many years ago and lived in Burton's Forge until she died."

"I understand the manuscript was written quite a while after John and Rachel Hazard died."

"After the whole family was dead."

"I wonder where Dame Goody got her information."

"Wherever she got it—it's the truth," the librarian snapped. All semblance of friendship was gone. Vonnie, it seemed, had questioned the authenticity of the town's prized literary work. The woman did not take kindly to that.

"Let me know when you're through," she sniffed, and left with another look of disapproval at Vonnie's getup.

Vonnie admitted that boots and riding britches were hardly the attire in which to visit a library, but she had driven Keith to Hazard House by her newly-discovered road that morning. He congratulated her on her finding it and then gone off with his tape recorder, telling her to come back for him around five. Thus dismissed, Vonnie could think of no better time to follow up the lead Jason Leopold gave her.

She opened the manuscript. The pages were yellowed but with care had been kept in very good shape. The title page was done in elaborate Spencerian. Obviously Dame Goody had been a woman of education. It read:

Notes on the Life of Rachel Hazard and Her Husbande, Being a Historie of the Household at Hazard House.

But while she could indite well, Dame Goody turned out wanting in literary ability. The rhetoric was childish—even illiterate in places:

Rachel Hazard comed North from the South with her husbande in 1859. She had the Mark and was beloved of the Prince . . .

The Prince, Vonnie mused. Could that mean Satan? Obviously it did because Dame Goody had written:

Rachel was teached to the many ways of Dark-
ness and was gave by the Prince his great gifts in
pay for getting many to worship . . .

Now here was an added disappointment: Dame
Goody, perhaps carried away by her material during
the writing, lapsed quite often into an unreadable
scrawl. Perhaps experts could have deciphered the
whole of the manuscript, but Vonnie was far from expert in that department. She turned several pages to
what seemed to be a second chapter. Now, Vonnie
could see the pattern and ran quickly through the
manuscript to verify her findings.

Dame Goody started each chapter in complete
control of her emotions. But, as she progressed, she
became more and more excited until her racing pen—
or quill?—was running helter-skelter across the page.
Obviously, Dame Goody did not view her material
objectively. What compulsion had forced her to take
up her pen in the first place? Was it an order from the
Prince? If so, he could certainly have called on a more
legible penman.

But perhaps Dame Goody's facts were more accu-
rate than her handwriting because the details Vonnie
could make out seemed authoritative:

The Pledge was in blood to tie to the Prince for-
ever . . . The signings was celebrate by a sacri-
fyce in the Circle and the Prince blessed the
blood . . .

Vonnie turned the page with the tip of her finger—as though the page were contaminated. What went on in that unholy place? Were the sacrifices human? Vonnie did not wish to even conjecture:

Rachel gave her husbande three children in great extasy . . .

What did that mean? Sex orgies? Vonnie preferred not to dwell on that either.

There was Johnathon and Davide and the girl childe Patience. Both sons when the pledging came for their own free will refused and were turned oute. But they had seen and heard and the Prince followed wherever theye went until their knowing was destroyed . . .

This seemed not too difficult to translate based upon what Vonnie had learned about the Hazards at the New York Public Library. The two sons, Jonathan and David, had defied their abominable mother and thus defied the Prince. Obviously their father had not protected them because they had been turned out. That left the matter of their tragic deaths as mentioned in the other history. Had this been brought about by the pursuing Prince—or a trusted lieutenant perhaps—because they knew too much? There had been no mention of murder in the genealogical record but then it had not been an in-depth study of the Hazard family.

Vonnie read on, skimming through the manuscript. Parts of it were revolting. There were sketchy descriptions of Satanic rites—all in all, however sketchy, a clear revelation into the black heart of Rachel Hazard.

Vonnie read a last, legible passage:

Ande so Rachel delivered up many souls to the Prince but not the greatest ande the Prince was angry . . .

Tired from fruitless eyestrain, Vonnie closed the manuscript and delivered it to the desk.

"Did you get what you wanted?" the librarian asked.

"It was most difficult to read, but it was revealing."

Then Vonnie remembered that she was also obligated to earn her salary and one of her duties was to sound out the natives. Glancing at the small plaque on the desk—something she'd overlooked, she said, "Mrs. Orton, my name is Vanessa March. We are here to look over Hazard House and the surrounding property with the idea of opening a ski resort."

There was a sniff. "Do you mean one of those places where fools tie slats to their feet and slide down hills?"

"After a manner of speaking—yes."

"What other way is there to put it?"

"Well, it would bring new people to Big Moose Lake. It would add to the prosperity of the town."

"I think we've got enough of that kind now."

"But without them, your town might not even be here."

"We'd make out. We always have. Outlanders coming and going in their fancy garb."

Mrs. Orton eyed Vonnie along with that statement but with a little less hostility. "You aren't naked, I'll say that for you. The disgrace is the naked ones parading around in next to nothing. Things have changed since I was a girl."

"A town ordinance could put an end to that—I mean to the near-nudity here in the village limits."

"Not with greedy men like Sam Bates and Frank Genessee on the board. They don't want to miss a thin dime."

"Well, at any rate, Mrs. Orton, people who come to ski are always bundled up."

"We've still got enough outlanders . . ."

Vonnie thanked the woman and went back to the jeep. In evaluating her first interview, she decided that Mrs. Orton was probably an exception to the rule in Big Moose Lake. And probably an exception without much weight. Sam Bates and Frank Genessee would no doubt outvote her if it came to a showdown . . .

Vonnie drove back quietly thinking, taking her time. As she rounded the bend which brought the lodge in sight, there was a definite surge in the region of her heart; this from the sight of the patrol car parked by the front entrance.

She hadn't been hoping for exactly what she would find there; but she insisted on that firmly, even while knowing it was a great big lie.

She parked beside it and went inside. On seeing her, Lucy Stone—alert as usual—jerked her thumb in the direction of the coffee shop across the lobby. Under the neat little neon sign she saw a khaki-uniformed back hunched over the counter.

She went up and said: "I've seen gold-bricking fuzz in my time, but you take the medal."

Bill Jackson spun around on his stool. "Where have you been?"

"In town. At the library."

He looked at her attire. "You've been shooting ducks in the library?"

"No, taking riding lessons."

"You're the darndest woman to keep track of."

"Well, you don't seem to be in any hurry about marrying me, so I'm looking over the rest of the local crop. Is this seat taken?"

"The rest of the crop was blighted at birth. Sit down. As to marrying you, I haven't made up my mind yet."

"I know. You're trying to decide between Lorraine and me."

"How did you guess?"

"I'm psychic. Have you made your decision?"

"It's a tough one. Lorraine would come nearer to filling my humble cottage."

Vonnie poured milk into the coffee a pretty little fugitive from some college brought her. "She has a towering intellect no doubt."

"Not exactly. A towering fanny. Lorraine weighs close to three hundred pounds. She's magnificent."

148

"Hmmm. Well, how can I compete? Shall I start eating five meals a day?"

Bill looked at her with veiled eyes and a quick change of mood. His grin turned to a soft smile.

"You put on a single pound more and I'll whack it off of you."

"Are you saying I'm just right?"

"I'm saying stay like you are."

"Mr. Jackson! I've never been wooed so romantically in my life."

"I saw you turning into the woods with a man in a jeep. What about that?"

"My boss. He's doing *his* thing. I took him to Hazard House."

"Come on! The road to Hazard House is clear around the mountain."

"Want to bet?"

"You're telling me you found your way in from this side?"

"A very nice road. The pavement is rough in spots but we made it."

"Look—you're way ahead of me."

It was a distinct pleasure to be ahead of Bill Jackson for a change; almost a delightful triumph. But then, like an idiot, she felt sorry for him.

"Abigail showed it to me."

"That kid? Well I'll be fried in goat grease."

"That might be an improvement. Are you off tonight?"

"Check. And you'd better be, too."

"I'll make a note of it."

After a pause during which Vonnie brushed some dust off Bill Jackson's shoulder, she spoke in a more serious tone.

"Bill, what do you think of a ski lodge at Hazard House?"

He shrugged. "What's to think?"

"You must have some opinion."

"None at all. Except I'm not going to be chasing pickpockets down a mountain on skis."

"You can wait for them at the bottom. But seriously, you know this country. Would a ski resort be a success?"

"I don't see why not. They come here in the summer so why not in the winter? The roads are pretty good and we usually have enough snow."

"Thanks. I'm supposed to be sounding out the local yokels on the project. Your name will lead all the rest."

"How would you like a good spanking?"

"Not 'til I get back from picking up my boss. It's hard to drive a jeep standing up."

Vonnie finished her coffee and as she started to rise she found herself spun around on her stool with Bill's hand behind her neck, and calmly kissed.

She was surprised but it was not the kiss so much as how it was done; as though Bill Jackson had been kissing her goodbye for years. Even as their lips touched and he drew back, his eyes turned vague.

"A road into Hazard House from this side. Well, I'll be—!"

"I'm sure you will. And thanks for the *big* thrill."

Vonnie left. At the door, she heard, just as vague, a "see you tonight," called after her.

As she drove toward Hazard House, she was again aware of how a few minutes with that crazy state trooper lifted her spirits. It was beginning to be annoying—as though she resented the power he seemed to have over her.

Another thing—this was not how a romance was supposed to be—a man taking a girl so casually for granted. There were supposed to be ups and downs in a romance; spats and making up again. Uncertainties that were pain and reconciliations that were minor ecstasies.

A romance was not supposed to be as calmly taken for granted as an old shoe.

Then Vonnie laughed and dodged an overhanging branch as Hazard House came in sight . . .

". . . Exactly what *will* they want in the report?" Vonnie asked.

She'd met Keith in front of the great, deserted monstrosity called Hazard House and he was studying it thoughtfully while pulling at one ear.

"A lot of data. One of your jobs will be to lay out a weather pattern back fifty years. Temperatures from day to day during the winter months. Snowfall depths—wind drift—that sort of thing."

"But I know nothing about meteorology!"

"Then find someone who does," he said absently.

"Do you mean hire a weatherman?"

"Who else? But whatever he asks, offer him less. We want to keep expenses down."

Vonnie was now beginning to get some idea of how widely her duties would range. It was a little daunting but it had an element of excitement.

"We'll need surveyors, too. We've got to have at least two proven ski runs; a fairly tough one and another for the less skilled—runs, and a place for one ski lift that will service them both."

He was peering up at the jagged contours on two sides of the cleared circle.

"A lot of trees will have to come down. I hope we don't bump into a hard-core crop of ecologists."

"I started polling the local residents and I think we should get as close as possible to the Chamber of Commerce in Big Moose Lake. I already have a couple of names. Sam Bates and Frank Genessee."

"Good."

"By the way, did you call your friend Walter Sims?"

There was a long pause until Vonnie wondered if he'd heard the question.

"No. I'll ring him tonight."

"How did you make out with Jason Leopold?"

"Okay. He may be of help to us."

Keith seemed to have steadied down. Vonnie was watching him closely while trying not to make it apparent. There was a grimness about him, giving her the impression that while his problem had not gone away, he'd resolved to hold it under control and get on with his work.

Another impression she was now getting had to do with Hazard House itself.

At this moment, it looked so different than at the time of her first visit. The sky was empty of clouds now. That certainly had a lot to do with it. No dark celestial framework for the mood picture she'd seen before.

But it was more than that; almost as if the house were consciously showing a different face: its shabby face. An image of self-pity from having been abandoned by those it loved.

Love? Hardly. After what Vonnie had heard and read, the word itself was grotesque in relation to Hazard House.

"It's got thirty-eight rooms," Keith said. "A lot of waste space, though. The hallways are four times as wide as need be."

He forgot Vonnie had seen the place, as he went on: "There's a big court on the first floor that's really something. Made to order for a restaurant with plenty of room left over for a lobby and a few guest rooms down there if they want to put them in."

"You never told me who owns the place," Vonnie said. "Did Enterprise Associates buy it?"

"They have an option that runs another six months. The owners live in California. They're descendants of old John himself through one of his sons, Christopher, who died in San Francisco while quite young."

This added somewhat to Vonnie's knowledge of the Hazards. One of John's sons had married and had at least one child before his death.

"Well, we'd better get back," Keith said, squinting at the sun. "Things look pretty good."

153

As the jeep climbed the rise toward the road, Vonnie said, "You mentioned needing surveyors. Do you want me to follow through on that?"

"You'd better. I'll go to New York tomorrow and talk to an architect I know. We'll need a proposal for rebuilding the inside of the mansion."

"Will you leave the floor in the court under the dome the way it is?"

"I think it would be a good idea, don't you?"

"It would really be a shame to tear up the floor. In fact, it might not be allowed."

"How come?"

"I found out that Jason Leopold keeps it clean. There is some kind of a clause in the original deed about that—or wherever such clauses are to be found. It says that the floor has to be cleaned and scrubbed every six months in perpetuity."

"That was mentioned at Enterprise. But they didn't seem to take it very seriously."

"Who pays Jason Leopold for doing the work?"

"The financial affairs are handled by a bank in New York. That clause is in the will along with a couple of others that aren't effective anymore. One of them said a big oak tree west of the house had to be cared for. Another ordered that a creek running along behind the house had to be kept dredged out and generally taken care of."

"What happened?"

"Lightning knocked the tree over, and the creek dried up when they put in a dam over near Lamphere."

That was interesting. Vonnie had attached a sinister

significance to the floor business without quite knowing why. But now it appeared that the eccentric John Hazard had merely liked the floor and the creek and the tree and wanted them to remain as they were.

Then again, she thought, perhaps not . . . The floor could still have been all-important—with the care of the tree and the creek thrown in to hide his true purpose.

There I go again, she told herself. Overanalyzing. I'd better get off the morbid side and start visualizing a beautiful ski lodge here in the days to come . . .

When they got back, Keith pulled up in front of the lodge but stayed behind the wheel. "I want to run into town for a few minutes," he said. I'll see you a little later."

With her services not needed, Vonnie stopped at the coffee shop for a quick cup in preference to a drink in the bar.

While drinking it, she pondered a problem she hoped would never come up: working as she and Keith now were, set up the possibility of a problem. At the office she went her way and he went his, after working hours.

But here, there were no defined working hours. They would be living next door to each other for twenty-four hours a day. So far, Keith had been away most of the time but if he settled down to work on the Hazard House, would he expect to monopolize her evenings also?

And, if that became the pattern, what was she going to do about Bill Jackson?

While she was pondering this, Lucy Stone looked in and called, "There's a man on the phone for Mr. Elwood. Do you want to take it?"

"I might as well," said Vonnie and went out to the desk.

The call was from Walter Sims. "Tell me," he demanded. "What's wrong with that boss of yours?"

"He didn't call you?"

"You did tell him to?"

"Why, yes. As soon as I saw him after you called."

"Well, tell him again. And you can tell him everything's okay. No problems."

"I certainly shall . . ."

She was resting on her balcony when Keith got back. He went into his own room and came out through his own balcony door.

"There was a call from Walter Sims," Vonnie said. "He told me to tell you that everything is all—"

"I know, I know," he cut in. "Called him from town."

Keith stood looking out across the lake, his head held high and his shoulders back. Vonnie saw the transformation instantly. It was so apparent that a comment seemed necessary.

"Well, whatever the news was, it must have been good."

He beamed down at her. "Let's have a drink," he said.

"I could use one. Shall I call room service?"

"Too slow. Let's go downstairs . . ."

"I'm afraid I've made it tough on you," he said when they were seated at a corner table with a scotch and a whiskey sour. "I didn't mean to, but—well, it's been pretty rough."

"I could see that. I only hoped there was something I could do."

"You did fine." He frowned and turned the stem of his glass in nervous fingers, trying to find words to begin . . .

CHAPTER NINE

"My wife, Valerie, had a nervous breakdown," Keith said.

"Then I can understand why you were upset," Vonnie replied.

"It was more than that." He paused to look deep into Vonnie's eyes, holding his gaze so long it became embarrassing.

"A lot more than that. She means so much to me. I don't know what I'd do without Valerie."

"She's a lucky girl."

"I did the best I could at home, but she finally had to go to the rest home for therapy. That's where I have been spending a lot of my time."

"I have a feeling that she's better now?"

This surprised him. "How did you know that?"

"By the way you've changed . . . You didn't have to tell me that you're deeply in love with her—your actions when she was in trouble showed that."

her if Keith suspended business. She suspected that there were few jobs in existence as erratic and unpredictable as the one she'd found.

So all in all, the talk had been satisfactory—up to a point. But however confidential and revealing Keith had been, he'd stopped far short of complete openness. The mystery of the metal box, Walter Sims's role in the drama, and what Keith feared Sims's findings would be, remained as obscure as ever.

Vonnie could only surmise. It seemed logical that Keith feared drug addiction as a trap Valerie had fallen into. But if that were true, what could Walter Sims have discovered from the drug-dealing equipment that could have had any bearing? It seemed more probable that the hypodermic had belonged to the tragic Sarah.

Also, Valerie's addiction, or not, would certainly have been ascertained at the rest home.

It was all very strange. She would probably never get the complete answer, Vonnie thought. But, then, again it was really none of her business. By way of consolation she told herself that doubtless hundreds of New York secretaries were puzzling over riddles their bosses chose not to solve for them. Her job was to make herself as valuable as possible to Keith and . . .

. . . "Where have you been?"

Vonnie was startled into almost knocking her glass over. She looked up at the towering Bill Jackson and retorted, "Good lord! Do you make a practice of sneaking up on people?"

"And how long have you been a lone drinker?"

"For years. I inherited the talent from my father."

"I phoned earlier. You weren't here."

"You may not believe it, but I do have a job."

"You were over at Hazard House with your boss."

"How did you know?"

"I bumped into one of the Burton's Forge men on the road. He'd come through that way and told me."

"Then if you knew, why did you ask me?"

"You don't want me to seem totally disinterested in your whereabouts, do you?"

"I think a little disinterest would be just fine."

"Are you working tonight?"

"No."

"Okay. I'm off at eight. I'll pick you up."

"Not tonight."

"Why not?"

"Because I have things to do. I want to write a letter to my aunt back home for one thing."

"That shouldn't take long."

"There are other things. I've been going all day and I'm tired. And I have some washing to do."

Bill picked up her drink and finished it for her while he appeared to ponder each excuse one at a time.

"Hmmm," he said, staring at the empty glass, "it was a real short romance, wasn't it?"

Really! Men could be so exasperating at times. "Bill! That's not true. Just because a girl needs a little time to herself—particularly a working girl—it doesn't mean that . . ."

She saw the grin start slowly and spread across Bill Jackson's face.

"Why you sneaky—!"

He did not let her finish that either. Still grinning, he was on his feet, planting a fast kiss on the top of her head.

"Write a long letter to your aunt and wash everything in sight. I'll call you."

With that, he strode off whistling, leaving Vonnie to kick herself figuratively for allowing him to do what he'd done. He had needled her into admitting to something she would have refused to admit seriously —at least at that stage in their relationship—that there was something between them other than casual dating. Thus he had won a victory in the duel which is a part of every romance, budding or otherwise. It was almost enough to make Vonnie order another drink to grumble into.

But instead, she did what any psychologist who knew her habit patterns could have easily predicted. She went upstairs, stripped off her working clothes, and got into the shower . . .

After a reasonable cooling-off period, she donned a loose, comfortable dressing gown and stretched out on the balcony. It was still too early for dinner.

Keith's balcony door was open and she could hear him moving about inside. This was vaguely uncomfortable. With her working day definitely over, it should not be necessary to remain in such close proximity to Keith. Somehow, it made her feel guilty— should she be in there helping him?

A request for a change in rooms would remedy the situation somewhat, but it was too late for that. Even though she liked Lucy Stone, she could still visualize her whispering to the help: "Vonnie March and her boss had a fight. She moved out."

No, better to stay where she was and suffer the guilt. She could live with it.

Vonnie closed her eyes. A half-hour nap would be just right. Then she'd dress and go down to dinner . . .

. . . "Hello."

Vonnie did not move a muscle. She did not even open her eyes. She just lay there and thought, Oh, no! Not tonight. I want to write a letter to Aunt Madge and wash some clothes and just relax.

"Are you asleep?"

"No, Abigail. I'm not asleep."

"Can I come in and sit down?"

"Of course."

At least she's a polite child, Vonnie told herself. I could have been burdened with a brat who'd be jumping on the bed and walking the balcony railings.

Vonnie opened her eyes and angled them to watch Abigail as she sat down cross-legged on the floor by the railing and smoothed her gray shift over her lap.

"Is that the only dress you have, dear?" Vonnie asked.

"No. I have three others."

"But they're all the same?"

"Yes."

"Would you like it if I bought you a new dress?"

"That would be nice."

"How about some blue jeans and sneakers? You

shouldn't be walking around in the woods barefoot."

"The boys wear blue jeans," Abigail said.

"Oh, I see."

"Sweaters would be nice."

"We'll go into town and see what we can do. How do you dress in the winter when it's cold?"

"Melissa bundles me up."

"Is Melissa your grandfather's wife?"

"I don't know. She's very nice."

"I'm sure she is."

Vonnie not only felt a stab of guilt for snooping, she was annoyed with herself. It was too much like a question that impossible librarian would have asked.

"Would you like to have dinner with me again tonight?"

"That would be nice but I don't think I will be here."

"Is your grandpa coming after you?"

"Maybe. I don't think so though. I think Bill Jackson will pick me up pretty soon."

"Did he say he would?"

"No. He'll just happen to come by."

"Abigail, you're the strangest child!"

"I'm sorry."

"Forgive me. I didn't mean it personally. You just keep surprising me. Did you just drop by or did you have a reason for coming?"

"I had a reason. Patience."

Vonnie felt herself cringing. So much of reality, however puzzling and frustrating, had intervened since her last brush with what Jonas Leopold refused to call the supernatural, that she'd almost forgotten the deeper frustration that the names Patience and Rachel brought.

"Honey," Vonnie said, "are you sure Patience isn't just a product of your imagination?"

"I don't think so."

"But you don't know for sure?"

"I'm pretty sure I know for sure."

It was like punching a pillow, or wading upstream against a gentle but relentless current. Why, Vonnie demanded silently, didn't Jason Leopold keep Abigail under closer scrutiny instead of letting her wander around involving other people who had troubles of their own?

"I'm sorry, dear," she said in apology for the thought. "Why did Patience send you?"

"I think she wants you to help her."

"But you aren't sure of that either?"

"I'm pretty sure."

"How can I help her?"

"She wants something that Rachel doesn't want her to have."

"But you've no idea what that something is?"

Abigail's deep, troubled eyes showed that she was trying very hard to understand exactly what it was Patience wanted.

"Patience is very unhappy. She has been waiting for you to come for a long time."

"But that's ridiculous, dear. She had no way of knowing that I would ever come—I mean it was pure chance that brought me here."

"Then maybe she was just waiting for someone who would be able to help her."

"That's even more ridiculous. I know nothing about the supernatural. I'm—well, I'm just not the type of person who could possibly help the dead. I—oh, this is all so ridiculous. Can't you see that?"

Abigail shook her head doubtfully. "I don't think that's the way it is. If it was, Patience wouldn't care about you. She wouldn't have sent the roses. And if Patience was not right, Rachel wouldn't have bothered to make them die."

"It's all just impossible!"

"Shall I tell Patience you won't help her?"

"How do you tell Patience things? How does she communicate with you?"

"I'm not sure. I just know when she's near me and I sit very still—"

"Do you consciously put yourself in her power?"

"I guess so. What do you want me to tell her?"

A sudden flash of recollection brought back Vonnie's conversation with Jason Leopold. He'd felt Abigail was in no danger, but he'd been far from sure. Then too, there had been his own acknowledged helplessness in protecting Abigail.

With that in mind, Vonnie's point of view changed somewhat. In pleading the shadowy Patience's case, Abigail might really have been asking help for herself. Suppose all this was in her mind? Turning her away could be disastrous.

Vonnie realized of course that in accusing Abigail of hallucinations, she had to admit certain mental distortions of her own. However, that probably had nothing to do with her decision.

"All right, dear. You tell Patience that I'll help her

if I can. But I've got to be given some idea of what's expected of me."

"I'm sure that will make her happy." Abigail got to her feet. "I've got to go now."

"Wait 'til I put on a dress and I'll walk you down to the lobby. Maybe you'll change your mind about dinner and have a bite with me."

Abigail waiting quietly at the door while Vonnie changed—too much like a well-trained puppy for comfort. As they reached the foot of the stairs in the lobby, Bill Jackson came through the front door.

"Hi," he waved. "Are you two living together now?"

"Abigail came visiting," Vonnie said.

"Lucky I came by, then. I can run her home." He reached out and Abigail put her hand trustingly into his. "Come on, chipmunk. You're getting to be entirely too much of a gadabout."

He escorted Abigail out of the lodge, but came back alone, before Vonnie reached the dining room entrance.

"Hey. Wait up. I came back to ask you about tomorrow night. Will you have your letter written and everything washed by then?"

"Probably. But I'm glad you came back. I wanted to ask you—did you know Abigail was here?"

"Didn't have the vaguest notion. I just stopped to maybe catch a glimpse of you."

"You're sure her grandfather didn't send you or anything like that?"

"Dead sure. What gives?"

"It's just what she told me. She said that when she was ready to leave, you'd be here to pick her up."

"So she happened to be right. Kids her age trust God and the fuzz."

"I know. It's just the way she said it. As though there was absolutely no doubt."

"She's a strange kid."

"You can say that again."

"Okay for tomorrow night then. If I don't see you before, I'll pick you up around eight."

Vonnie agreed by not disagreeing. Bill gave her a quick, piercing look and squeezed her shoulder. "You're tired. Get something to eat and then get to bed and get a good night's sleep."

"I'll do that."

Vonnie glanced about, afraid that Bill would kiss her there in public. When he didn't, striding off toward the door, she resented that also.

I guess I'm just tired, she thought . . .

CHAPTER TEN

The date with Bill had to be broken.

Keith announced it the following morning: "You're invited to dinner."

"Isn't it a little early?"

"I mean this evening. I was talking to Valerie last night and she wants you for dinner. We've got to go in anyhow to clear up a few things that came in at the answering service. So we'll do that, have dinner, and still get back fairly early."

When Vonnie hesitated, he said, "You can make it, can't you? You don't have anything else on?"

If it had been a matter of going in only for the dinner, Vonnie would have probably begged off on the grounds of having a date. As it was, they were going in anyhow, so she could hardly refuse.

"No. I'll be happy to meet Mrs. Elwood."

"Good. We'll start right away."

Vonnie had dressed for another trip to Hazard

House so she went upstairs from the dining room and spent a few minutes debating what to wear. A sensible midiskirt and a simple white blouse with a tan sweater? In other words, look as mousey as possible?

It may have been resentment at being practically ordered to appear on such short notice or the mood brought on by not sleeping too well the night before. At any rate, Vonnie demanded to know why she should hide her best side just because she was going to meet the boss's wife.

So, with a defiance which was really unjustified, she donned the sleek pantyhose which accentuated the nakedness of her legs, slipped on the miniskirt, and selected a black turtleneck sweater and a minijacket that didn't disguise anything—thinking as she dressed: I'm sorry if this outfit isn't quite for dinner at the boss's home but I'm a working girl just in from the country. It will have to do.

She met Keith in the lobby, where she rated a couple of blinks from him and two other male guests passing by.

"Tell Bill I'm sorry I can't make it tonight," she told Lucy Stone. "Maybe he'll call and it will save him a trip to the lodge. Tell him I'll explain later . . ."

The trip to Manhattan was pleasant enough, what with the weather so satisfactory and Keith practically a new man since his tragedy had been averted.

He talked of this and that relative to the job, nothing she had to concentrate on very hard. One point was interesting: he thought they could wind it up in about three weeks if no unforeseen obstacles got in the way.

That meant Vonnie might be out of a job in less than a month if he stuck to his resolve of a long vacation. She was tempted to bring that up but decided to let things work themselves out.

At the office, Keith wrote checks against a pile of bills they found in the mail. Vonnie sent these out together with four letters in response to other letters and calls to the answering service.

As the time wore on Vonnie found herself growing more tense. This angered her. Why on earth was meeting Keith's wife such a big deal? She wasn't trying to steal him from the woman!

By four-thirty, they were through. "Okay," Keith said. "Let's head uptown. I'll let Valerie know we're coming."

Vonnie made a final trip to the washroom while Keith called. She checked her makeup, put a couple of strands of her burnished hair back in place, and then, in defiance of herself as much as anyone else, made a face in the mirror.

"Vanessa March," she said, "you're an idiot . . ."

Valerie Elwood was at the door to greet them, and Vonnie caught her breath. This woman was stunning! Keith took her into his arms immediately and Vonnie, thankful for the interlude, tried to compose herself. She realized now—a little belatedly—exactly what she'd been trying to do: not outshine or triumph over his wife in any way, but definitely to be on par with her. She hadn't wanted to win but she certainly hadn't wanted to lose—as she appeared to be doing.

The sense of defeat was within herself. Valerie Elwood had an aura, charisma that even exceptional physical beauty could not match. Vonnie's immediate feeling of inferiority sensed this immediately.

Valerie wore a straight silver sheath without a single piece of jewlery. Her hair was raven black drawn into a bun. This hairdo would have been disastrous for nine out of ten women, but it complemented Valerie's classic features. She had a long narrow face with Garbo's gauntness in her cheeks. Her mouth was a red slash but it belonged.

All this created an image shouting sex allure and regal unattainability in one striking whole.

And to this was added a graciousness comprised of dignity and warmth.

She extricated herself from Keith and turned to Vonnie, not waiting for any introduction and brushed velvety lips across her cheek.

"Vanessa, dear, I'm so delighted that you accepted my invitation."

"It was sweet of you to invite me."

"Come. We'll have drinks in the living room. Then I'll leave you for a few minutes. I've been away and our staff is not back yet. So I'm doing the cooking."

As she led Vanessa down the steps, she laughed—a sound like liquid silver. "Our staff! Sounds very impressive, doesn't it? Actually, we have a cook who sleeps out and a very faithful full-time maid."

"Do you feel up to a martini, darling?" Keith asked.

Again, the laugh. "Of course. I don't have an *alcohol* problem, Keith."

The subtle accent on the word alcohol was the faintest acknowledgment that hers was another problem. Vonnie wondered if she knew he had told her about the breakdown. Somehow, she felt that Valerie did not.

As Keith was making the drinks, Valerie folded herself gracefully to the floor before the lounge where she'd seated Vonnie, and said, "This is a wonderful opportunity to satisfy my curiosity: Keith is always so dreadfully busy I never learn a thing."

"I'd be happy to tell you anything I can," said Vonnie.

"Tell me all about that fantastic mansion Keith mentioned. Hazard House I believe it's called?"

Vonnie was relieved; had feared Valerie might be after her own personal history. "Well, what can I say? It *is* fantastic."

"Will it make a good ski lodge?"

"I'm sure it will. It has over thirty rooms with a crazy Moorish tower right in the middle."

"How unique!"

Keith brought a martini and a whiskey sour. After tasting hers, Valerie closed her eyes in appreciation. Then she opened them, "Keith, darling," she said, "I'm surprised at you. How did you know Vanessa wanted a whiskey sour? You didn't even ask her. You're a fine host!"

"That's what she always drinks. It's okay isn't it, Vonnie?"

178

"Oh, yes." Smiling down at Valerie, she added. "I'm a very light drinker. I mean, until I came east, it was only wine."

It was a clumsy moment, but no one's fault that Vonnie could see. Keith could have asked her what she wanted but he hadn't. Valerie could have overlooked the implication that they'd done a lot of drinking together, but she hadn't done that either.

Valerie's silvery laugh dismissed the whole exchange—the tone of minor triumph read into it by Vonnie.

"This Hazard House," Valerie said, "I understand is far back in the woods where one could easily get lost."

"Vanessa took care of that. She met a little girl who showed her a road no one knew existed. It will save a bundle."

"How marvelous!"

Keith had dropped to the floor beside Valerie. Her hand went automatically into his. Sitting above them on the lounge, Vonnie felt herself on display, but she was more keenly aware of the slip Keith had made. Calling it a slip was no doubt a result of her own uneasiness; of a guilt she had no right to feel. After calling her Vonnie, he'd shifted to Vanessa. Had Valerie noticed that? If so, she gave no sign.

The conversation remained in "safe" areas for some fifteen minutes after which Valerie excused herself to go to the kitchen.

"Another drink?" Keith asked.

"No—please. I'm nursing this one."

179

"I think I'll go help her."

"I wish you would. You two see so little of each other you shouldn't lose a minute . . ."

Vonnie was glad to be alone. It gave her a chance to fight the uptight feeling which was making the dinner a nightmare for her. There was no reason for it, she told herself savagely. Why am I acting like a sneaky husband-stealer when I'm innocent of any such idea?

Of course, it was the impact of Valerie's personality; her stunning impact. Or was it? Vonnie had met beautiful women before. So why this terrible sense of awe and guilt?

What is the worst that could happen? she pondered. Lose a job that's temporary in the first place? So relax; stop acting like a ten-year-old.

The respite did her good. When they sat down to dinner, Vonnie was more at ease than she'd been all evening. And was no doubt why she saw more clearly; why she now became aware of the tension in the room—because her own tension had blurred her receptivity.

And tension there was. Slowly she realized that Valerie was acting, beautifully and skillfully. Acting out the part of the gracious hostess, but under a tension shared with Keith. Both were in silent rapport—tight as fiddle strings—which, in essence, left Vonnie far outside . . .

The dinner was excellent: boned chicken delicately flavored after the French cuisine; white wine Vonnie barely sipped; asparagus tips in butter sauce to have impressed even Aunt Madge; and small French pastries for dessert. Probably one of the finest dinners Vonnie ever ate, despite its being the one she least enjoyed.

A little while after coffee, Valerie herself paved the way for a graceful exit:

"You two have such a long way to go, I'm sure you want to get started."

"You're sure you're all right here alone?" Keith asked.

"Why, darling, of course I am."

"I can stay over; Vonnie could drive back alone."

It was back to *Vonnie* again. She wished Keith would stay with one name or the other. "There's no reason Keith shouldn't stay over," said Vonnie, "things are going very well up there."

"I wouldn't hear of it. Keith has his work and I'm not a clinging wife."

"Then let me thank you for the evening. I don't know when I've enjoyed myself so much."

Valerie's great liquid eyes said *Liar*, but with such a humorous glint that it was forgivable.

"You are too kind," Valerie said. "We must get together again very soon."

"I'll look forward to it . . ."

The miles back to Big Moose Lake were covered mainly in silence. A barrier, vague, but still a barrier, had sprung up between them.

Vonnie said, "You have a lovely wife. You're a very lucky man."

"She's one in a million all right," Keith replied, then they lapsed into a silence which lasted most of the way.

It gave Vonnie a chance to evaluate the dinner, to make a decision. She had acted childishly and was grateful that it hadn't shown on the outside. As the green miles rolled past she made a firm decision: to accept Valerie at her face value. To have done with all the ridiculous analyzing, dissecting and concluding which was probably without any foundation whatever. A more compassionate attitude was certainly in order. Valerie had gone through a harrowing experience and had the strength to recover and go on with her life. Therefore she merited admiration, not suspicion.

With that decision Vonnie felt better. She settled back into her seat and dozed. Only one question dancing faintly about in her mind:

What was the secret of the metal box? . . .

"Where did you go?" asked Bill.

"The—the city," Vonnie replied.

"With your boss?"

"I took him along," said Vonnie acidly. "I thought he might get lonesome by himself around here."

"You sound out of sorts."

"Hold on a minute."

Vonnie shifted the phone from one hand to the other and reached for her lighter.

"Okay," she said.

"What did you do?"

"I lit a cigarette! Any objection?"

"I think maybe you're smoking too much but that's not what I meant. I meant what did you do in the city?"

"Keith took me to dinner at his apartment. Mrs. Elwood is a wonderful cook."

"Hmmm. So he took you home to see Mother."

"Mrs. Elwood is his wife, stupid! Not his mother."

"Oh. She wanted to look over the competition?"

"Bill! I'm in no mood, and what you're saying isn't funny!"

"Sorry. Rough day, huh?"

"It was a long ride both ways."

"You're down, aren't you?"

"As a matter of fact, I am."

"Kind of in the dumps?"

"You might put it that way."

"Tell you what—I'll come up and sit on your balcony with you a while and cheer you up."

"No. Keith is—"

"What?"

"My boss—"

"Oh."

Vonnie caught herself up quickly. So Keith *was* in the next room. So what? He was neither her father nor her guardian.

"Come on up, Bill. I'd like to see you."

"Fine. I'll bring a nightcap . . ."

Vonnie was in her shortie nightgown. She slipped a floor-length housecoat over it, and just in time. She was fluffing her hair when Bill knocked.

He had a tumbler of scotch in one hand and a shaker in the other.

"Good lord!" Vonnie exclaimed. "Were you planning an all-night drinking party?"

"No sweat, angel. This is a double of scotch—"

"A very generous double."

"—and two sours in the shaker. Got a glass in the bathroom?"

He went in and brought out a tumbler even as he spoke, and then went out onto the balcony.

Vonnie followed, noting gratefully that Keith's balcony door was closed and the light was out.

"Don't talk too loud—I think Keith is asleep. Let's not wake him up."

Bill sprawled out in one of the chaise longues and sighed expansively. "I had a rough day too. Glad it's over."

"Lots of traffic tickets?"

"No. I passed a sedan with no plates on Salt Lick, the other side of town. I took out after him with the siren on and he pulled over all right, but he let go with a .45 as I was walking up to him."

Vonnie, stretched out beside him, straightened and laid a quick hand on his arm.

"Oh, Bill! You could have been killed."

"Uh-huh," he retorted casually. "He was a lousy shot. Off on a trip. I'd psyched him a little because I did have my holster open."

"Did you shoot?"

"Didn't have to. I got close enough to lay my barrel across his skull."

"Oh, Bill—"

He lowered his glass and turned his head from

dreamily eying the dark lake. He seemed honestly surprised at her concern.

"You could have been killed."

"I suppose so," he conceded.

"Does that sort of thing happen often?"

"Very seldom. Most folks are peaceful and law-abiding. They hardly ever haul out a cannon and start blasting."

It was all so strange. From what she'd seen of Bill, she could not conceive of him laying a pistol barrel across anyone's head. She'd seen nothing of him but gentleness and cheerfulness.

Also, there was the casual way he spoke of the incident; no different from a fisherman telling how many trout he'd caught that day.

Of course she knew that Bill was the police and at times had to face danger in his role as protector of law and order. But to hear it mentioned so casually . . .

"But you said you were down, angel. Any particular reason?"

"No. Anybody can droop occasionally."

"Sure. No problem. But I wanted to ask you—do you work a five-day week?"

"Well, I did in the city."

"Then it should be the same out here, no?"

"Why did you ask?"

"I've got a cabin up in the country."

Vonnie laughed. "Up in the *country!* What's this? A crowded urban center?"

"It gets a little crowded here in the summer. I've got a spot on Gar Fin Lake about eighty miles northwest."

"From one lake to another. It's a little like the mail-man taking a long walk on his day off."

"This is no lake. It's just a little-bitty puddle. In Gar Fin, the bass get on one another's backs and punch you in the nose."

"I take it you have the weekend off."

"That's the score. How about coming up with me and hooking one of those monsters?"

Vonnie's first thought was to decline. Then realized she didn't have to be that abrupt.

"I'll see what the routine is and let you know."

She was sure Keith would want to be home with Valerie over the weekend—she was sure enough to vouch for it, that very moment. But she wanted time to think. A country weekend with a man? Actually, the way Bill put it, a *wilderness* weekend with a man. It was something she did not want to decide on the spur of a moment.

Bill was not especially talkative, probably through conscious effort. They sat looking out across the lake, Vonnie's hand in his. Then, with his scotch tumbler empty, Bill yawned and climbed to his feet.

"Tired," he murmured. "Time to hit the sack."

Vonnie followed him in and he turned before they reached the door and took her in his arms.

Vonnie surrendered willingly; perhaps a little too willingly. This thought occurred to her as she felt the warmth of his lips and beat of his heart against her breast. There was the heady masculine smell of him and the deep, passionate stirring in herself, sweetly exciting as it rose toward the surface.

But not here. Not in her room. No cheap hotel romance. But with that seeming instinct for psyching her, Bill released her an instant before she would have been forced to break the clinch herself.

"Get to bed," he ordered.

Moments later she heard him, faintly whistling on his way downstairs.

Vonnie went to bed but stayed awake long enough to make one definite decision: No weekend in the wilds with Bill. It was a decision with some regret . . . it would have been exciting . . . fun. The uncertainty, if nothing else, would have made her blood race. The wondering. If a stark situation arose, how would she handle it? Or would one even arise?

She thought she knew Bill very well for the time involved. But until you have been with a man under *all* situations, she conceded, you can be in for surprises. So the trip was out!

Basically, however, her problem had nothing to do with Bill, or Keith, or anyone else. It was within herself. What was she *really* looking for in life?

She had the intelligence, if not the experience, to know that standards had changed since Aunt Madge's day and were constantly changing—and rapidly. Many things were tolerated, if not accepted, today which would have totally ostracized a girl not too long ago. Many perfectly respectable career women had given up all thought of marriage—were actually content without it—and had put themselves on par with men so far as casual love was concerned. Nor, did she believe, they were looked down on for that reason. The emancipation of women was a practice rather than a theory. Women's lib was a growing movement, with its followers openly admitting to the same sexual freedom as men. They were women who not only practiced such broadmindedness but defied anyone to look down their noses at them.

Vonnie could not help admiring such brave souls, but did she want to join them? Once the decision was made, it could be exciting to look forward to a life of varied male companionships; to ever-varying vistas and relationships.

Was the orthodox pattern: marriage, children, and one man for life already outmoded?

Putting all moral values aside, Vonnie tried to decide, objectively, if the other, the free-wheeling future, was for her.

Then, because she didn't know the answer and, characteristically, didn't want to think about it, she told herself she was being moody, morbid and stupid, lying to herself and pondering intangibles when she should be getting some sleep. So she blanked her mind and began to doze off.

But vetoing the weekend with Bill still held . . .

ent with it. ollected openly admitting to the xual freedon as men. They were women who y practiced such broadmindedness but defied to look down their noses at them.

CHAPTER ELEVEN

When Vonnie awoke next morning, she wondered if any pattern could be established with Keith as to the start of their working day. Functioning as they were, in a vacation setting, that could be difficult.

She went down to breakfast, resolving that she would speak to Keith about it. She had heard no sound from his room so she called from the house phone in the lobby.

Lucy Stone bustled in. "Good morning, Vonnie. Mr. Elwood left a note for you."

It merely said: *I've gone to Hazard House. How are you coming with the meteorology thing? Take my car if you need it.*

Keith

Vonnie was sure the word should have been *meteorological* but she got the point.

Also, she was to learn. Keith had already set the pattern for their working partnership. After telling her what he expected of her, he would leave execution of the duty up to her. There would be little or no supervision.

In the coffee shop five minutes later, Lucy Stone arrived and invited herself to sit down.

"Those college kids," she exclaimed. "Milt's been half an hour late for three mornings in a row. But if you complain you lose them and have no help at all. So what can a person do?"

"Just grin and bear it, I guess," Vonnie sympathized.

The waitress brought two coffees with Vonnie's orange juice and toast and Lucy said, "I declare. You New Yorkers don't eat enough to keep a bird alive."

"Dieting gets to be a way of life, I guess."

"I'd think you'd collapse. By the way, did you hear about Bill's gunfight?"

"Yes. He mentioned it last night."

"*Mentioned* it. That's about what he'd do. Why he sticks to that dangerous job when he doesn't have to, I'll never know."

"Do you mean he doesn't have to make a living?"

"Oh, he could never remain idle, but he could take time out to find another career. His parents left him very well off."

"He's fortunate. Does he have any relatives in this area?"

Lucy shrugged. "A few poor ones he helps out. There's an aunt on his father's side—Luella Keenan. She was crippled by arthritis a few years ago. Oh, she gets around all right and can do for herself. But if he hadn't installed her in his house up on Gar Fin Lake, I don't know what she'd do."

A light was turned on in Vonnie's brain but she gave no outward indication.

Lucy gulped down the rest of her coffee and bounced to her feet. "Have to be off," she said. "A million things to do."

Vonnie finished her breakfast and had hardly stepped back into the lobby when the young room clerk called, "Phone for you, Miss March. You can take it next to the booth."

Vonnie went to the phone, said hello, and heard a familiar voice:

"Sleep good?"

"Like a top. Where are you?"

"Home. Just got in. I was out on an emergency call."

"I have something to tell you."

"Fire away."

"You—are—a—sneak."

"Oh, come on now—"

"And something else. It's okay for the weekend."

"You talked to your boss?"

"No. I talked to Lucy Stone."

"And she said it was all right?"

"You know very well what she said. But about the weekend—don't get your hopes up too high. I'll never marry you. You're too devious."

"I wish I knew what you were talking about."

"We'll go into that later. In the meantime, I've got

192

to cut you off. I'm busy. I've got to find out about the weather."

"That shouldn't take long. Just look out the window. It's beautiful. In fact, it's too nice to sleep. I think I'll come on over there and—"

"You'll do nothing of the kind. You're a growing boy and you need your rest. What I meant about the weather was that I've got to get a meteorological report on this area as a part of the survey we're making. We've got to make sure this lovely August weather you've got doesn't last the year around."

"It doesn't. Come winter it gets colder than a witch's—well, it gets cold. You have my word for it."

"Not nearly enough. I've got to find a meteorologist who can lay out some convincing data."

"Hmmm. Why don't you go over to Williams College?"

"Where's that?"

"In Lewiston—about thirty miles north. Follow Salt Lick straight through town and keep going. You'll see the sign."

"I never heard of Williams College."

"Few people have. It's small, underfinanced, understaffed, and underfed. They've got a weather station there, though, and give a course in what you said."

"Heavens! What would I do without you?"

"Wither on the vine, I'm afraid. Ask for Chester Vance. Tell him I sent you—no, wait a minute." There was a pause. Then: "It's okay. You'd never fall for a guy who left the braces on his teeth too long."

"You never can tell. I impress very easily. What does Chester do?"

"He sucks his gums and teaches students that when clouds come up it rains—sometimes."

"I think he's just the man I'm looking for. Thanks."

"Don't mention it. I'll meet you for dinner. And see that you're there this time . . ."

Vonnie hung up and returned to the desk. "If Mr. Elwood comes looking for me," she told the clerk, "will you please tell him I'll be back by midafternoon —either that or I'll phone."

The clerk made the note and Vonnie went out the front door to hear a familiar "Hello" as she turned toward the parking lot . . .

"Abigail! Isn't this awfully early for you to be so far from home?"

"I was up early."

"Did you come with your grandfather?"

"No. I came alone."

Vonnie saw no point in asking the obvious questions —why Abigail was allowed to wander around unsupervised. She would get no more satisfactory answers than she'd gotten before. There was a more personal reason; she did not want to inquire further. She was in no mood to hear Abigail say that Patience had sent her.

"I've got to drive to Williams College—in Lewiston. Have you ever heard of it?"

"Oh, yes. I went there one day."

"Do you know someone at the college?"

"Grandpa does. Professor Heinz. They're friends."

"That's nice. Perhaps I'll see you tonight, after I get back."

Abigail regarded her solemnly, the deep pools of the child's eyes seemingly aglow with hidden knowledge.

"You don't want me to go with you, do you?"

Vonnie wrestled with her frustration. "Abigail, you have such a weird way of putting things. Of course I would have no objection. But I'm on business for Mr. Elwood. I'm a working girl."

"Mr. Elwood took your jeep. I saw him. His car is over here."

Abigail started off toward the parking lot. Vonnie hurried to catch up with her.

"But Abigail . . ."

The child turned gravely. "You said you wouldn't mind."

"Yes, but what about your grandfather?"

"He won't mind either."

"Well, all right. Come on."

Of course he wouldn't mind. It was nice to have someone else around to take care of your children . . .

All was silent until they were moving along the main street of Big Moose Lake. Then Vonnie glanced down at her quiet little passenger with a frown.

"Abigail," she said. "I can't stand that rag you're wearing for another instant. I think I promised to buy you a dress."

"Yes."

"Well, let's get it over with."

"That would be nice."

Vonnie pulled up to a meter, deposited a nickel, and led Abigail into Bennett's Department Store. Shrewdly estimating sizes, she sorted through a pile of dresses on the children's and came up with a neat middyblouse and skirt.

"How do you like this one?"

"The red belt is very pretty."

There was a curtained dressing room. Leading Abigail inside, Vonnie put the dress on the child, appraised the fit for a moment, and said, "It will do. Now take it off. I'll be right back."

When she returned, she was carrying a pair of blue jeans and a durable red T-shirt.

"Put these on."

Either through luck or skill, the fit was again right. Picking up the dress, Vonnie said, "You can take this home with you," and led Abigail out to a table piled with sneakers. Snatching a pair of child's socks from a shelf, Vonnie sat Abigail on the table. Then, thinking better of it, she said, "I just can't put socks on those dirty feet. You can take the socks home with you too."

A pair of sturdy sneakers finished the job and Vonnie surveyed her handiwork. "That's better," she said grimly.

Up front, at the exit turnstile, she handed the price tags to the clerk, paid the bill, and marched out of the store with what looked like an entirely different child. She had not felt so satisfied with herself for days . . .

Williams College looked to be exactly what it was, a modest little seat of learning which would never send a winning team to the Rose Bowl or to Madison Square Garden but might very well turn out some well-educated youngsters. In spite of its meager staff and sparse financing, its four buildings were clean, every window sparkling, and its lawns could have been used for putting greens.

Vonnie went to the administration building where a girl behind the registrar's desk directed her to Hazard Hall.

"Did you say Hazard Hall?" Vonnie asked.

"Yes. It's the building on the right as you go out."

Vonnie followed directions. On a bronze plaque beside the entrance she saw her first likeness of John Hazard.

At least a purported likeness. Actually, with his beard and bushy eyebrows he could have been Ulysses S. Grant or any of the hairy leaders who dominated the era in which he flourished.

The legend read:

> *John Thomas Hazard, the far-seeing humanitarian who realized that only through education could our nation achieve true greatness.*

While Vonnie stood reading the plaque and wondering about this new side of the builder of Hazard House, a surprised voice called out: "Well for heaven's sake! Who do we have here?"

Vonnie turned to see a fussy-looking little man with pince-nez glasses, enormous ears and remarkably shabby clothing drop to one knee and peer at Abigail.

"It can't be! But it is! There's no doubt about it! Little Abigail all dressed up like a boy."

"Hello, Professor Heinz," Abigail said gravely.

The man rose and peered at Vonnie. "I am Herr Heinz," he said, making a crisp Prussian bow.

"So I understand," Vonnie replied. She introduced herself and Heinz said, "Abigail and I are old friends. Can I be of service?"

Vonnie stated her purpose and Heinz said, "You will find Herr Vance in Room Twenty inside on the second floor. But while you visit him, may I have Abigail?"

"I see no reason why not," Vonnie replied.

"My office is just inside—on the first floor. I promise to take good care of my little friend."

They entered the building and Vonnie went on upstairs to find that Bill had been right in not worrying about Chester Vance as romantic competition. He was a bean pole, close to seven feet with a face vaguely like Abraham Lincoln's but totally devoid of the beauty.

He reared to his full height and thrust out a hand which engulfed Vonnie's up to the wrist.

"I'm lucky to find you here, what with vacation," she said.

He sucked on his teeth for a moment and replied, "I came back early this year. We have so much to do with such a small staff."

Vonnie stated her business. Vance thought it over. "You say Bill Jackson sent you?"

"He suggested I talk to you. He said you might be

198

able to recommend someone competent for the assignment."

"I think I'm probably as competent as anyone. I have access to the material."

"That would be fine. I didn't think you'd be interested personally."

"I need the money," Vance said frankly. "You don't get rich in the academic world."

"Then it's agreed."

"I'll do my best. Can you tell me exactly what you want?"

Vonnie explained the survey in detail.

"I'd say fifteen years back would be enough to impress them—with a forecast based on long-term expectations."

"Then I'll leave it up to you."

"A week?"

"That will be fine."

Vonnie left and went to Heinz's office. It was more of a laboratory—she found Heinz and Abigail seated on either side of a high barrier separating two tables. As Vonnie entered, she heard Abigail say "A square."

Heinz made a note. "Next?"

"A diamond."

Abigail was calling the faces on the cards Heinz was turning behind the barrier on his side of the table. Vonnie waited until he was finished.

"I've been wanting to work with this child," Heinz explained. "Jason has promised again and again to bring her over. He has not kept his promises."

"He's a very busy man," Vonnie said, "Does Abigail have strong ESP powers?"

"This test is disappointing. But there are the conditions . . . not conducive to bringing out her true abilities. I'd like to keep Abigail but I suppose that is out of the question."

"You'd have to talk to Mr. Leopold about that. I'm in charge only temporarily."

"Tell Jason to call me if you see him. Would you do that?"

"Certainly. Come Abigail, we must be getting back . . ."

With Abigail hardly on the chatty side and Vonnie preoccupied with matters pertaining to her job, the trip back was made in silence—at least three quarters of it.

But as Vonnie rounded a bend some three miles from Big Moose Lake, all that changed.

Vonnie felt a sudden chill for which there was no explanation. Then she glanced down at Abigail to see an entirely different person.

Again, the child had not changed physically. None of her features had been actually reconstructed, but it was as though a small demon out of hell leered back at Vonnie.

"Abigail—what—?"

The creature beside her drew back her upper lip in the vicious snarl of an animal. Both of her small hands had turned into claws.

"Abigail! Stop it!"

Vonnie's foot went for the brake but missed. It hit the accelerator in a clumsy, desperate movement, and the powerful engine lunged forward . . .

At the same moment, Abigail struck, diving up from her seat like an enraged tigress set upon destroying Vonnie. There was far more than childish strength in the body that hurled itself upon her. The fingers, turned into claws, raked at her eyes as Abigail attacked with no thought of self. It was like fending off a maddened animal—a tiger cat loosed, there in the confines of the car.

There could be only one result: a matter of how long Vonnie could stave off disaster.

She held out for a surprising length of time, rocketing at eighty miles an hour before her foot found the brake. She pushed the ravaging Abigail away as the brakes screeched. But an uneven stretch of road was her undoing. The car careened off to the left across the center line. InstinctivelyVonnie swung it back. It swung up on two wheels as it changed directions.

When it came down again, one side over the low embankment flanking the road, the car turned on its side; then clear over to land again on its side and rest there.

Vonnie was still confined by her seat belt while Abigail had wriggled out of hers prior to the attack. Vonnie struggled back from half-consciousness and reached out blindly.

She heard a childish cry of terror and twisting around she saw Abigail wedged against the back window.

"Help me . . . please. Help me!"

The seizure was over. Whatever had taken possession of Abigail was no longer there. She was now a frightened child begging for help.

The fear of fire leaped to Vonnie's mind as she reached for the door above her. Loosening her seat belt, she managed to reach the handle; but it would not move.

"Just lie still, dear," she said. "I'll get you out. The door is stuck a little."

Vonnie never prayed more fervently in her life: *Don't let the car burn! Please don't let it burn! And please, please, let the door open.*

Half the prayer was answered. Sparks had not reached the gas tank. The car lay there, an inert monster, its upper wheels spinning lazily to a halt.

But the door was jammed. With some of her fear diminishing, Vonnie gave way to anger. Why hadn't Keith the sense to buy a four-door sedan instead of one of these two-door firetraps? She struggled with the handle, but to no avail.

The window was electrically controlled. At last Vonnie's fingers found the switch that lowered the glass. She drew back. Suppose the window did not respond? Instead, the switch might activate electricity which would set them on fire.

"Abigail," Vonnie said, "Are you hurt? Are you in pain?"

"My arm is twisted. I can't move it."

"Don't try. Don't struggle. I'll keep working at this door . . . someone is sure to come along."

It was a matter of minutes before Vonnie heard brakes squeak up on the road. A moment later, the face of a frightened girl appeared, peering down through the window, her expression frightened at what she expected to find.

"We're all right," Vonnie called out. "Can you open the door from outside?"

The girl's voice came back faintly: "I'll try."

A brief second later, her stricken face again appeared in the window. She was showing the handle in her fist. It had been damaged in the roll-over . . . had broken off in the girl's hand.

"I'll get help," the girl called.

Vonnie heard her struggling up the incline. Her motor roared; Vonnie and Abigail were alone again.

Abigail had cried out only once. During the escape struggle she'd remained silent.

"Does your arm hurt badly, dear?" Vonnie asked.

"No. My shoulder aches a little."

"We were very lucky . . ."

With time to think, Vonnie realized that the child would not remember attacking her. Vonnie was positive when Abigail asked "Was there another car?"

"No, dear. I just hit a bad spot in the road and lost control."

"Somebody will come," Abigail assured her.

". . . Very soon now. Just lie quiet."

It was strange, faced now with the fact of a near-disaster, how calmly Vonnie could accept the truth: Rachel had tried to kill her. Even as she reasoned against this, she had to accept it.

If what happened was a simple schizophrenic seizure in Abigail, the manifestation would have been different, less demonic. Nothing in the child's mind could possibly have manifested so murderously.

Proof that Patience's protection had its limits. Obviously, Rachel was eager to destroy Abigail, her only channel to the material world. And in order to destroy Vonnie also.

There was a part of Vonnie's mind which took the other side of the debate: she was shaken up, she'd been scared out of her wits—therefore she must be thinking nonsense.

No, Vonnie told her analyzing brain firmly: Rachel *was* here . . . she tried to kill me.

The sound of a siren broke into Vonnie's thoughts. Louder and louder, screeching at the top of its power, then it began to die. Brakes screamed . . . there was the rattle of rock and shale on the incline.

A moment later Bill Jackson was peering in the window.

A rewarding moment for Vonnie, the look on his face. Stark concern far outstripping anything if he were confronting an accident involving strangers.

He *is* in love with me!

"Vonnie! What in hell! Are you all right?" he shouted madly.

"Yes. We are both all right. Will you quit jabbering and get us out of here?"

His face disappeared to show up again at the windshield. The moment was over. Now he could have been assessing the situation through the objective eye of a trained police officer.

"Twist around and put your feet against the windshield," he ordered.

"Why?"

"Shut up and do what I tell you. Wedge yourself in with your back against the seat, with your feet against the glass."

Vonnie obeyed. A most undignified position, but she managed it—thanking her stars that she had pantyhose on. Otherwise, with that big oaf gaping, it would be doubly embarrassing.

"Okay, now draw your feet back as far as you can and hit that glass. It ought to pop out. If not we'll smash it."

Vonnie gritted her teeth, closed her eyes and kicked. A sound of glass against metal and her feet went right on through.

"I could have done that anytime," Vonnie said.

"Why didn't you then?"

"I wanted to see how clever *you* were."

"Come on. Crawl out. Then I'll go in to get Abigail."

There was further proof as Bill helped her out of the trap: he could control his expression—he'd put on an overall scowl—but he couldn't keep his hands from shaking. He tried to hide his anxiety once by changing the scowl to a faint grin and murmuring, "Nice, very nice."

"Keep your hands where they belong, *sir*," Vonnie warned him sternly.

A second trooper was on the scene now. He eased her to a nearby rock where she sat, watching Bill's feet disappear into the car.

A minute later he handed Abigail out to the other trooper.

With Abigail clear, Bill said: "What happened? Another car?"

"No. I just lost control."

"Great! Do you make a practice of dumping cars on a wide-open stretch of road?"

"It can happen."

The other trooper shook his head as he surveyed the car. Then, looking at Vonnie and Abigail, "Lucky . . . lucky," he murmured.

"More luck than brains," said Bill. "Take over, will you, Mel? I'll run these two into town for body checks."

He picked Abigail up in his arms. "Hang on to my belt," he said to Vonnie. "And *don't* fall down . . ."

CHAPTER TWELVE

"Mr. Elwood said to tell you he'd call you, honey," Lucy Stone reported.

"That was all?"

"Yes. He seemed terribly agitated."

"Thank you."

"I heard about the accident. I'm awfully sorry, but I'm glad you weren't badly hurt."

Bill Jackson had brought Vonnie back to the lodge after a sojourn in the emergency rooms of the local hospital. X-rays gave Vonnie and Abigail a clean bill of health.

Bill said, "Those scratches on your face and Abigail's sprained shoulder seem to be it. That makes it a good accident. You know what they say—any accident you walk away from is a good one."

"Thanks, Bill, for everything."

"All in the line of duty. I'll take Abigail home and call you later."

"Do that. I'll be in my room."

"When you're ready," Lucy said, "I'll have dinner sent up to you."

"Thank you." Vonnie fled upstairs.

The only thing she wanted was to be alone for a while. The whole project had collapsed, was the only verdict she could render. The natural and the supernatural had both conspired to wreck the Hazard House project. She vaguely remembered Jason Leopold's warning that Rachel might resent any incursion into Hazard House.

She realized that now. From personal experience and not strong arguments on anyone's part she had come to see Patience and Rachel as living forces.

But even after the accident, after the shocking trauma of seeing Abigail turn into a murderous little monster, that was only a part of it. It was the whole, the overall assignment which she saw going down the drain.

Regardless of what Jason Leopold had said, she was sure she would escape all danger by leaving Big Moose Lake. In fact, Rachel would no doubt settle for that.

But was only Rachel responsible for the other elements of the failure? Was she, Vonnie, in any way creating Keith's problems? That seemed impossible.

Lying in the dark, Vonnie pondered. She reviewed the entire problem until her brain was fagged. Then, when the phone rang, she reacted like a twanged bowstring, realizing that she'd been subconsciously waiting for Keith's call all evening long.

It was not Keith; it was Lucy Stone, announcing

Bill Jackson, on the way up with dinner. Vonnie's first reaction was to say no—"Please tell him I'm not hungry."

But then the peremptory knock came, followed by Bill's opening the door and his casual query: "Are you decent?"

She was, having slipped on a robe before lying down. But, somehow, it did not seem important now. All those maidenly worries and restraints now seemed so childish.

If not wearing anything she'd have put on a robe: that would have been that.

"I'm not, Bill, in the least hungry."

"I know, so I made it light. Some veal scallopini cut with a razor. Some lemon jello and coffee."

"You're too good to me."

"I'm trying to keep you in good shape for the wedding."

Bill laid the dinner out on a folding table he got from the closet. "Okay," he said, then turned. "Where are you?"

He followed Vonnie out onto the balcony. A moment later he held her shoulders, was turning her face to the light.

"Now hold it. Why the tears, baby? The accident is all over."

Vonnie burrowed her tear-streaked face into his shoulder and clung to him.

"Oh, Bill. I'm so miserable!"

"Easy, angel. It was a shock, I know, but—"

"It's not the accident. It's just everything. I'm jinxed!"

210

"Not in my book. Come on, and tell it all."

He picked her up with as much ease as he'd have lifted Abigail, then eased himself down onto one of the chaise longues and stretched her comfortably in his lap.

"Okay. Let's have it."

"I just—I just don't know where I stand."

"That doesn't tell me much. Did you fall out with your boss?"

"No, but I don't know where *he* stands, either. We came up here to do a job but so far we've gone absolutely nowhere. He has other things on his mind. For a while he was a lot better and I thought everything was straightened out. But now he's off again. He has some terrible personal problem."

"You take this job of yours pretty seriously, don't you?"

"Yes, I suppose I do."

"You've got to remember it's just a job. You're working for him and getting paid. But your duties aren't to take on his personal problems, too, are they?"

"No, I suppose not, but well, there's more—the things that are happening to me."

"Tell me about them."

"I can't."

"Why not?"

"Because I know you too well—you're practical."

"What does that mean?"

"You'd laugh."

"If that's what you think, you *don't* know me very

well. I wouldn't be likely to laugh at anything that's causing you trouble."

"Then you'd say I was neurotic."

"I might, but why should that stop you from telling me what's bothering you?"

"It's—oh, it's so crazy. But that accident today. I didn't hit a bad place in the road. It was Abigail. She turned into a little demon. And I do mean a demon. She wanted to kill me. These scratches on my face. I didn't get them when the car rolled over. It was Abigail's fingernails. She tried to scratch my eyes out."

When Bill didn't answer, Vonnie said, "See? I told you you wouldn't believe me."

"It's a little difficult to swallow, that's all. The idea, I mean. That little character a schizo. What's she got, a dual personality?"

"Not exactly. Not according to Jason Leopold."

"It's really not as hard to accept as all that. Not when you consider the kid. She's definitely on the odd side. But in the other direction, as gentle as a kitten."

"That's the point. Abigail herself *is* as gentle and sweet as she seems."

"Then you're saying she's possessed?"

"That sounds so strange, coming from you," Vonnie said.

"Why, for God's sake?"

"Because—well, because you're so completely matter-of-fact. So down to earth. So practical."

"You forget I'm a New Englander. We burned witches and chased warlocks up tall trees."

"Did you ever hear about John Hazard's wife, Rachel?"

"Sure. She's part of local folklore."

"What do you know about old John himself?"

"He was some kind of a nut, but he made a lot of loot."

"I got a surprise today. There's a plaque dedicated to him at Williams College."

"Uh-huh. He endowed the school. Started it."

"A man as evil—as brutal—as John Hazard gave money to a school? Why, he drove his own sons from his house!"

"No. Rachel did that. John Hazard had only one weakness: his wife. She was the evil one."

Vonnie suddenly threw her arms around Bill and kissed him. When he got his breath back he asked, "And what was that for?"

"Because you continually surprise me. Every time I think I know you, a different side of you appears."

"Hold it—how many sides do you think I have?"

"Well, being a square, you'd have to have four. Ouch!"

"That's to show you how deeply you hurt me."

"All right. I deserved it. But, next time, pinch somewhere else."

"But that's the nicest place."

Vonnie buried her face in his neck and whispered, "Darling, how is it you can lift me out of the dumps no matter how deep I go?"

"It's my native charm."

"Don't ever lose it."

"I won't. But tell me about Jason Leopold. What have you talked to him about?"

"Several things. He said he'd help Keith with Hazard House. And about Abigail."

"What about her?"

"Things I'd never have believed if I hadn't seen them. He says Patience Hazard and Rachel use her to —well, to come back from the dead."

"And you believe it?"

"Oh, Bill! I don't know what to believe."

He stroked her hair and played absently with her ear while he mulled the idea over in his mind. "The Hazards are a big part of the local lore. And Leopold is about as weird as they come. He's done a lot for the Burton's Forge people, though."

"At the college today, a Professor Heinz was trying Abigail out on some cards. He was testing her ESP."

"Has she got any?"

"He said the conditions were bad, or something like that."

"He's head of the psychology department over there. As much of a kook as Leopold, only he tries to be a little more scientific about it.

"One thing I don't get. Why are you involved in this hocus-pocus? Why did Abigail climb all over you?"

"According to Leopold, Patience and Rachel are still around. There's something that's unfinished. Patience picked me out to finish it for her."

"What is it?"

"I don't know. When I first got here, there was an incident in an old graveyard between here and Hazard House. Abigail took me there. It's where Patience is supposed to be buried."

Vonnie went on to give Bill the details, thinking the while of how wrong she had been about him. She'd expected such total disbelief.

One thing remained constant, however. Bill was facing the situation with the same matter-of-fact, practical attitude that was part of his basic nature.

"Then, according to Leopold's theories, there's been a change," he said.

"A change?"

"Sure. Abigail's attack on you proves it. Patience is supposed to be able to protect Abigail—to hold the line. So if it was Spook Number Two, Rachel, who possessed Abigail, then Patience is losing the fight, isn't she?"

"It looks that way. I wonder what Jason Leopold would have to say about it?"

"I don't know, but I'm sure of one thing: We're keeping you away from that kid. That way, we keep both spooks away from you."

"The poor child."

"Sure, but unless or until the authorities take over, she's Leopold's problem."

"He sent me to the public library after a manuscript by a woman named Goody. I could only read parts of it but she wrote about blood sacrifices when Rachel was alive."

"Those jokers were a pretty rough bunch. I wouldn't put it past them. But now you've got to get to bed and get some sleep."

"What shape was the car in?"

"Not bad. We had it hauled over to Sid's Garage.

Sid said around three hundred dollars. When your boss left did he take that jeep you rented?"

"No. Abigail said he did, but he must have rented another car."

"And you've no idea when he'll be back?"

"No."

"Okay—tomorrow morning we head for Gar Fin Lake. You need a change of scenery."

"I don't know. The way things are, I ought to wait. I might hear from him any time over the weekend."

"If he calls, he gets the message: you work only five days a week!"

Vonnie did not feel like arguing about it. Also, she wanted very much to go. She felt that a change of scene would help a lot. She dreaded the two long days there at the lodge with nothing certain, with ticklish situations—everything up in the air.

Bill, still holding her in his arms, got up and carried her inside. Then, as though she were a sleepy child, he sat her on the edge of the bed, stripped her robe off, smoothed down her shortie nightgown and put her into bed.

His kiss was brisk and businesslike rather than romantic. Then he said, "Now go to sleep. If you can't, ring Lucy and she'll send up a sleeping tablet."

"Goodnight Bill—and thanks again."

"For what?" he replied, closing the door softly after himself . . .

. . . Vonnie tried to sleep, but the room kept rolling over and over like the car going down the incline.

So, half an hour later she called down and asked Lucy for a sleeping tablet.

Lucy came herself, bringing two white pills.

"I never took a sleeping tablet in my life," Vonnie said, "so I don't know whether these will work or not."

"They'll work all right, dear. You had a frightening experience and you need your rest."

"Thank you. You're very kind . . ." The tablets were wonderful. Every muscle in Vonnie's body relaxed. The bed vanished, she was floating. Time became timeless . . .

. . . The door opened and Lucy came in again. She still carried the tray upon which she'd brought the tablets but now it had turned to gold and supported a gleaming knife.

The room changed also. It turned into the domed room at Hazard House with many people in a circle around the astrological design on the floor.

Lucy Stone was the priestess who stood in the center of the circle. Something had been added—an altar stone, the length and width of a coffin.

Vonnie was a prisoner held by intangible chains. A force other than bonds restrained her.

The sacrificial altar was overlaid in silver. Its lights danced off the brilliant golden robe worn by High Priestess Lucy Stone.

The knife in Lucy's hand was jeweled, with a gleaming, curved blade. Now a young man was brought to the altar—a slim, defiant young man clad only in a breechclout.

There was no sound. Vonnie's ears were stopped. She was not permitted to hear the powerful words at this conclave of the Prince.

But the attitude of the principals was unmistakable. The young man was a picture of defiance. He sneered at the priestess who was obviously feared.

Lucy Stone's regal mien bent somewhat as she talked to the young man. She was obviously trying to convince him since he appeared to be daring her.

She was patient. Vonnie was reminded of Satan tempting Jesus on the mountaintop.

To no avail. The young man sneered at each symbol of her power and to Vonnie he was not so much refusing every offer as implying this was all an impotent display.

Finally Priestess Lucy's patience came to an end. A shouted word and the young man was stretched on the altar without further ceremony and Lucy Stone stepped forward and plunged the knife into his heart.

His dying expression reflected surprise, utter consternation, but not pain. He had not believed it would end this way.

Then he was dead . . .

Vonnie struggled against her bonds. Her escape looked so simple, yet it was impossible. Someone was with her—either there in her room at the lodge or in the ceremonial hall at Hazard House. A presence and communication of a kind; some desperate effort to make her understand.

Finally, as the young man's body was being carried away, Vonnie's struggles were successful. Now the presence could only plead with her to stay, the plea coming clearing in wordless despair:

There is more. There is more. Wait . . .

Vonnie came awake with an upward thrust that brought her bolt upright. She was wringing wet from head to foot. Her nightgown clung to her as though she'd just stepped out of a shower.

But something had cleared; a confusion in her mind had retreated. Where there should have been terror, there was, instead, an oddly objective contemplation.

She could account for this in only one way: Bill Jackson, from whom she had absorbed his sound, practical outlook. Also, there was Leopold's attitude: nothing was supernatural.

Vonnie left her bed and went to turn on the shower. As she stepped under it, she considered what had happened. It was real. It *had* occurred. The whole nightmare originated from within—a conglomeration of all the frightening things that had invaded her since she came to Big Moose Lake—or were external entities in part responsible, which invaded her mind to make their presence known. It all added up to a fear for her own safety.

Vonnie was sure of one thing:

No so-called supernatural entity can injure me but to upset my reason. If that occurs, I would only be injuring myself through my own weakness. Therefore I have only to keep cool and watch my own mental balance. She had won a victory. Instead of cringing, terrorized, she stepped calmly out of the shower, toweled herself and put on a clean, dry nightgown.

The bed was soaked, so she pulled the cover over the sheets and wrapped herself in the spare blanket from the closet and lay down again on top, having achieved a quiet satisfaction and found herself to be completely normal—in every respect. The sleeping tablets had worn off but she knew she could drop off to sleep without them. Only one faintly disturbing thought seeped into her mind as she began to doze:

Is all this a false strength?

Then she was asleep . . .

CHAPTER THIRTEEN

Bill was on the phone at eight-thirty the next morning. His voice was cheerful, good to hear.

"How did it go?"

"Fine. I couldn't sleep so I got a couple of tablets from Lucy."

"They worked?"

"Did they! I never saw anything like it."

"Good, then we're ready to take off."

"Bill—I was thinking . . ."

"Oh, come on. You're not backing down, are you?"

"No. I'm looking forward to it. But this is only Friday. It isn't actually the weekend yet and—"

"And your conscience is bothering you. Right?"

"Something like that. I am being paid and the way things are, Keith might need me."

"I can't argue with a salaried working girl, I guess."

"How about a compromise? That is, unless you'd rather go on without me."

"Don't be silly."

"All right. Let's leave at four. That will clip only an hour off my working week."

"And you'll still probably feel as guilty as hell."

"No. I promise to forget Hazard House exists."

"Okay. There are some things I can do. What's your program?"

"There are things I can do, too," Vonnie replied—though she couldn't for the life of her think what they were.

"Then I'll pick you up at four."

"I'll be waiting . . ."

There were a couple of things Vonnie thought of. After breakfast she called the office in New York. The answering service girl came on the line:

"No, Miss March. Mr. Elwood didn't leave any message for you."

"Have you heard from him at all?"

There was a pause while Vonnie could sense the girl's mind working. It was a good service, trained to think in terms of the subscriber's benefit. So it probably seemed strange that Mr. Elwood's secretary would be hunting for him. Perhaps Miss March was no longer Mr. Elwood's secretary . . . was merely making a nuisance of herself. Perhaps why the voice was less cordial, sharper, more impersonal when the girl said: "I'm sorry, Miss March. Mr. Elwood has left no messages for you."

Vonnie broke the connection, wondering what could possibly have happened. Had Valerie Elwood slipped her cable again? Should Vonnie check with

Information for the number of that clean, white rest home? At last she did.

Again a female answered. Vonnie told the woman who she was, said, "I thought perhaps you might have heard from Mr. Elwood."

"I'm sorry."

"Perhaps you can tell me if Mrs. Elwood is a patient there."

The pause was even more pregnant than at the answering service; the cut-off silence coming feeling even sharper.

"I'm sorry, Miss March. We can give you no information concerning a patient."

"Thank you."

The woman hung up but Vonnie felt she'd learned something. The woman had said the wrong thing. Her negative reply might certainly be an acknowledgment that Valerie Elwood was back.

At least Vonnie could assume so until it was proved false. It explained perfectly Keith's absence. Yet, there was nothing but wait for word from Keith.

Though Vonnie felt that the Hazard House assignment had gone up the spout, she did, however, take a less depressed view of the failure. It was one of those things. It could mean she'd be looking for a job sooner than she'd expected . . . Nothing very important really.

But she hadn't seen Hazard House in more than passing. Under other circumstances, the place could have been a tourist attraction, so why miss the opportunity to really see it?

The jeep was still in the lot and soon Vonnie was

pushing it through the green copse—now pretty well beaten down—and pointing it along the road to Hazard House.

As she breasted the rise and started across the huge open circle in front of the mansion, she was struck by her own reaction. The mansion generated no sense of the macabre, no feeling of awe or shadowy aspects from the invisible. It was merely a huge monstrosity built by an unbalanced man who might better have used his money in other ways. The Moorish dome was now more ridiculous than impressive.

So she entered; the great, lonesome hulk was a curiosity and nothing more.

And with a tourist's eye to economy of motion, she found the stairway and went clear to the top, planning to work down.

It was quite a disappointment: the interior was as casually put together as the exterior; the only diversion: guessing what would come next. Corridors opened up, ran a short distance, with rooms on either side, then ended abruptly for no apparent reason. To possibly continue beyond was futile, since some of the corridors were actually dead-ends, forcing Vonnie to backtrack and start again. She thought of the problems the foolish place would present to an architect wanting to rebuild the floors into sensible patterns.

Most of the rooms had been stripped, either by vandals, over the years, or by the last Hazards to occupy it. Yet, the pieces which did remain were certainly antiques of great value.

As it turned out, Vonnie found her biggest surprise of the day outside the house rather than inside. As she was about to descend to the floor below, she glanced out one of the circular windows carrying out the Oriental *motif*. On that side, the forest had been cut back to make room for a smaller building whose foundations were still visible, though its main structure was gone.

And there, just at the edge of this clearing, at the left, a man was digging a hole! A sight so shocking that Vonnie did a double-take—she passed, paused, then returned, doubting what she had seen.

It was true all right. He was heaving shovelfuls of earth out of a hole so far only ankle-deep. His back to Vonnie, she could not identify him if, indeed, she had ever seen him before. Curiosity drew her down the nearest stairway, through the front door, and around the house.

Peculiarly enough, the sight of a stranger working so industriously in that lonely place intensified the eerie menace of the house even more than the brooding loneliness. Vonnie approached the corner, half-expecting to find no one there.

But he was real enough. When she came close, she stopped in even greater surprise: "Professor Heinz!" she exclaimed, "I certainly never expected to find you here."

Heinz turned and peered at her like a blind owl. He was completely at a loss until he pawed toward a grassy spot by the hole, found his pince-nez and fastened them to his nose.

"Oh, Fraulein March. I am delighted to see you."

"And surprised?" Vonnie laughed.

"Perhaps."

"This seems a long way from Williams College to take your exercise."

"Oh, I come here as often as I can get away."

"Are you digging for hidden treasure?"

"In a way . . . in a way. I've made a study of Hazard House and the period in which it was built. There is here much of interest."

"I agree with you on that score. What do you expect to unearth?"

"One can never know," he replied after some hesitation. (From this Vonnie gathered a reluctance to be specific.) "Much has been lost since Hazard House was built."

"I'm sure it has. The place must have been a treasure trove. But it looks as if already most of the furniture is gone . . . was stolen."

"A great deal, yes, I'm sure. But on this rugged terrain, much which was too heavy to carry very far," he said contentedly.

Heinz seated himself on a rock and Vonnie found one nearby. "You say you've made a study of Hazard House. Did you ever discover any deep, dark secrets?"

She deliberately kept her voice light, to evince only casual interest; perhaps overdoing it to the point of sounding amused.

If so, Heinz didn't seem to notice or care. He said, "There *were* dark doings here; no doubt about that. And the dark after-shadows of such things often remain."

"I've discussed it with Jason Leopold, Herr Heinz, so I am not unfamiliar with the situation—with the beliefs."

"A good man, Leopold," Heinz conceded.

"He certainly is. But what is your opinion of his theories—that Rachel, John Hazard's wife, and Patience, his daughter, still linger here?"

"It is entirely possible, fraulein—entirely possible. As the great Shakespeare said: 'There are more things . . .'"

"I'm familiar with what Shakespeare said, but I'm more interested in your opinion. Do you think Patience and Rachel can really use Abigail as a means of returning to this plane of existence?"

"Oh? It is *not* beyond the realm of possiblity, you know . . ."

"But that is not your reason for being here, is it? I mean the phenomena which have taken place at Hazard House, they really don't interest you, do they?"

"Oh, yes. So very much."

Obviously Heinz was interested only in avoiding argument and discussion. Of that Vonnie was sure. If she claimed Rachel could materialize in the flesh to help him dig up the grounds, he would no doubt have agreed that that too came within the scope of Shakespeare's more things in heaven and earth than were dreamed of.

"Herr Heinz," Vonnie continued, "do you expect to prove or disprove Jason Leopold's theories by digging in the ground?"

He thought that over like a bright little bird considering a worm about to be devoured. "Yes . . .

228

yes, Fraulein March. You could say that. You could definitely say that."

Vonnie felt she could carry her line of inquiry no further without the professor realizing he was being cross-examined as before a grand jury.

"Well, I hope you find what you're looking for, Professor. And it's been very nice meeting you again."

"It has been delightful, Fraulein."

"I must go now. I have an engagement."

"I hope we shall meet again."

"I hope so," parroted Vonnie, then turned to walk swiftly back to the jeep.

On the way out of the forest, she pondered Heinz's role in this drama. Was he a major, or a minor, character? Either way, he was willing to toil and sweat for whatever he was after . . .

Vonnie and Bill arrived at Gar Fin Lake well after dark. The headlights centered on a log house rather than a cabin, with lights blazing cheerfully from all the windows. It was a two-level dwelling with a rock base reaching up some four feet and the rest of weather-browned logs. The roof was of dark material—slate, Vonnie thought—and there was a wide chimney with white smoke crawling lazily skyward.

As the lights beamed on the front door, it opened and a woman in a wheel chair came down a ramp built beside the stairs at one side.

"My Aunt Lou," Bill said. "Guess I forgot to tell you about her."

"I knew all about her already," Vonnie volunteered.

"You did?" Bill asked in surprised innocence. "How come?"

"I'm clairvoyant."

The wheel chair, run by electric batteries, was now beside the car. Bill said, "Hi, Aunt Lou. This is Vanessa March, a friend of mine."

Vonnie got out of the car and said, "I'm *Vonnie* March, and I'm delighted to meet you."

"Delight," Aunt Lou said. "Let's get in out of the damp. It's a little chilly up here so I built a fire in the fireplace. Makes it cozy."

Vonnie extended a hand to push the chair but it was already gone, flying at full speed back toward the house. When Vonnie started to follow, Bill held her back.

Speaking in a low voice, he said, "Look—don't try to help her. Not in *any* way. That's her thing. You try pushing her chair and she'll bite your head off."

"I'm glad you told me. I'd like to keep my head for at least a few more days . . ."

Inside, the whole first floor was a single room with an open kitchen at one end. A balcony ran clear around the second level with rooms giving off the front and a glassed-in terrace to the rear—where there was probably a view of the lake, Vonnie thought.

Louella Keenan was not difficult to read. Her face was like a page from a fine book. It was a face ravaged and made strong by suffering, which gave it a rugged beauty.

Vonnie having removed her coat, Aunt Lou looked her over with open frankness.

"She's a pretty thing."

"Don't be afraid of embarrassing her, Lou. Say it. She's beautiful."

"I'm surprised she'd have anything to do with you."

"I have my points. I'm overbearing. It works."

"Overbearing is right," Vonnie said. "He won't even let me pick out my own swim suit."

In Big Moose Lake where Vonnie selected a fetching bikini, Bill had put it back and picked out a simple, black knit suit. "This shows enough," he'd said.

Aunt Lou was still regarding Vonnie critically. "Good bones. Solid stock for child-bearing."

"She's complimenting you," Bill said quickly.

"Well—thank you."

"I suppose you two are hungry."

"What have you got?"

"Fried chicken. Make a drink and sit down. I'll get it on the table."

Vonnie felt terribly self-conscious watching the woman fly back and forth from the kitchen, setting out the meal. She looked helplessly at Bill, but he merely grinned and raised his glass in salute.

With dinner over, Lou not only cleared and washed the dishes, but with the fire low, she rode outside to the woodshed and returned with two logs in her lap. Running the chair almost into the fire, she deposited the logs and brushed her hands off briskly. "That's better," she announced, and Vonnie was awed by a woman with a greater zest for living than many who were possessed of two sound legs.

"Back in a minute," Bill said, "I want to check the boat," and was gone out the back door.

Alone with his courageous aunt, Vonnie made a tiny blunder. The woman had lit a cigarette and was looking about for an ashtray. It was across the room and Vonnie said, "Let me get that for you."

"No!" The word came sharply. She rolled the chair to the far table, got the ashtray, and came back.

"You'll have to put up with me," she said. "I guess I'm a little eccentric, but I have a fixed rule: *I do for myself.* And if I carry it to extremes it's because I want to keep in training. You see, Bill gives me this lovely place to live. He doesn't need it. He'd get rid of it otherwise. So that's enough. I won't be a burden to anybody and if you start being a burden in small ways, you get to be a burden in big ways."

"I understand."

"I'm glad. And now I think I'll retire. Your room is the first one on the south end. Sleep well."

"Thank you. I'm sure I shall."

Vonnie watched as Aunt Lou steered her chair to the stairway. A section of the floor turned out to be a stairway lift. It began to hum and Lou and her chair were lifted to the second floor . . .

Bill was back a few minutes later. The fire was dying now—into a bed of lovely red embers. Bill stretched, yawned, and said, "How about a nightcap?"

"I don't think so, thanks."

He dropped down on the couch beside Vonnie and drew her close. "Did you two get acquainted?"

"Yes. She told me how she feels. I think she's a wonderful person."

"You're right. With all the pain and suffering she's had, I've never heard her utter a single word of complaint."

They fell silent. Bill drew Vonnie's face around and kissed her. Vonnie clung to him, grateful for the protection of his arms and the warmth of his lips.

"Getting around to loving me?" he whispered.

"I'm thinking about it."

"Think hard."

Five minutes later, he picked her up as though she were no heavier than Abigail, carried her upstairs and deposited her at her door.

"Do you want me to come in?"

"That's up to you."

Even as she spoke, Vonnie saw Aunt Madge's stern face and that stubby finger lifted in warning.

"But how do *you* feel about it?" Bill asked.

"I don't know. I'm pretty inexperienced in such things. What would you advise?"

"You cheat!" he whispered. "The mouse asking the cat what it wants for dinner."

"Poor kitty," Vonnie soothed.

"If I had a paddle, I'd spank you, but not with my bare hands," he replied, panting slightly.

Then he kissed her again, set her down, and vanished into his own room . . .

It was a glorious two days. Worries and problems and Big Moose Lake were far, far away. They swam and hiked and lolled on the shore. Vonnie had never been so happy.

Hazard House with its mysteries did come up on Sunday afternoon. The three of them were having a drink on the lawn beside the lake—a farewell drink.

Vonnie couldn't recall exactly how it came up, but Aunt Lou said, "If you want to find out about John Hazard and Rachel and their goings-on, you've been talking to the wrong people. You should consult Melissa."

"Melissa? Oh, yes."

Vonnie remembered the tall, gaunt woman who lived with Jason Leopold—she had taken Abigail that night when they'd returned her to Burton's Forge.

"Scandals never die so far as Melis' is concerned. Get her started and she'll talk up a real witch's brew."

"She teaches school in Burton's Forge, I understand."

"That she does, but she spends most of her time filling those kids' heads with tales about early times that would make *Macbeth* sound like a Sunday School picnic."

"But she must be qualified or the school would not be accredited into the educational system."

"Oh, she's qualified all right. I went to school with Melis'—a long time ago, that was. She is not from Burton's Forge, you know. She came from down Lamphere way and was training for teaching. She did go away and teach for a while, but then I heard she was back. What she saw in that weird Hungarian, I'll never know, but she took over his cabin and she's been in the Forge ever since."

"They're all a bunch of weirdos," Bill said comfortably.

"Don't misunderstand me," Aunt Lou went on. "Melis' was all right. Still is. I liked her. Still do. She just made a strange decision, that's all."

Aunt Lou's parting advice on the problem of Hazard House was: "If you want the way smoothed for a ski lodge, go to the Big Moose Lake Chamber of Commerce. They'll get behind you and any stupid ecologists will get stamped into the ground for fertilizer."

"I was beginning to suspect that," Vonnie said.

"Well, you suspected right . . ."

They finally left after dark. Their conversation lapsed after a few miles. When Vonnie's lids drooped, she took a comfortable hold on Bill's thigh with her left hand and snugly drifted off to sleep . . .

Later she was awakened by a sharp "Yipe" and a slight wavering of the car.

"What's the matter?" she asked.

"That's what I was going to ask you, angel?"

"What happened?"

"Oh, nothing—except that you just tried to claw a handful of me out of my right leg."

"I'm sorry."

"It's okay. I'd just like a little warning next time."

"It must be the suppressed tigress in me."

"At least it'll lessen the work when we're hitched. You'll only have to broil *my* steaks. You can eat yours raw."

"You put up with an awful lot from me, darling," Vonnie said, passing a soft hand over his cheek.

"Don't I ever? What happened? Did you have a boogieman dream?"

"I'm not sure. I can forget a dream before I'm half awake."

"You better take a memory course. Some of your dreams might be interesting . . ."

Vonnie settled back down. But she did not go to sleep. She hadn't been truthful with Bill; she remembered the dream very well.

It had been a continuation of the sacrifice scene except Lucy Stone was no longer presiding. A tall, fierce-faced black woman had taken her place.

But the most frightening part was toward the end—no doubt when Vonnie had clawed Bill's leg. Somewhere in the darkness, merged with the invisible power which held her there, a desperate voice cried:

"Do not go. Do not go. There is more—more—oh, more. Help me. Help me . . ."

CHAPTER FOURTEEN

Bill had stretched his off-time to the very last minutes, so when he deposited Vonnie at the lodge, he had barely half an hour to get into uniform.

It was going on midnight and Vonnie was ready for a night's rest and sure she'd need no sleeping tablets to send her off.

This proved true. She slept so deeply that she did not feel the hand pulling at her shoulder until the cry in her ear finally penetrated.

"Please wake up. Please! Patience wants you."

"Abigail—oh, Abigail. Quiet, child. At least let me wake up."

Vonnie sat up and snapped on the bed lamp. There was Abigail's pale little face: the symbol of all that she'd fled from over the lovely weekend at Gar Fin Lake—and what she had now come back to.

"Patience is waiting for you," Abigail repeated. "She wants you to come."

"She wants me . . . to come . . . where?"

"To Hazard House."

"Abigail! Doesn't Mr. Leopold pay any attention whatever to you? If he's so concerned about you, why does he let you wander about at all hours?"

"He's spending the night at Lamphere. Somebody's dying over there."

"All right, but what about Melissa?"

"She was asleep when Patience came for me. I couldn't wake her up. Then Patience told me to come here and get you. She'll be waiting at Hazard House."

"This is positively insane!" Vonnie exclaimed. "Now you sit right there, in that chair, and don't move until I get dressed."

Vonnie got into slacks and a sweater, noting that her bed clock read two-fifteen: also, that Abigail was again in her gray, shapeless shift.

This alone was depressing enough. It seemed that she'd made no progress whatever with the child.

"All right. I'm ready, come along."

Abigail put her hand obediently into Vonnie's and they went downstairs. The lobby was empty. No doubt a touch of the button on the desk would have brought Lucy Stone instantly, but, as it was, no one saw the pair leave.

Vonnie piled Abigail into the jeep, started the motor and gunned the vehicle resolutely onto Salt Lick Road.

After a short silence, Abigail said, "This isn't the way to Hazard House—I mean the short way."

"Never mind. You just sit there and be a good girl."

Vonnie remembered the road to Burton's Forge from her visit there with Bill. Even so, she got confused at one of the intersections, but refused to ask Abigail for directions. Things, however, had come to a point where she no longer trusted the child. Given an opportunity, she might put her onto a road leading back to Hazard House.

Vonnie made the right choice and came down along the narrow, rutted lane and into Burton's Forge. The settlement was totally dark save for the lamp shining from Jason Leopold's hut.

Approaching it, she was forced to ask herself about the strange Hungarian. She respected him implicitly because of his impressive background. Not only that, but admired him for his courage—coming here to live among these people, and to help them.

She was now about ready to revise these evaluations. What had he actually done for them? They were still living here in squalor. He'd instill them with no ambition to better themselves. Rather, it would seem, they had pulled *him* down to *their* level.

The man's life was his own, she conceded, but she, also, had a right to her own judgment and her opinion of Jason Leopold had taken a sharp turn for the worse.

Stopping in front of the hut, she took Abigail firmly by the hand and marched to the door. She knocked. There was no response. She knocked again.

"It won't do any good," Abigail said, "Melissa is asleep."

"Well, what does it take to wake her up—an avalanche?"

Vonnie pushed on in. By Burton's Forge standards, the place was probably well furnished. But by hers it was a hovel.

This was both the living room and bedroom. A lamp stood on a table beside the bed on which the gaunt woman was stretched.

"Melissa?" Vonnie called softly.

No response.

Vonnie crossed the room and bent over the woman. From this close it didn't take long to see why she slept so deeply.

Vonnie straightened. "My God! She's dead drunk!"

"Melissa drinks sometimes," Abigail said solemnly. "And, when she does, she certainly goes all out."

Vonnie bent over and retrieved a bottle from the floor. She leaned close to the lamp to read the label. She stood there amazed.

"Napoleon brandy? Good lord! That stuff must cost at least twenty dollars a bottle. Did Jason Leopold rob a bank or something?"

Abigail came over and looked at the bottle doubtfully. "Usually, Melissa drinks wine."

"Well, she certainly lived it up tonight. The whole bottle. I wonder if it's safe to just let her sleep it off."

Vonnie took the woman's pulse. It seemed okay. She wondered why her late arrival woke no one else in the settlement. Surely everybody wasn't dead drunk. One thing did seem obvious, though: the people of Burton's Forge minded their own business.

Vonnie could have knocked on a few doors and possibly roused someone, but there didn't seem any point to it. She saw no way in which anyone could have helped even if they'd been so inclined.

That brought up another problem; what to do with Abigail. Left alone, the child would probably head straight back to Hazard House and the psychic creature who had come from the grave to give her orders.

"So what?" Vonnie muttered. "It is not my responsibility."

But even as she spoke, she knew that it was, for the obvious reason that she could not walk away from it.

"Are we going to see Patience now?" Abigail asked.

Vonnie was suddenly on her knees, holding the child close. "Oh, darling! You're in such trouble. You need help—lots of help. And there isn't anyone!"

Abigail did not react. She stood like a soft little statue, the shadows from the flickering lamp playing across her expressionless face.

Feeling a little better, Vonnie got to her feet. "Come on, dear. We're definitely going *somewhere*." At the door she paused. "You'd better turn that lamp off. All it needs is a small spark to send this place up like tinder."

Abigail turned down the wick and blew into the chimney. She'd had long experience with lamps. Then Vonnie took her back to the jeep . . .

A half hour later, Vonnie was on the phone: "Hello. Is this the State Patrol Station?"

"Vonnie! What's up?"

"Bill! I didn't think I'd be lucky enough to catch you right away."

"What's wrong?"

"I've got Abigail on my hands."

"That kid again?"

"She came to my room after midnight. I took her home—back to Burton's Forge, and—"

"You found your way to that rat's nest in the middle of the night?"

"That's not important. The important thing is that Melissa is dead drunk. Somebody was feeding her brandy—"

"Brandy! Those people drink ten-day-old wine. It's all they can afford."

"Napoleon, no less. Anyhow, she's out for good. And—well, I couldn't leave Abigail there."

"Where are you?"

"In a phone booth on Salt Lick Road. It's a red one at the intersection of—"

"I know where it is. Sit tight. I'll be right there."

Vonnie went back to the car. Abigail sat wide-eyed, waiting. Vonnie got in beside her and drew her close.

"Abigail, why didn't you wear the nice clothes I bought for you?"

"I'm sorry. When Patience woke me up and told me to bring you to Hazard House, I just forgot and put on my old dress."

"Tell me more about Patience. When she takes you over, don't you remember anything that happened?"

Abigail raised troubled eyes. "I don't understand."

"Never mind. It doesn't matter. Just tell me how Patience *told* you to come after me."

"I was asleep and then I woke up and she was in my room."

"What did she look like?"

"I don't know. It was dark."

"What about Melissa? Did she hear Patience?"

"No. She was already asleep. I think she's talked to Patience, though—or maybe it was Rachel?"

"What makes you think so?"

"Because I've heard her talking to somebody."

"But you didn't see who it was?"

"No. They turned the light out—so I wouldn't wake up, I guess. And Melissa has been going off into the woods the last couple of days. I think she's been meeting Patience."

"Are you sure that the voice you heard in your room tonight was a woman's voice?"

"What do you mean?"

"Could it have been a man trying to make you *think* he was a woman?"

"I don't think so. Why would a man do that?"

"I don't know myself. I'm in a total fog. I thought maybe it was not Patience because you weren't allowed to see the person. It was in the dark. Why would Patience not want you to see her?"

"Oh, I have seen her."

"Where?"

"Near Burton's Forge day before yesterday. It was after sundown and there were a lot of shadows, but I saw her. I'm sure it was Patience. Then, after a while, Melissa came out of the woods. I think they'd been together."

"How was Patience dressed?"

"In white. That was all I saw."

"I don't know," Vonnie sighed helplessly. "I just don't know!"

"Are we going to see Patience pretty soon?"

"Not for a while, dear. Why don't you try to take a little nap?"

There wasn't time. Headlights appeared from the direction of Big Moose Lake at that moment and, a short while later, a patrol car pulled up alongside the jeep. Nothing had ever looked so good, so comforting, to Vonnie.

Then Bill's head poked in out of the darkness. "Hello, scatterbrain."

"That's a fine thing to call me!"

"Look, you're sitting out here in the middle of the night with a kooky kid. If that isn't scatterbrain, what is it?"

"Bill—don't scold me. Don't—don't do anything. I'm too upset. How can things like this happen?"

"Beats me. You say Leopold's away and Melissa's dead drunk."

"That's the situation."

"I guess something'll have to be done. The kid will have to go to Children's Welfare. Maybe they can find a decent home for her."

"Oh, Bill!"

"What do you mean, *Oh Bill*? She'll certainly be better off than she is now."

"But talking about it right in front of her . . ."

"Oh, sure. I thought she was asleep. Well, I guess the thing to do right now is to go to the Forge and give Melissa the treatment. Snap her out of it."

245

"Is she an habitual alchoholic?"

"I guess Lou didn't tell you that. Melissa's been on the juice for years. That's how she lost all her jobs."

And ended up at Burton's Forge . . . and not through any urge to help the underprivileged . . . but because she couldn't make a go of it anywhere else: the thought depressed Vonnie even more.

. . . Also why Leopold had ended up there: rejection by the outer world.

None of that helped at the moment, however, Vonnie thought.

"Even if we do get her on her feet, she'd be in no shape to take care of Abigail," she announced.

"Then what is the answer?"

"I'll keep her with me."

"But you've got a job to do. You can't haul a kid around with you."

"Maybe not, but we're talking about right now— tonight. And I'm not going to let the child go back to that drunken wreck."

Bill smiled and pushed a lock of Vonnie's hair back. "The little mother of all the world. Okay. Let's head for town . . ."

Bill's patrol car escorted Vonnie back to the lodge and he petitioned Lucy Stone for a cup of coffee while Vonnie took Abigail on upstairs.

She sat the child down and said, "Now look, dear, I want you to go to bed and go to sleep."

"But—"

"No buts about it. You must do as I say. Now go

into the bathroom and wash those dirty feet. You didn't even wear your sneakers."

"All right. But will we go see Patience tomorrow?"

"Perhaps."

Properly washed, Vonnie put Abigail into one of her nightgowns and into bed. "I want to go downstairs for a few minutes," she said. "Will you promise to stay in bed and go to sleep?"

"Yes."

"And I'm sure you always keep your promises, don't you?"

"I'll keep my promise."

Vonnie turned out the room light, leaving the one on in the bathroom. As she closed the door, a great wave of frustration swept over her. That poor child! She had so much dammed up inside her. Someone must knock down that wall and let it escape or it would destroy her.

And it must be done soon . . .

Bill was still in the coffee shop with Lucy. She wore a dressing gown and her hair hung in two braids giving her a lovely, old-fashioned look.

When Vonnie joined them, she poured another cup as she handed it to her, said, "Well, I hear you're running around the country rescuing lost orphans."

"Something of the sort."

"That Melissa! Something ought to be done about her."

"I think something ought to be done about Burton's Forge."

"What, for instance?" Bill asked.

"I don't know. But something. There must be other children up there who aren't getting a square deal."

"There's the way things *should* be," he declared, "and the way they *are*. Do-gooders are busy as hell rushing around doing good for people—but most of them want a little credit! You know: Some television time . . . a few spots in the press. And, tell me, who's interested in spotlighting a country pigsty like Burton's Forge?"

"What about the local officials? Don't they feel any responsibility?"

"They see that nobody starves. And Burton's Forge isn't something that just happened. It's been around a long time. People have been born and grown up there. Some leave and work out all right. Others just stay. How do you help people who don't want to be helped?"

"Do you mean they prefer that kind of a life?"

"If you went up there and tried to change them, you'd find out," Lucy said.

"Bill, you're not saying that things should be left alone, are you? That Abigail should be left with that weird pair, to grow up like an animal?"

"Of course not. But the reason we'll be able to do anything is not from any official urge to help the kid—it's because she's making trouble."

"Trouble! Why Bill! That's cruel."

"Maybe, but it's the truth. Abigail would rot in Burton's Forge as long as she stayed there and didn't bother anybody. But now she's called official attention to herself; so something has to be done."

"Not quite," Lucy said. "Now something *can* be done."

Vonnie remembered Lucy's attitude when Abigail first came to the lodge. A Burton's Forge brat bothering her guests. Perhaps, Vonnie thought, being *shamed* into helping the helpless was also a factor. But she was more interested in Trooper Bill's viewpoint.

"I didn't think you were so cynical," she said.

"I'm not cynical. It's just how things are. You take on the job of uplifting the lowly and you'll find there's no end to it. You either leave it alone or make a career out of it."

"What shall we do with Abigail? All we solved was the overnight problem."

Bill frowned. "You said she seems to have a fixation on Hazard House."

"That's how it is."

Lucy finished her coffee and yawned. "Well, I don't know about you two but I'm going to try and get a little more sleep before the grind starts again. See you come sunup."

With that she left the coffee shop and Vonnie gave Bill a briefing on the night's activities. "This is the first time," she said, "that Abigail has spoken of Patience as being a flesh-and-blood person."

"Her hallucinations seem to be taking solid form."

"I'm not enough of a psychologist to know what the next step is, but I doubt if it's good. That is, if they are hallucinations."

"Do you mean you really think there's somebody in the act who walks and talks and breathes?"

"I don't know what to think."

"It might be a good idea if I had a look at Hazard House. Maybe some hippies or outland characters have found the place."

"I don't think I told you, but someone has found it —a Professor Heinz from Williams College."

"Never heard of him."

"He's a friend of Jason Leopold. I found him digging out behind the mansion."

"Digging? For what?"

"He was very evasive. I questioned him pretty closely but got nowhere."

Bill was scowling. "I don't think I like the idea of your going over there alone, at least not until I've had a chance to look the place over."

"When will that be?"

"How about this afternoon?"

"I'll be ready . . ."

Vonnie went up to bed to find that Abigail had kept her promise. The child was sleeping peacefully.

Vonnie went out on the balcony and looked across the quiet lake. No scene could have been more serene. Soon dawn would come to silver the lake and then the guests would start splashing around in it and trying to catch its fish and polluting it with poisons from their outboard motors.

Waxing more philosophical, she thought of all those guests, those privileged, quietly asleep in their beds, ready with the morning to spring out and start enjoying their privileges again.

Good Lord, she thought, how morbid can a person get? And how patronizing? Just because a few people get the opportunity to enjoy themselves, I find cause to be critical. Probably most of them have worked hard all year to earn the vacation they were now spending at Big Moose Lake Lodge.

She realized that she wasn't really so critical, she'd merely found something to occupy her mind—to crowd out her unwanted thoughts—until she could get to sleep.

She went back to bed to drift off without too much trouble . . .

When she awoke, the sun was well up and the day's activities outside were well under way. Then she sat up and looked around. She called out; there was no answer.

Abigail was gone . . .

CHAPTER FIFTEEN

As disappointed as she was at finding Abigail gone, her greater distress was not hearing from Keith. Actually, not only the Hazard House project worried her, but her own job also. Even if Keith returned soon, she did not care to work for a man with such erratic habits.

However, she saw no reason to leave until he did show up and she could collect the back pay he owed her and give him formal notice.

As she dressed to go down to breakfast, she conceded that Abigail's disappearance was convenient for the moment. The child had probably gone home. Or was lurking around Hazard House, in which case she and Bill would no doubt find her. In the meantime, she saw no reason for a desperate search.

Bill felt the same way: When he arrived, after Vonnie's breakfast, he said, "The kid's been taking care of herself for quite a while. She'll turn up again . . ."

They used the patrol car to go to the mansion because he was still on duty. "This is an official complaint," he said, "so the state might as well pay for the gas."

The jeep had the hidden road pretty well beaten down by now, so the going wasn't so bad. When they got there, Bill looked up at the mad architectural mistake. "A small army could hide in there for years. It's a good thing the place is impossible to get to or there wouldn't be a whole window in the place."

They went inside and found the astrological diagram under the dome, shining clean. "It looks as though friend Leopold just finished his semiannual chore," Vonnie said.

Bill shook his head in wonder. "The things some people do to keep from being forgotten."

"Do you think that was why John Hazard put those stipulations in his will?"

"Either John or Rachel. Show me where that guy was digging."

Vonnie led him around to the hole where she had found Professor Heinz working. The hole was now some three feet deep but it looked as if the professor had given up.

"What do you suppose he was looking for?" Bill asked.

"I can't imagine. And he certainly wasn't about to tell me."

Bill turned away and looked up at the house. "Well,

as long as I'm here I'd better go through it. Why don't you wait in the car?"

"Can't I go with you?"

"I'd better do this alone. If I have to make a report I wouldn't want to involve you."

Bill disappeared into the house. Vonnie waited on the porch for a while. Then her own curiosity began stirring, what with the boring wait, and she wandered into the great hall. Studying the astrological figures for a while, she wandered toward the west end of the hall.

She found a stairway she had not previously seen. It was narrow and mysterious, in no way proportionate to the grand staircase in the center.

She started up. Halfway to a turn on ahead, she hit a loose step. A loud creaking protest caught in the upward stairwell started to echo.

She was almost back where she'd started before the echoes died.

Annoyed at her own timidity, she retraced her steps upward and turned at the halfway landing. The stairs went on from there, to a narrow corridor off which several closed doors gave promise.

None were locked. All were disappointing, each opening into empty rooms. Where the last of the building had been going on: two of the rooms were not finished—bare, aged lathing awaiting the plaster which was never applied.

How long would construction have gone on if John Hazard had lived, Vonnie wondered? She'd heard of a house in California where a millionaire's widow, for some pathological reason, had kept adding to their mansion for twenty years after her husband's death—it was said to stretch over acres. Perhaps the same thing would have gone on here.

Vonnie mounted another stairway to the third floor and found a similar situation; more unfinished rooms.

Now an even narrower stairway led up. Into one of the smaller turrets which graced the roof, perhaps. At any rate it looked interesting.

Above this one there was only a small landing with a door directly ahead. She turned the knob and pushed; the door resisted. She braced herself and pushed harder.

—And found herself hanging in space above an old rock garden far below.

The door gave so suddenly she completely lost her balance. Only by the grace of God did she grasp the edge of the now-open door while clinging to the knob with the other. She was stretched precariously, far forward, on all her weight supported only by her hands and her toes—no leverage to pull the door inward.

Any effort would have pulled her feet off the landing, left as she was, spreadeagled in space. Her chances of getting back were gone. She could only cry out and hope.

"Bill, Bill! Help! Help! Help me, Bill!"

Where could he be? Could he hear her? If he was anywhere on the upper floors of the far wing her chance of being heard was remote.

"Bill! Help me!"

Her voice echoed and re-echoed down the empty stairwell far below. Bill couldn't possibly hear.

The rocks below loomed menacingly. No chance of missing them if she fell.

Then faintly, from far off in the mansion, she heard an answering cry; wordless, but lilted like a question.

"I'm here. Over here, Bill. In the west wing!" Vonnie shouted back. "Hurry! Hurry please! I can't move!"

It was then she saw the face on the stairway. She was so positioned that by moving her head, she was looking backward, under her right shoulder. The angle caused her to see a tilted image—almost upside down—and her strained position blurred her sight. But the face of a woman was advancing upward. Toward her, coming step by step, with a hatred that was all too obvious.

The face was hideous; matted hair enclosed it. There was madness in the eyes and in the twisted mouth. Dirt caked the brow and cheeks, exposing a picture of pure, maniacal, murderous madness.

Vonnie screamed and on the moment came a pounding of feet carrying Bill from the corner of the house below.

"My God! What are you doing up there?"

"Hurry! I can't move! Help me."

"How did you ever get there?"

"Through the main hall. Turn left. Some stairs. But hurry!"

Bill raced back as he'd come and Vonnie again stared down the stairwell. The apparition was still there. But had come no closer. The woman had stopped on hearing someone below and now was undecided. One step upward, then she stopped again.

Vonnie's arms were weakening, about to give up. She would hold on as long as she could but it could not be for long enough. Bill would never get there in time. Finally she must fling herself outward—or trust to her grip on the doorknob and the edge of the panel. It would never be enough; not nearly enough . . .

The image on the stairs was blurring now as strain filled Vonnie's eyes with tears. Then the image vanished in a whirling near-unconsciousness.

Faintly she heard footsteps pounding up the stairs. She did not see but she knew it was Bill there when her grip loosened, and she hung head downward—a flying bat—over the rocks below.

"E-e-easy now. I've got you by the ankles. Don't kick. Don't fight. Just put your hands against the wall while I pull you up . . ."

An aeon of agony later she was in his arms, feeling his rage. "*Damn* you! I told you to stay in the car! Who do you think you are, pulling a trick like that?"

"I'm sorry," Vonnie sobbed. "I'm so sorry. I pushed it open, the door came open. It led to nowhere. I didn't know."

For a time he held her, realizing that his fear for her had put him into that rage.

"Go ahead," she whimpered. "Call me anything you want . . ."

"All right . . . easy. It's all over now. It was just—"

"I know," Vonnie replied, her sobs turning into half-laughter. "I was there, remember? But you thought you lost me."

259

"You insane little idiot," he snarled tenderly, and kissed her so hard it numbed her lips.

"Sit here on the step for a while, until you get your strength back." Vonnie obeyed, leaning weakly against him. He said, "That took guts, honey—to hang on and not panic. I'm real proud of you."

"Thanks," Vonnie murmured feebly. "Flattery will get you everything. Just keep it up."

"You're a crazy broad," he chuckled.

Vonnie straightened suddenly and looked down the stairwell. "Oh, I forgot . . . That woman!"

"*What* woman?" He stared at her incredulously.

"She was on the stairs, coming toward me. A terrible, a demented hag. She was . . . awful."

"Now, wait a minute. Let me get this straight. "You say there was a woman—"

"Yes! Right down there," said Vonnie, pointing. "She was coming up to push me out."

"How do you know? Maybe she was coming to help you."

"If you'd seen her you wouldn't say that!"

"But, honey. There was nobody on the stairs when I came up."

"Then she's in one of the rooms, hiding."

"I'll look. You wait here."

"Oh, no! You're not getting rid of me again. Where you go, I go."

"All right, but stay back . . ."

There were four doors on the third level—below the staircase where Vonnie almost dropped. Bill opened each to find each room empty. A mouse could not have hidden in any of them.

Also on the floor below that. Nothing but empty rooms, marking only John Hazard's insatiable compulsion to build and build and build.

"Nobody anywhere around," said Bill as they searched the last room.

"Then she must have hid in one until you passed, and then ran away."

"But, honey . . ."

"Bill! Don't tell me I'm going batty!"

"Nothing of the kind. If you say you saw a woman, well—then you saw a woman."

"But you don't believe me."

"I believe that you think you saw someone."

Vonnie clung to his hand as they walked out into the great hall. She passed the other hand over her eyes.

"All right. I'm not going to fight with you. Maybe I *was* seeing things."

"It's just that I covered the whole place. I didn't see a living thing—not even a spider."

"You searched this whole house during the short time we were apart?"

"It was a good twenty minutes."

"What did you do . . . *run* up and down the stairs and through the halls?"

"I did a thorough job."

"Bill—would you take an oath, on your honor, that there's no one in this house but you and me?"

"Well, it is a big place. There may be some nooks and crannies—"

"—And hidden rooms and blind stairways and revolving walls."

"Honey, you're trying to make a mystery where there isn't any. Why would anybody *want* to hide here? There's no future in it. The Devil himself would be afraid to hang around this mausoleum at night."

"Maybe that's why Rachel stays here," Vonnie murmured. "She's hiding from the Devil."

"What did you say?"

Vonnie looked up quickly. "Did I say something?"

"Look—I'm getting you away from here right now. I didn't know you were so damned impressionable."

Vonnie was suddenly contrite. "I'm sorry, Bill. I've taken up your whole day when you should have been out protecting the citizens who pay your salary."

"You pay part of it so protecting you comes under that head. Come on. Let's go back to the lodge. I'll buy you a stiff drink . . ."

Vonnie was not sorry to leave Hazard House. As she got into the car, she told herself it was forever. She'd had enough of the place, of Patience and Rachel and all the other psychic monstrosities conjured up out of Abigail's mind.

The way to attack this problem was to do something for the child; get her out of that environment. Perhaps put her under psychiatric care for a time.

Vonnie tried to wash the last vestige of that horrible face from her mind, content now to accept Bill's explanation because it *was* an explanation—and this was more than she could produce for her version of what had happened.

As they approached the lodge, her earlier resolve to wait for word from Keith before quitting her job began to weaken. Why should she? His actions in ignoring her were lacking in even basic respect. She would no longer work for Keith under any circumstance. An interesting job was fine; but there was such a thing as carrying an interesting thing too far.

With that decision made, all else became academic. There was nothing to hold her at Big Moose Lake Lodge. She would return to New York City, start looking for another job and let Keith get in touch with her at his leisure.

She was sure he would because he was honest, if nothing else, and would certainly pay her whatever he owed her.

There was one comforting aspect to the whole dramatic fiasco. Her coming to Big Moose Lake country directed attention to Abigail. Bill would follow through now on that . . .

Bill! How could she have possibly made all those plans without considering him! She was in love with him. She knew that now. And he had proven again and again that he was in love with her.

Now other possibilities sprang to her mind. Suppose, when she told him her plans, suppose he would propose? What then? What would her answer be?

Love was all well and good, but was she ready to settle down into married life? She had not come to New York for the sole purpose of meeting a man. She'd come to seek a career and if she turned from that now it would amount to failure.

It was all too complicated. If she and Bill had anything lasting, he would not let it die even if she were in New York and he remained where he was.

Anyhow, the decision did not have to be made at that moment . . .

When they got to the lodge Bill bought her the drink he'd promised. Then he left, promising to run over to Burton's Forge and check on Abigail.

"If that woman is still drunk, you bring Abigail right back here, Bill. We'll figure out something."

Bill promised and left. Vonnie lingered in the bar for a while then went upstairs to relax and try to clear her mind.

Ten minutes later, her phone rang.

It was Keith . . .

CHAPTER SIXTEEN

"Vonnie—I'm sorry. I've treated you miserably. I've been meaning to call . . ."

"And I've been waiting to hear from you," Vonnie replied with frost in her voice.

"You see, what happened . . . Well, Valerie left me."

"Oh, Keith! I'm so sorry!"

"It—it was just one of those things."

"But everything seemed so right the other evening. She's a lovely girl. And you two were so devoted."

"I know." Pain and bitterness clogged his voice. Now Vonnie needed no further proof that his love for Valerie was Keith's great problem. With his obvious love for her she could not imagine a more terrible tragedy.

"Have you been talking with her . . . trying to straighten things out?"

"No—no. You see, I don't know *where* she is. She may have gone to Florida. She has an aunt down there she likes a lot and she went there once before when we've had difficulties."

"Then you will be able to talk to her."

"I called. Her aunt said she wasn't there. But the way she said it—you see she's a little hostile toward me. I think she was trying to keep us apart."

"Then the thing to do is for you to go down there and insist. She's your wife. You have a right to talk to her."

"I'm going to try again on the phone in a few minutes." There was an uncertain pause. "Vonnie . . ."

"Yes, Keith."

"I've been thinking about that job up there . . ."

"I know. I've been thinking about it too. I was wondering if you'd planned to cancel your contract?"

"I don't want to. I put up a bond and it would cost me money. I need the fee too, so it would be doubly rough welching out on it."

"How much time do you have?"

"Ninety days—and I could probably get an extension."

"Then everything should be all right."

"It's just that I know my capacities and limitations, I guess." A short, humorless laugh came over the wire. "They're not the greatest and I just can't seem to do two things at once—Valerie, and the job . . ."

"I understand, Keith. The thing for you to do is take one job at a time. Valerie comes first. Go after her. Make things right. I think if you brought her up here with you, it would help. Maybe it's just being away from you . . ."

"Okay—I'll try," Keith said.

"In the meantime, do you want me to stay here or go back to New York?"

"You'd better stay there. Before long they'll be inquiries from the Associates. They'll be trying to get in touch."

"Don't worry about it. I'll keep them happy. I'm very good at talking a streak and saying nothing."

"I'm depending on you."

"I promise not to let you down . . ."

It had been a good talk. It had cleared the air. Certainly, it had killed all of Vonnie's uncertainties about the job—at least for the time being. Walking out on Keith while he was in trouble was unthinkable.

But yet there was something that disturbed Vonnie; something most annoying because she could not put her finger on it. She felt that, somehow, Keith was not telling the whole truth.

Then she denied that to herself. Of course he wasn't lying. He was certainly pessimistic over the possibilities of a reconciliation. Vonnie could tell from the hopelessness in his voice when he agreed to see Valerie even if the aunt stood in the way.

But there was *something* . . .

Vonnie decided it was not hers to worry about. She could hope that Keith got straightened out but there was no way she could help him directly. And if he hadn't told her all of it, well, that was his privilege.

There are things people just can't talk about—especially when they are as much in love as Keith.

In a way, the call freed Vonnie. The weather data was being compiled and Keith had said something about a surveyor, but she decided she could do nothing about that. She could no doubt find the man, but Keith would have to be there to tell him what to survey.

So all Vonnie could do was wait—hover about and be ready to take possible phone calls and play it by ear. In a sense, it was an admirable job; do nothing and get paid for it. Vonnie, however, would rather have had it the other way. But as long as the time was hers, Vonnie saw no reason why she shouldn't try to enjoy it.

So after Keith called, she put on her bathing suit and a robe and went down to the lake. There were miniature cabanas set up along the man-made sandy beach and Vonnie was surprised to find one with Keith's name on it. Obviously, Big Moose Lake Lodge did things up right.

Vonnie made herself comfortable and shortly a young man who reminded her a little of Walter Sims, the weatherman, arrrived in a white coat to be of service. Vonnie ordered a whiskey sour for the sheer novelty of it.

Then, when the waiter returned, he brought a message along with the drink:

"Miss March, there's a man in the lobby. He asked for Mr. Elwood and then for you."

"What does he want?"

"He didn't say. His name is Lukas Dean."

One of the Associates, Vonnie thought; one she hadn't met. Her first thought was not to be discovered basking lazily in the sun. Then she refused to be that timid. So Keith was away—in New York on business. So she had the day off. What was wrong with that?

"Send him down here," she said . . .

Lukas Dean didn't look like a smart Associates executive. He was a slightly paunchy, middle-aged man in a blue suit which lost its press easily. His collar was a little too tight and his mustache just too irregular to indicate a smart dresser.

"Miss March?" he asked in a gravelly voice.

"Yes. Won't you sit down?"

He eased his bulk into a chair and smiled pleasantly. "Nice around here. Very nice."

"It's restful. May I order you a drink?"

"No—no thanks. He glanced ruefully down at his paunch. "Watching my calories. Booze has too many of them."

"What can I do for you, Mr. Dean?"

He handed her a card; it didn't tell much. It simply read:

Lukas Dean

Concessions.

Hardly enlightening.

"I wanted to see your boss, Keith Elwood."

"I'm sorry. He's in New York."

"What we do, Miss March, is handle concessions,

like the cigarette and candy machines in resort hotels and motels—that sort of thing."

"Then can I assume you're interested in the concession at the Hazard House ski lodge?"

"That was the general idea."

"Well, I'm afraid you've come far too early. Mr. Elwood isn't here to build the resort or manage it. He's here merely to see if a ski resort is feasible in this area."

"I know." Mr. Dean smiled, causing his mustache to twitch slightly, and said, "But we find it's always a good idea to be around as soon as we hear of something going up. The concessions in a place like this would be valuable and we like to earn our way in a sense. We go on the theory that the early bird gets the worm."

"Well, in this case, you may still be too early. The worm isn't born yet. It may never be."

Lukas Dean shrugged. "Then I'm only out my time and that's what I'm paid for. I understand the site is up in pretty rugged country."

"Hazard House? Yes, it is."

"Thought I might take a look at it."

Vonnie hesitated. Was Mr. Dean trying to further interests of his own—interests counter to Keith's? Even so, she could hardly bar him from looking at an old house in the wilds.

Sensing her reluctance, Dean said, "We've had a lot of experience in these things. Maybe I could give Mr. Elwood the benefit of that. A tip here—a suggestion there."

Vonnie decided she was being too suspicious. "Hazard House *is* in rough country, but there is a road. You wouldn't have to climb over rocks."

"That's fine. A big step in the right direction."

"As you go out of the lodge, you turn left. About two miles down, you'll find some fresh bushes that have been cut through by other vehicles. That's the road. All you have to do is follow it."

"Well, thank you a lot, Miss March. I'll go up and have a look."

Vonnie watched as Dean walked away; a tired man who went methodically about a job he didn't care much for but had to do . . .

Vonnie had been discovering that at the lodge she was not one to take her ease in very long stretches. An hour or so of inactivity and she became restless.

Also, she worried a little about Abigail. She'd had no word of the child from Bill or anyone else. That concern, besides her own restlessness, finally sent her back to dress and down Salt Lick Road headed for Burton's Forge in the jeep. Bill was sure to advise against the trip, but he wasn't there at the moment to direct her destiny.

She pulled up in front of Jason Leopold's hut and felt many eyes on her as she walked toward the door. Some of the natives were about. A woman was sawing wood across the road from Leopold's hut. Her knee on the sawhorse holding the log and her hand on the bucksaw she posed there like a statue, her eyes fixed on Vonnie.

Down the road two women who had been walking

side by side, also froze and stood staring, but Vonnie felt the majority of eyes were peeking at her from behind dirty, colorless shades.

When she'd reached the door, her resolve to rescue Abigail from this squalor was even more firmly fixed.

Melissa opened the door to her knock. The woman was nowhere near the bad shape Vonnie expected. Evidently downing a bottle of brandy did not incapacitate her for very long.

"Hello," Vonnie said. "Perhaps you remember me. I brought Abigail home one night with Bill Jackson."

"I recollect," Melissa said. She made a vague pass at her hair and smoothed her gray apron. "Would you like to come in?"

"Thank you."

Vonnie entered and Melissa swept a pile of clothes off one of the chairs. "Please sit here. I'll make a cup of tea."

"Thank you. Is Abigail around?"

"Oh, that child. A person can't keep track of her. She was here an hour ago. Now I guess she's off somewhere."

Melissa's earlier breeding was reflected in her speech if not in her appearance. Vonnie felt sorry for her. Here was a woman who had tried but had not the strength to make it with the Establishment. Surely a great waste.

Water was already boiling on the stove and Vonnie watched as Melissa poured it over two tea bags.

Vonnie said, "I was talking to a friend of yours over the weekend. Louella Keenan, Bill Jackson's aunt."

"Lou Keenan? For heaven's sake! How is Lou?"

"She seems to be in excellent health."

"The poor soul. She was once so active. Then that arthritis knotted her up. But she's a tough one; wouldn't stay down."

"I admired her a great deal."

Melissa set a steaming cup beside Vonnie. "Are you going with Bill?"

"Oh, no. He's just a very nice person and he's driven me around some. He took me up to meet his aunt over the weekend."

"Bill Jackson would be a good catch for any girl."

"I actually met him through Abigail. She came to the lodge and we were having dinner. Abigail of course knew him and he came over and introduced himself."

"I understand you and your boss are here to do something with Hazard House?"

"Yes. Mr. Elwood is looking it over with the idea of turning it into a ski lodge. A New York syndicate hired him to make the survey."

"That house has seen a lot of history."

"I saw that interesting design on the floor of the court under the Moorish dome."

"Isn't that the most outlandish thing you ever saw?"

"It's fantastic. And the astrological circle is fascinating too. I understand Mr. Leopold has the job of preserving it."

"Yes. It pays Jason two hundred a year but I haven't the least idea where the money comes from."

"I think it was left in trust by John Hazard. His

wife, Rachel, must have been a fascinating character."

"Oh, yes. That's really what the place is—Rachel Hazard. There's blessed little of John in it. From the moment he met that woman he was doomed. Rachel was a Haitian. Black as the ace of spades—but beautiful as a dream, according to the story. She was the devil's daughter, no doubt about that. Had a working agreement with Satan himself according to the yarns."

So far, no indication that Melissa believed anything of what she was saying. It was just as Lou Keenan said: Melissa liked to spin a yarn.

"I was quite intrigued," Vonnie said. "Mr. Leopold mentioned a manuscript in your public library—a sort of history by Dame Goody. So I went down to have a look at it."

"I studied it once, a long time ago. Very hard to read, most of it."

"I had the same difficulty."

"According to some research I did," said Vonnie, "Rachel and John had three children. A daughter, Patience, and two sons. One of the sons went to San Francisco and had children of his own. His descendants own Hazard House now."

"It certainly hasn't done them much good. The taxes were always paid though so I guess they got it clear."

"Both sons died through accidents I understand."

"The one in 'Frisco did. The other one, young John, was murdered by his mother, or so the story goes."

"How terrible."

"That Rachel was a terrible woman. The yarns say

that she demanded a pledge to Satan from her whole family. Young John refused. His brother did too, for that matter, but he escaped to the west coast. That was Christopher. The long arm of Satan caught up with him, though."

"But you say Rachel actually murdered the other boy?"

"Put him on an altar and stabbed him through the heart, or so it's told."

This didn't surprise Vonnie either. Something in her New York research hinting at dark ceremonial doings at Hazard House when Rachel ruled it.

"What about Patience?" Vonnie asked.

"The daughter? She signed the pact but tried to recant. This brought Rachel's wrath down on her, but finally she died."

Melissa sighed. "They all passed on in the end—to whatever reward or punishment they deserved."

Vonnie finished her tea and set the cup down. "Well, I must be running along. I just wanted to see how Abigail is getting along."

"That child just roams and roams. She seems to meet some of the strangest people."

Melissa's eyes dropped as she made that comment. They shifted, then she turned away. It was the first gesture Vonnie had seen that marked her as other than some ordinary woman with a drinking problem which had dragged her down.

Yet even that gesture was most vague; one Vonnie certainly would not have noticed if she had not been looking for it. For that reason, Vonnie felt she had no right to attach any importance whatever to it. It had probably been her own imagination.

Vonnie smiled. "I hope I'm not included in that category."

Melissa was quick to apologize. "Oh, no, Miss March. I think it's fine that Abigail can meet *nice* people. The poor child doesn't get much opportunity. And she *is* exceptional. A very smart child."

"I'm well aware of that. Thanks for the tea. And tell Mr. Leopold hello for me."

"That one!" Melissa snorted. "He's all over the place doing things for everybody but his own . . ."

As she turned the jeep in the narrow road, conscious of the scrutiny of the Burton's Forge people, she decided that Melissa felt no great loyalty to the man she lived with. She referred to him with open contempt.

Vonnie drove back. At six, Bill turned up without his uniform and they dined together. Afterward, they walked along the shore of Big Moose Lake hand-in-hand, from time to time stopping to make chaste love.

Vonnie sensed how easy it would be to pull out all the stops with Bill—a situation she could either bemoan or be thankful for, Aunt Madge's early training. Many modern girls who took the joy of the moment and were in no way losers, considered themselves completely respectable.

Then what did hold her back? She tried to imagine Bill as an attractive, magnetic male but for whom she felt only friendship. Would that have changed things? Possibly. It was clearly a question for which no clear answer existed.

There was one thing—if Bill had been more aggressive things might have turned out differently. He obviously wanted her passionately. Then was he, too, restraining himself because *she* was such a special person?

There was no answer to that question either.

On the walk back Bill said, "By the way, I may have set up something for Abigail."

"Why, that would be wonderful!"

"I talked to Aunt Lou. She said she'd like to have the kid up at Gar Fin Lake."

"But your Aunt Lou . . ."

"I know. She's crippled. You didn't see that stopping her though, did you?"

"Hardly. But an active child. Do you think she could cope?"

"It might be the best thing in the world for her. She has no one and she makes a lousy recluse. I know damned well she just sits up there and waits for my visits."

"Then why doesn't she live down here with you?"

"It's her choice. She's so deathly afraid of being a burden to someone. I've tried to tell her I'd be happy to have her down here. Do you know what her answer is?"

"No—what?"

Bill grinned and toyed with Vonnie's fingers. "I'm afraid it would shock you."

"Try me."

"Well, she said a virile young bachelor needs a love life—like a girl friend in to spend the night once in a while. So he doesn't want a useless old aunt messing up the picture."

"She didn't say any such thing!"

"Scout's honor. Aunt Lou's a pretty broadminded old biddy."

Bill was evidently not trying to make any personal point with Vonnie, however, because he went right on:

"I think Abigail and Lou would hit it off. And if anybody can get through that kid's outer shell, she'd be the one."

"Would Melissa object? Or Jason Leopold?"

"I don't think there'd be any trouble with Jason. About Melissa? I don't know. I mean I don't know if she'd let go voluntarily. Abigail could be gotten away from her through the courts without any trouble, but I'd just as soon not go to that extreme if I could help it."

"Of course not."

"Then, too," Bill mused. "*We* could take the kid."

Vonnie came to a dead halt. "What are you talking about, Bill Jackson?"

"Well, like we might get married."

"Just like that, eh?: we might have a drink when we get back to the lodge . . . it might rain on Thursday . . . we *might* get married? Wow!"

"Oh, so you're one of those broads who wants to make a big deal out of it? A panting proposal on the guy's knees? Kisses like she was a holy relic?"

"You're the most exasperating man!"

His answer came slowly and when it came, his tone was more serious. "What about it, Vonnie? Do you think we could make a go of it?"

Matching his changed mood, Vonnie said, "I don't know, Bill."

"You have thought about it, haven't you?"

"I'd be a liar if I said I hadn't. Somehow, I've kind of gotten the idea you're in love with me."

"Is it one-sided?"

"No, Bill, it isn't. I'm in love with you. I'm sure it isn't just a chemical attraction, either. But somehow it's too soon."

"Do you mean we've got to stall around for a year or so to see if it's genuine?"

"No. I mean too soon in my personal program. I could have gotten married quite easily back home, but I wanted to see something of the world. I wanted a try at a career. So I took the plunge and came East to the Big City. And now, if I get married less than a month after I got off at the airport, it wouldn't make much sense, would it?"

"You've got a point."

They walked for a while before Vonnie said, "Bill, I think complete understanding is important."

"I'll buy that."

"All right. Do you want me the other way?"

"Of course I want you." He stopped to scratch his head in perplexity. "I know a couple of guys, old schoolmates, who do it that way. They found girls they liked and set up housekeeping—with everything except a marriage license."

"There are also girls who want it that way. They want a man but they don't want to be tied down. They want to be able to pack up and leave any morning they wish to."

"You know—I envy those guys."

"And you'd have Aunt Lou's blessing if you went their way."

He thought that over carefully. "Uh-huh. If I told her you and I were moving in together, she'd give a big cheer and throw a party for us. But, way down deep, she'd be hurt."

He straightened his shoulders and assumed a grim expression. "Of course, none of that means a damn thing. I live my life for myself. Not for anybody else."

Vonnie laughed and pulled his face around and kissed him. "Sure you do. Hard-hearted Bill. That's my boy."

"How would you like a good spanking?"

"It might be fun."

With that they went in to the lodge and sat on the balcony for a while in a kind of understanding silence that made Vonnie say to herself: Good Lord, we're a couple of old married people already. This is a fine romance.

But when Bill left, she felt differently. The slightest gesture from him would have melted her defenses and she would have locked the door and kept him there until morning.

He sensed this as he kissed her. "It's a good thing I have to go to work, angel . . ."

281

When he was gone, Vonnie did some more thinking. There were the things she'd heard about Bill: He did not need his job; their married life would *not* have to be spent tied down out in the country—she would liked to have gone into it, but she did not like the impression that she was bargaining in any respect . . .

The next morning another visitor came asking for her. A Frank Kaiser from New York City who arrived in a truck with his surveying instruments and a partner named Tom Wendell.

"Mr. Elwood sent us, Miss March. He said to see you."

"Then you know what you're to do?"

"Oh, yes," said Kaiser. "It's just a question of where we do it. Mr. Elwood said you'd show us."

Kaiser was the younger of the two, and a personable young man who smelled strongly of peppermint. Wendell was older and appeared to be the second man of the pair.

"Your truck looks sturdy enough. I'm sure you can make it to Hazard House without trouble," Vonnie said. "Why don't you just follow along behind my jeep?"

"Good deal," Kaiser said, stripping down another stick of gum.

Vonnie was gratified that Keith had gone ahead with the assignment; he probably forgot he'd told her to find the surveyors. But no matter, the job was progressing.

When they reached Hazard House, the men went

into conference, peering up at the slopes and inclines and laying out the procedures they would follow.

No longer needed, Vonnie wandered about in search of any other holes Professor Heinz might have dug. As she poked around she kept thinking how much simpler things would be if everyone were honest and aboveboard. Why didn't Heinz say what he was after! She found some excavations but none from which he might have extracted anything of value. Then she wandered back inside, where the tile design on the hall floor gleamed in the sunlight coming down from the dome.

It was all so incongruous: that one spot of clean, bright artwork surrounded by the dust and neglect of generations.

It was really quite beautiful, but knowing its history colored it in Vonnie's eyes; gave it a grim, bleak image in her mind. Was human blood actually spilled on that floor? Did a scream from the victim sacrificed echo up into that dome?

She wandered into the untended wing beyond. As she went farther, the dust thickened. She came to the place where the dust was disturbed: There had been a struggle in that place.

But more? The results lay in the shadow by the wall. She approached, then suddenly realized that she had stepped into blood.

She looked beyond one of the pillars, into the deeper shadows.

Then she screamed . . .

CHAPTER SEVENTEEN

"Holy God!" roared Kaiser.

Wendell said nothing. He leaned against the pillar and with his head bowed.

Vonnie dashed from the carnage there on the floor. She sat down on a ledge to regain control of herself.

It was the abruptness of it; the sudden coming upon a dead man—stepping into his blood—though the blood was dried and dark.

Any girl would have screamed.

The scream swiftly brought the two surveyors who were now discovering more than they'd bargained for on this job.

"Do you know who he is?" Kaiser asked.

Vonnie nodded without looking around. "He came to see me at the lodge this morning . . . His name was Dean . . . he was interested in concessions."

Kaiser had now gotten the courage to bend closer to the corpse. "That's odd," he said.

"What's odd?" asked Wendell.

"If he's an ordinary businessman how come he is carrying a gun?"

"Maybe he had enemies."

"Out here, miles from nowhere?"

"Maybe they followed him."

"Maybe we've got to get the police. Why don't you drive Miss March back and call the cops?"

"Okay." Wendell seemed to welcome any chore which would take him from the scene.

But Vonnie objected: "No. I want to stay. One of you go for the police. You can take the jeep. Call the State Police and ask for Bill Jackson. He's familiar with this mansion. He'll get here quicker. Tell him I'm here—Vonnie March."

"Okay, Tom," Kaiser said. "You handle it."

When Wendell left, Kaiser came and sat down beside her. "This is a pretty rough thing for a girl to stumble over. I'm sorry."

"Thank you, but I'm all right now."

"What kind of a maniac would commit a murder like that? Slash the victim up that way?"

Vonnie's answer came only in thought: A maniac who has been dead for generations and who's found a way to come back. Of course it was only in fantasy: The dead do not return to murder the living . . .

In less than an hour Bill Jackson arrived with another trooper—the longest vigil Vonnie had ever kept. The second trooper went straight to the body while Bill went to Vonnie's side.

Under other circumstances he would have taken her in his arms and she would have melted into them.

But he only took her hand and led her gently toward the door.

"Out of here, angel," he said in a low voice. "You wait in the patrol car."

When Vonnie was safely deposited, Bill began: "The guy on the phone says you knew the dead man."

"Yes." Vonnie repeated her story, by which time the other patrolman came up to Bill with Dean's wallet.

"That guy was a private detective. Licensed in New York. There's his card."

"A private detective!" Vonnie exclaimed. "He told me he was interested in getting the concession at the ski lodge."

"His cover, I guess. What do you suppose he was after?"

"Beats me," Bill said. "I'll phone him in."

Bill got somebody on the patrol-car phone and reported what had happened. He gave all the known details on the dead man.

When he disconnected, he said, "There'll be a medical inspector out here as soon as they can. In the meantime we'd better comb this place."

"Start giving it the works," said Bill. "I'll be right along."

Alone with Vonnie, Bill took off his cap, wiped his brow and scowled into the cap. Then he said, "Honey, this makes that woman you saw on the stairs look more alive than before."

"I'd just about decided she was strictly a figment of my imagination, of which you convinced me. Now I'm sorry to have her come up again."

288

"One thing. Was she after you or after that guy?"

"She could have hardly known he was out here. That is if she really does exist. It could have been someone else."

"We'll know all about it in time. But right now, you're going to be covered."

"I'll be safe enough at the lodge. No one would want to kill *me*—maniac or otherwise. I don't have any enemies."

"Yes, well anyway, I'll take you back now. Jinks can handle things here until the medical examiner and a couple more cars show up."

"I thought you and he were going to search the mansion."

"That will be taken care of. There's no immediate rush because Dean has been dead for quite a while. You say he showed up here before noon yesterday?"

"I didn't actually see him make the trip, but this is where he said he was going when he left the lodge."

"We'll get your statement later."

"I've got to get in touch with Keith somehow and tell him what's happened."

"You can do that also, back at the lodge. The New York cops will be looking him up too if he doesn't show up here pretty quick."

Vonnie shuddered; a reaction was setting in. "That poor man! How could *any*body do such a thing?"

"I'm sorry as hell that you saw it, honey. Let's get going. I'll tell Jinks and be right back . . ."

They met a patrol coming when they were halfway to Salt Lick Road, the two vehicles on the narrow road had difficulty passing each other.

At last Vonnie was back at the lodge and quite ready for a shower and some rest.

"I'll see that your jeep is brought back and I'll drop by later. Don't talk to anybody unless he's got a uniform, and then refer him to me."

He kissed her, said "Lock the door," and left.

Not much later, there came a knock and voice in the corridor. "It's Lucy, dear."

Vonnie hesitated. She was sure Bill's order didn't include Lucy Stone.

Vonnie unlocked the door and Lucy came in. "Oh," she said, "you poor darling. Bill told me. To stumble on something like that. I'm glad you weren't alone out there."

"I'm glad too."

"I want you to do me a favor, dear. Don't talk to anybody around here who might get wind of it."

"Bill said the same thing."

"With him it's official, but with me it's a matter of business. Bad publicity for the lodge."

"They'll find out sometime, won't they?"

"No doubt, but talk makes rumors and rumors get bigger and pretty soon they'd have the murder right here on the premises."

"I'm sorry you've been caused so much trouble, Lucy."

Lucy was instantly contrite. "Oh, honey! Don't misunderstand me. You had nothing to do with that murder."

"I may have been the last person to talk to Mr. Dean before he died."

"That still didn't kill him. A private detective!

What could he have been after anyway, way up here?"

"Bill said they'd find out eventually."

"I'm sure they will. Is Mr. Elwood due back very soon?"

"I hope so. If he calls and I'm asleep—anytime—be sure and wake me up."

"All right, honey. Now you rest a while. And like Bill said, lock the door after I go out . . ."

Alone, Vonnie did not feel like lying down. In a sense, she had become a prisoner in her room. She could have gone down to the lake, to the Elwood cabana, but Bill would not have approved.

Finally, she threw herself onto a chaise longue on the balcony to puzzle things out. She remembered something that was said: that Rachel would not want things at the mansion changed.

This yanked her mind up sharply: she was *not* going to waste brain power on such neurotic foolishness! If she didn't watch it she would be as confirmed a bearer of old-wives' tales as Melissa.

Melissa. Vonnie rolled the name around in her mind. How much of what Abigail said about Melissa and the mysterious visitor was true, and how much the stuff of Abigail's strange dreams?

One thing had not been the stuff of dreams: that bottle of expensive brandy. Nobody in Burton's Forge would have had the money for such a luxury, nor would they have known where to purchase it.

Vonnie continued to mull. The least she could do was leave word with the answering service to have

Keith call her immediately; it was vitally important. That might do some good. And went back to while away the time gazing out over the lake.

Just after sundown there was a knock and Bill Jackson came wearily into the room, followed her out to the balcony and sank into the other lounge.

"A murder's always got so damn much detail to it," he grumbled.

"Did you find out anything about Mr. Dean and who he really was?"

"No problem there. He was a New York City private eye."

"Who was he working for?"

"We don't know that yet. The city cops say he was a one-man outfit. Didn't even have a secretary. A little hole-in-the-wall office. They're going over it now."

"The poor man."

"He had a clean record. No marks against him. Just a guy trying to make a living the hard way."

"Do you suppose he was actually what he claimed to be?"

"What do you mean?"

"Working for someone who had him checking on concession possibilities at the mansion. After all, he didn't use an alias."

"I doubt it, although it's possible. Anything's possible I guess."

"You didn't find anyone when you searched the mansion, I don't suppose."

Bill shook his head. "There was nobody in there."

"Then what I saw *was* an hallucination."

"You mean the woman on the stairs? Probably, but not necessarily. There's plenty of hiding places out in those woods. We know somebody killed Dean and that there was nobody in the house. So, they'd either took off for good or hid out where it would take the whole national guard to find them."

"Bill, do you think it will ever be solved?"

"Sure."

"Not all murders are."

"In the cities maybe, where there are so damned many. But up here in the country it's different." He smiled and reached for Vonnie's hand. "Up here, people are curious. They like to have their curiosity satisfied and when it comes to murder, they expect their police to end their suspense."

"How was Mr. Dean killed?"

"With a knife. That is, he was killed that way. Afterwards he was—well, we won't go into that."

"Then it must have been someone who hated him terribly."

"Not necessarily. It could have been someone who hated—period. A homicidal maniac."

"It's just too incredible!"

"If we knew more about Dean personally, it would help. We know he was a pro because he had a gun permit and the gun was still in his shoulder holster. A man like that in a strange place would probably have been on the alert, thus no one could have slipped up behind him. But you can't tell. It might have happened, or else it was someone he knew and trusted enough to have his guard down."

"Then you have no suspects at all?"

"We questioned that guy you said was digging out behind the house."

"Well I hope you got more out of him than I did."

"There was no fooling around on that score. He told us what he'd been looking for."

"Well, don't keep me in suspense!"

"He claims he was looking for some old bones—trying to verify some local legends. It's a hobby of his, so he claims."

"Any particular bones?"

"Uh-huh. He claims the historians are wrong, that both of John Hazard's sons did not leave home. Only one. He thinks Rachel killed the other one as a sacrifice when he wouldn't sign some kind of a crazy pledge to the devil."

"And he's trying to find the body?"

"That's what he claims."

"And you believe him?"

"Why not? It's something a kooky old character like Heinz might do. We'll keep an eye on him, of course, but so far he has been of no value. He claims he's never seen a soul at Hazard House except you."

"And he didn't see me until I practically stepped on him. He's blind as a bat without those glasses."

"And the typical absent-minded professor. The Legion could be having a convention in the place and he'd probably not notice."

"What's the situation with Abigail?"

"I guess Melissa's riding closer herd on the kid. Have you seen her around?"

"No. Haven't you talked to her?"

"Not yet."

"Don't you plan to?"

"Maybe, but it's hardly worth while. We know she was nowhere near Hazard House while Dean was there. We checked that. And if we questioned her, with that imagination of hers, she'd probably tie us up in knots."

"You're looking for a flesh-and-blood killer, aren't you?" Vonnie mused.

"Oh, come on now. You aren't hooked on that stuff about Rachel coming out of her grave!"

"Of course not. But I told you about Abigail—how she came here and told me Patience wanted to see me and that Patience had talked to Melissa and that Patience met her out in the woods."

"We checked that. It was all the kid's marvelous imagination."

"Then where did the bottle of expensive brandy come from?"

"She explained that. The stuff wasn't brandy. That bottle's been around for years. Leopold brought it from Europe with him and the brandy had been drunk long, long ago. Melissa keeps her wine in it."

Vonnie sighed. "I guess there's a simple explanation for everything, isn't there?"

"Except who killed Dean."

"I think when you find that out, it will be simple too."

"I've got to run along now. I'll see you tomorrow or if I'm busy, I'll call."

"Please let me know right away if you reach Keith. I doubt if he knows any of this happened."

"He does if he checks with his answering service. We left word there."

"Poor Keith. He's star-crossed. One tragedy after another . . ."

After dinner and by the time she was ready for bed, the shock of the murder had pretty well worn off. In fact Vonnie was ashamed of herself, for having become, as she termed it, a basket case.

She slept well and awoke to a lovely day and the monotony of waiting for something to happen.

There was no call from Keith and when Bill phoned her he said they thought Keith was somewhere in Florida looking for his wife.

The tone of Bill's voice caused Vonnie to ask, "You don't suspect Keith of anything do you?"

"I'm not sure. If stupidity were a crime I'd have him in jail as soon as I could lay hands on him."

"He hasn't handled himself very well," Vonnie admitted reluctantly.

"You can say that again."

"He's terribly upset."

"Aren't we all? Now, you stay put at the lodge and amuse yourself. I'll see you tonight . . ."

Amusing herself was easier said than done. Vonnie found this out as the hours dragged by. She felt herself to be in the static center of a whirlpool of activity, going nowhere, learning nothing.

Then the call came.

It came through the switchboard. Vonnie answered. She heard Melissa's voice, tight, frightened.

296

"Melissa! What's wrong?"

"Miss March. I'm in a phone booth. Call me back from a public phone—please!"

"Of course."

Melissa gave her the number and Vonnie ran down to the lobby to the public phone. She thought Melissa was probably calling from that red booth she herself had used to call Bill.

Melissa answered instantly. "Miss March, I have a message for you from Mr. Elwood. Your employer."

"Yes—yes! Where is Keith?"

"He's badly hurt. He has to see you. Can you come to Burton's Forge?"

"Certainly. I'll get in touch with Bill Jackson—"

"No! Don't do that. You must come alone."

"What kind of trouble is Keith in? Why is he avoiding the police?"

"Bad trouble. I think you can persuade him to come out of hiding—that it will do him no good. But he says he has to talk to you alone."

It all came clear now. For reasons beyond Vonnie's comprehension, Keith had become personally involved at Hazard House—and had killed Mr. Dean? It all seemed possible now.

"Is Keith hurt?"

"Yes, yes. Please hurry."

There was now no thought of anything but to get to Keith and convince him of the sensible thing: that whatever he'd done, hiding out was the wrong answer.

Vonnie in her jeep left without being noticed. The sun was quartering down the afternoon sky when she reached that red phone booth; she was right. Melissa was waiting there. She had been hiding behind some bushes and came out with a shawl over her head, clutched tightly at her throat.

Vonnie stopped and Melissa climbed in.

"Go straight on ahead," Melissa directed.

"Where is Keith? Hiding in the woods?"

"He's at Hazard House."

"But this isn't the way."

"It's one of the ways. We can't use the road Abigail showed you. We'd have to pass the lodge. Turn in next to that big boulder."

Negotiating the turn and the rocky path beyond took all Vonnie's attention. The jeep clambered valiantly over every obstacle and soon Vonnie found herself on a narrow trail skirting the base of a high, circular bluff which supported the mountain above.

"I don't understand any of this," Vonnie said. "I didn't know Keith even knew you."

Melissa clutched her shawl with one hand and braced herself with the other and stared straight ahead.

"He got in touch with me through Abigail . . ."

"Where is she now?"

"She's at home, locked in. I don't want her roaming around."

Vonnie threw a brief glance at Melissa; at the stern, worn profile; her cheeks sagging from alcoholic abuse.

"You're terribly frightened, aren't you?" Vonnie said.

"I'm not used to this sort of thing."

"I understand. How badly is Keith hurt?"

"He'll live . . ."

"What was he doing up here? Everyone thought he was in Florida."

"He'll tell you all about it when he sees you."

A few more tortuous roads, with the jeep creaking at very turn of the wheel. Then Vonnie said, "Why are you doing this, Melissa?"

"Why?"

"For a man you can't possibly know very well, why didn't you just call the police?"

"We do what we have to do," Melissa said harshly. "Turn that way, it brings us out at Hazard House."

Vonnie turned bravely into what looked like a wall of solid foliage and came out behind the mansion a short distance from where Professor Heinz had been digging.

"Is Keith inside?" Vonnie asked.

Melissa nodded. It seemed to Vonnie that the woman's fear had increased. Perhaps she saw herself more starkly now, as a law breaker, and the thought weighed her down.

Vonnie parked near the columned porch and they went inside.

"This way," said Melissa.

They mounted the grand staircase to the second floor and then left. Vonnie wondered if Keith came after the police search or whether he'd managed to stay hidden.

Melissa pointed to a door. "In there, and to the right."

Vonnie went in. The suite consisted of two rooms separated by an arched opening. In the next room, she saw a pile of rags on the floor and a few crusts of bread.

Melissa had not followed. "There's no one here," Vonnie called back.

There was no answer.

Vonnie returned to the door and back into the corridor. It was empty.

"Melissa!"

The name was echoed again and again through the empty hallways.

"Melissa. Where are you?"

The stairs went down half a floor at sharp right angles. When Vonnie reached the landing she saw a figure outside, through the landing window. It was Melissa running—toward the woods behind the mansion.

Vonnie pushed the window up. Miraculously, it lifted some six inches. Vonnie knelt down and put her face to the opening and cried "Melissa! Where are you going? Wait!"

The woman froze and looked back over her shoulder, her face was a mask of terror. Then she ran on, disappearing into the woods.

A drenching wave of fright swept over Vonnie which she fought to control. She'd been tricked! No doubt, but for what reason? Why had she been lured back to Hazard House?

The sun stood at the edge of the tall pines to the west now. Vonnie saw the sturdy jeep parked by the porch as the goal she must reach to escape. She straightened to dash down the stairs.

Below, on the next landing, an apparition barred her way . . .

CHAPTER EIGHTEEN

It was the woman from the narrow stairway. The face Vonnie had seen while stretched out inches from death gripping the knob of the door, which led to nowhere.

But the creature was no vision this time. She was real, down there in the shadows below, the knife in her hand catching light from the window.

She was not so wildly disheveled now. Her hair, while still unkempt, was not a rat's nest shaped around her head. And the white that Vonnie had seen only dimly before, now turned out to be a turtleneck sweater and a skirt.

"Valerie! I was looking for Keith. I came here with . . ."

Vonnie's explanation dribbled away. It was so uselessly inane—explaining anything, to the so obviously mad creature standing poised below her.

There was an answer of sorts, however; a throaty, happy crooning chuckle of evil gloating which branded the madness.

Valerie Elwood raised the knife and started up the stairs.

Vonnie fled back to a door at the far end of that corridor and flung it open. Valerie's mad face appeared behind her just as Vonnie slammed the door.

She thought desperately of something to push against it but there was no furniture in the room. She could only shove her own weight against it and brace her heels, while clutching the knob to keep it from turning.

Her pursuer hit the door like a maddened animal. Screams of rage from the corridor heightened and Vonnie knew she was dealing with a savage beast that had once been a beautiful woman . . .

Valerie's strength was far beyond normal; a well of power only maddened ones are be able to tap. The door trembled on its hinges; the entire wall shuddered.

Again that insane weight was flung against the door and again Vonnie knew she could not hold the mad-woman off; she did not have such strength.

No way to escape except the windows which gave onto a roof ledge outside. Vonnie held out against one more assault and during a pause, while Valerie set herself for another rush, Vonnie raced to the window.

The glass broke against her shoulder, she pushed the shattered edges out and felt a long slash down her arm as she fell out down onto the ledge.

The decorative extension on the bottom of the

steep slant above was barely more than a foot wide but it was level. Enough to walk along if it only would support her weight.

It creaked perilously as Vonnie inched along. But this brought her to another window and she was about to break the glass and enter when she remembered the cunning of the insane. Valerie might well have sensed each move and would be waiting inside with her knife poised.

Then she saw that Valerie had not been that clever; but insanely tenacious. She had followed Vonnie out on the ledge through the window Vonnie had broken.

Fearless in her blind rage, Valerie came on, chuckling her mad, discordant delight of a murder to come.

Vonnie then edged swiftly to the next window, used her knee on the pane, and reentered the house at the cost of further cuts.

She ran till she found a long, dim corridor. Never had she been so thankful for darkness. Now she had only the first floor to go—and out into the forest.

She ran, turned at the angles in the corridor, and ran again. Only to come sobbing to a deadend wall. (This was one of those architectural jokes with which the mansion was honeycombed.)

She could only start back. Now she did not run, but went very softly, her terror increasing with each moment. She expected to die of fright if Valerie Elwood's mad face materialized out of the gloom.

Very softly she tried each door as she went along. No room had a second door to help her escape. Each room would be another trap for Vonnie until Valerie

Elwood traced her down and drove that knife into her heart.

Strange thoughts flashed through Vonnie's mind: To die quickly would not be so bad. But then she remembered Mr. Dean: What would Valerie do with the knife?

Every second made the situation more perilous. It gave the insane Mrs. Elwood that much more time to hunt her down. Perhaps the thing was to run? . . . Retrace her steps . . . Make a dash for it?

Too late for regrets now.

Then Vonnie opened a door in this house of endless doors—and saw another at the far side of the room. She ran to it, panting, hoping that it led to the paradise beyond. In a sense it did—to another corridor, in a house of eternal corridors.

She turned, for no reason, but it was the wrong way! By sinister magic, Valerie Elwood's ghostly figure was facing her at the far end.

Vonnie turned, fled in the opposite direction. As she turned in the corridor to look back, *there was no sign of the madwoman.*

My God! Vonnie sobbed. My mind is going! Are phantoms helping her? Help me! Please, God. Help me.

And her prayer had been heard because this corridor ended in a down stairway. Now the forest was closer. Closer than ever. Close enough. She exulted: free at last.

And things remained that way until Vonnie was halfway down, when there stood Valerie Elwood waiting at the bottom.

"No!" Vonnie screamed. "No! You are not real!"

Valerie Elwood's delighted laughter and the way she slashed the air with the knife proved otherwise. Vonnie fled back up the stairs.

This time, Valerie Elwood followed her.

Searching for a way through the malignant maze of doors she slid into a corridor which dead-ended at still another. As she turned the knob she glanced back. The demented one was behind her now, but did not seem in a hurry. Seconds later, Vonnie knew why.

They were in a corridor with a stairway in the center that led upward; a narrow staircase.

To Vonnie it seemed familiar. Then all the seeming vanished. It *was* familiar. It led to that deadend door which opened on the rock garden four floors below.

With the craft of purest madness, Valerie Elwood had herded her victim to the slaughter-pen of her choice, just as cattle are directed into their pens.

There was no going back. With Vonnie on the top landing, with no place into which to escape, Valerie Elwood slowly moved upward—to the kill she'd been deprived of by Bill Jackson's arrival.

There was no retreat for Vonnie. Nothing but to stand and fight, she swung on her pursuer and yanked at her wrist just below the upraised knife.

Now Fate did favor Vonnie. In the shape of Valerie's particular design. To drive the knife into Vonnie's throat, could have succeeded quickly, her violence in madness far outweighing Vonnie's panic.

But Valerie had special notions—to force Vonnie against the wall with the cold steel flat against her throat and use her other hand to turn the door knob.

Her intention? To send her victim crashing onto the rocks below.

Vonnie was able to strain away, making it difficult for her assailant to find the knob. But find it Valerie did, her face reflecting mad triumph.

The door swung open. Valerie, now using her wild strength to advantage, edged Vonnie toward the death drop.

Then a harsh voice roared up the stairwell. "Vonnie! Turn to the wall so I can shoot!"

Valerie Elwood's slitted eyes opened wide. Like a runner thrown off pace, she became confused, her pressure on her victim's body lessened.

Vonnie's panic heightened now. The knife: It was flat against her throat and Valerie had only to turn the blade inward and slash across with a sweep of her arm.

Finding new strength herself, Vonnie heaved at the weight pressing against her. This brought her against the wall as Bill had ordered; and he did fire his gun.

Valerie teetered on the open sill, flung her arms in the air, lunged at Vonnie in a last desperate thrust, and fell screaming to the rocks below.

Vonnie, off balance, teetered toward the stairwell. Below, she saw Bill's arms stretching upward. But too far away. To reach them, she would have to be Superwoman, or a bird, and she was not. Her heel got caught and she crashed downward. A pain shot through her arm.

The last thing she saw was Bill's stricken face just as her head was slammed against the wall and the world exploded inside . . .

She was lying on something soft, the world a vague place around her. She could move her eyes, and she saw patrol cars grouped about, beyond the pillars along the edge of the porch.

She felt no pain; that was the odd part. She saw the cast on her arm and felt the pressure of the binding around her ribs, but there was no pain; not even in her head which she remembered splitting wide open as she fell toward Bill.

Then there was his face again, close to hers.

"Nothing hurts," Vonnie stated.

"They gave you a shot. The ambulance is ready. We're going to take a little trip."

Another face appeared, above a white coat this time. "One more for the road," said White Coat cheerfully and there was a slight sting on her unsplinted arm.

Then everything was so serene and lovely as she drifted off to sleep . . .

CHAPTER NINETEEN

"She survived the fall," Aunt Lou said. "Talk about children of the devil! She was banged up more than you were. Both arms and one leg broken. Her ribs a mess. But she survived and they'll be able to put her back together again."

"The poor thing," Vonnie said, then to herself; I wonder if she would want it that way? Being brought back to keep on suffering?

"Everybody has been so protective," Vonnie went on. "I haven't the least idea of what's been going on all this time."

"All this time?" Aunt Lou said. "It's been two days. And B.J. has been the watch dog. A person would think you were made of fragile china."

"I don't even know where Keith is."

Bill Jackson had been sitting back in the corner of the hospital room with his chair tilted against the wall, his cap over his eyes. Without moving, he said, "Elwood is being held for the grand jury."

"But he didn't do anything criminal!" Vonnie cried. "He was just broken up about his wife."

"They found him in Florida. He was convinced she was hiding from him down there. Or at least he tried to *convince* himself that he was convinced."

"That's a crazy thing to say."

"Now that we've pieced the whole thing together I think he may get off as being temporarily insane. He was so gone on that wife of his that he kept covering up for her. He refused to believe everything wouldn't come out all right."

"Maybe he had reason to believe it."

"He had reason to believe otherwise. We checked with his friend Walter Sims over at the college. You see, jealousy was Valerie Elwood's thing. But she was so damnably clever. She fooled some of the experts about her homicidal tendencies."

"*Tendencies!*" Aunt Lou gasped.

"Quiet," Bill growled. "Keith knew she hated his other secretary, thinking there was something between them. When the poor girl died of an overdose Keith suspected that his wife had come to the office and given it to her. That was why he sent the hypo kit to be tested for her fingerprints. They weren't there, though."

"So that was the mystery of the metal box!" Vonnie exclaimed.

"It didn't prove anything except to Keith Elwood. That's where he was at least culpably negligent . . . Imagine having to bring you home to dinner and in-

313

troducing you to her! Assuming his suspicions were groundless—even when he knew they weren't?"

"How could a man become so enslaved by a woman that he'd act that way. It's impossible!" Aunt Lou said.

"Oh, I don't know about that," Vonnie countered. "What about John Hazard? Doesn't the legend say he let his wife kill their own son?"

"It's only a legend. The amazing thing to me was the fantastic determination of that woman; coming up here; finding Hazard House on her own. Then finding Melissa and terrorizing her into luring you there when her first attempt to murder you failed."

"We owe little Abby a real debt," Bill said. "She's not as zany as we thought. At least she decided Valerie Elwood was up to no good and phoned me when you were lured to the mansion. Otherwise, Valerie would probably have done you in."

"But what about Mr. Dean—that detective. Was he looking for Valerie?"

"Yes," Bill said grimly. "And he found her. When his wife vanished from their apartment, Keith didn't want the police in on it, so he hired a couple of private eyes to help him hunt. One of them went to Florida with Elwood; but Dean suspected that Valerie was up here and came hunting."

"How awful!" Vonnie murmured.

"Bill," said Aunt Lou. "We're wearing Vonnie out."

"No," Vonnie said. "You haven't told me about Abigail. "What was done with her?"

"She's being well taken care of at Williams College

314

—temporarily," Lou replied. "They're observing her to see if she needs psychiatric help or any mental therapy. Then the child is coming with me."

"That's wonderful. Abigail turned out to be one of my greatest problems."

"All right, Bill," Aunt Lou said. "It's time you got me back to Gar Fin Lake . . ."

Vonnie was released from the hospital the next morning and Bill chauffeured her to the house on Gar Fin Lake where Aunt Lou was waiting to make her comfortable. Her arm was still in a sling but it was only a minor fracture, and the bandage on her cracked ribs would come off soon.

It was pleasant enough at the lake and Aunt Lou could not have been more attentive. But finally, the good lady had to ask the direct question:

"Vonnie—what's wrong?"

"Wrong? Why, nothing."

"Don't try to fool a wise old woman. Is it Bill?"

"No—not really."

"Do you love him?"

"Yes—I guess I do."

"Then what's the problem? Marry him."

"It's not as simple as that."

"It's as simple as a two-dollar license and an official muttering a few words over you."

"Aunt Lou, there's something we've avoided talking about. Abigail and her psychic attachments—Patience—Rachel . . ."

"Oh, that. I don't think we've avoided it. The subject just hasn't come up."

"But it's important!"

"Yes. Bill thought it was too. He had some long talks with those experts over at the college. But I told him in the beginning how things were. And those people agreed."

"Then tell me."

"It was quite simple. Melissa was the culprit there. She filled those children's heads with all the gory tales about Hazard House." Lou paused and considered deeply. "Of course we do have a problem with the child. Schizoid, they called it; highly impressionable. But it can be corrected."

"I hope so."

"I think what worries you, dear is—how can I put it—the reality of the unreal? You're wondering if Patience and Rachel really exist?"

"Something like that. Abigail's seizures were so real . . ."

"Of course they were. She was acting out Melissa's absurd stories. Many children live in worlds they create from bits and pieces that unthinking adults give them."

"Perhaps. But there's the matter of those wilted roses. When I told Bill about the incident, he pooh-poohed it. Still . . ."

"Didn't he tell you?"

"Tell me what?"

Aunt Lou laughed. "He did a little checking with Lucy Stone."

"Do you mean there was a natural explanation?"

"Yes," Lou replied slowly, "but I wonder if you really want it."

"I don't understand you."

"All of us are children in a way. We like to cling to our fantasies."

"Aunt Lou! I'm surprised at you. Are you saying I'm neurotic?"

"You're a highly sensitive person, dear—you can't get around that."

This momentarily diverted Vonnie. She had to admit that there was truth to what Lou had said. She thought of her dreams. They had been so real. But it was comforting to realize that none of the nightmares had come prior to the time she'd researched Hazard House in the New York Public Library.

They could well have been creations of my own subconscious, she thought hopefully.

"You were telling me about the roses."

"Oh, that. Well, it's not absolutely conclusive, but you see Lucy Stone orders roses to put into the guest rooms. An order had come very early in the morning the same day you arrived. The way it's done there, a flower truck from town pulls up the back way and they put the roses in a cooler near the kitchen. Well, there's a freezer right beside it and the delivery boy was new and that's where he put the roses."

"Do you mean that was where Abigail got them to bring them up to me? Out of Lucy's freezer?"

"There's little doubt of it. And they had to be frozen stiff at the time. You know what happens to a frozen flower when it thaws out."

"Then Abigail embellished it with her story of how Rachel could wilt a rose with a glance."

"Perhaps Melissa told her that or she may have dreamed it up herself."

"How absurdly simple."

"So many things turn out to be absurdly simple when we look them in the face. And by the way, did you hear that that weird Professor Heinz found what he was looking for?"

"I haven't heard a thing."

"It seems his interest was proving some of the old legends factual—historically that is. Anyhow, he dug up a skeleton he claims is that of Rachel Hazard's other son. You know the story has it that she murdered him because he wouldn't sign a pact with the devil."

"So that was what Heinz was looking for."

"Of course, it's not proof. They're checking the bones, trying to date them, but even if the time is right, they could be someone else's bones. An Indian, an old settler."

"I guess none of it really matters anymore, does it, Aunt Lou?"

"Of course not. We can't brood over the past. It's tomorrow that counts. What we do with it . . ."

Tomorrow. What to do with it.

A few days later, completely on her feet again, Vonnie had Bill drive her back to the lodge.

Lucy was all questions and Vonnie answered them as best she could.

"And what are you going to do now, darling?"

"I don't really know," Vonnie replied.

"Are you going to marry Bill?"

"He wants me to."

"But I gather you haven't made up your mind."

"No. I wish I could."

Happy with the prospect of having a story of her own, Lucy glanced about for invisible eavesdroppers and then said. "Do you know what Bill told me?"

"I'm dying to find out."

"Well don't tell him I told you. Act surprised when *he* tells you, but he checked into the Hazard House situation. That syndicate your boss worked for is dropping the whole thing. They're going to let their option run out. When they do, Bill is thinking of picking it up and building that ski lodge."

"Oh, no!"

Lucy was distressed. "You mean you wouldn't want to help him?"

"I never want to see the place again."

"I suppose that's logical. Have another cup of coffee, dear. There's something I must do. I'll be right back."

Instead of waiting, Vonnie strolled out of the lodge and down toward the lake, her mind filled with uneasy thoughts. Then as she glanced toward the parking lot she saw something that had obviously been someone's oversight.

The jeep was still parked there.

Acting almost as an automaton, Vonnie got into it, backed out of the lot, and turned into Salt Lick Road . . .

Twenty minutes later, she was back at Hazard House. The heavy, quiet gloom of the place was unchanged. Vonnie went slowly across the porch and inside where the sun shone down on the tile symbols below. Vonnie stood staring at them. But she was looking more with her mind than with her eyes.

Was there anything here—anything really here—for the mind to see?

Vonnie felt a slight chill. But instead of allowing it to remain, she straightened and brushed it aside with a deep breath.

"Patience," she whispered. "Are you here?"

Vonnie waited for stirrings; stirrings of any sort; the movement of air; the brush of psychic presence against her consciousness.

All was still.

"Was it your brother, Patience? Did the finding of his body change things where you are?"

Silence. The empty stillness of a void.

"Or are you anywhere, Patience?"

There was the peremptory sound of an approaching car. Vonnie waited.

The car stopped outside and heavy feet ran across the porch.

"Vonnie! What are you doing here?"

Vonnie turned. "Talking with old friends."

The words formed into a question deepened Bill Jackson's frown. He studied Vonnie's face. Was that a faint smile? And if so, what did it mean?

"Vonnie. You've got to get a hold of yourself. That damned mumbo-jumbo is for kooks. Can't you understand that?"

"Of course, darling. All we kooks understand it."